ESCAP
JUP

'The lava is heading straight for the colony. The fissure is still growing . . . We have to evacuate. This whole place is going to crack like an egg!'

Without warning, the chamber shook violently, throwing Michael and Kumiko to the floor. Kumiko shrieked as a roof support gave way and collapsed nearby, sending a cloud of dust swirling into the air and dragging electrical cables from their fittings. The lighting flickered and sparked, and as Michael dragged Kumiko away from the live cables, a section of the chamber wall split with a loud explosive crack.

'The outer wall!' Michael yelled, watching horrified as dust and smoke was sucked through the crack into the weak, poisonous atmosphere of Io beyond. Their time had run out. If they weren't crushed to death by falling debris, they'd suffocate as the remaining air was sucked out of the chamber.

ESCAPE FROM JUPITER

David Ogilvy

BBC CHILDREN'S BOOKS

A Film Australia/NHK co-production in association
with the Australian Broadcasting Corporation,
made with the participation of the
Australian Film Finance Corporation Limited.

Published in the UK by BBC Children's Books,
a division of BBC Enterprises Limited
Woodlands, 80 Wood Lane, London W12 0TT

First published in Australia by ABC Books, 1994
First published in the UK by BBC Children's Books, 1995

ISBN 0 563 40430 2

Printed and bound in Great Britain by Clays Ltd, St Ives plc
Cover printed by Clays Ltd, St Ives plc

CONTENTS

CHAPTER ONE

DISASTER

In the black depths of space, the planet Jupiter, floated defiant and impressive. Bathed orange by rays from the distant sun, and circled by 20 lunar satellites, it seemed remote and inhospitable.

High above Io, one of Jupiter's tiny moons, the loud drone of a giant space liner's engines eased. *Zargon 12* was nearing the end of its unscheduled detour to Io's remote mining colony, a cluster of red-stained, oddly shaped spherical domes set into the sides of a deep ravine on the moon's volcanic surface.

On board, Kumiko sat in her cramped compartment scowling at computer-generated images of their destination. She'd spent much of her life accompanying her geo-physicist parents to mining operations throughout the galaxy, and hated it.

She flopped back miserably into her seat and stared unhappily at the computer screen in front of her. 'The lunar satellite of Io is the third largest of Jupiter's moons and lies some 778 million kilometres from the sun,' said an enthusiastic voice, sounding like a demented travel guide. 'The dedicated band of colonists settled on Io, 27 in all, are primarily involved in mining. Theirs is an exciting challenge, conquering the frontiers of space ... '

Kumiko flicked the off button and the sound went dead. 'Yet another holiday gone the way of the dinosaurs,' she muttered to herself, annoyed that their scheduled return to Earth had been so abruptly postponed.

'I don't know why we have to come to this dumb rock in the first place,' Kumiko complained bitterly to her father, as they were getting ready to disembark from the space liner.

'Because Kumiko,' Tatsuya replied with mock seriousness, 'The company decided to send your dumb father to do some dumb tests in the dumb mines. Urgently.'

'But it's prehistoric!'

'Think of it as an adventure. And there are other children down there,' her mother, Akiko, added cheerfully.

'Yeah. And I bet they drag their knuckles on the ground,' Kumiko sneered miserably. 'They live in caves down there!'

In the centre of the colony's hydroponics lab, surrounded by lush plants, Michael was hunched over a cluttered bench top sorting through a collection of rock and soil samples.

He had lived all his 13 years on Io, and the hydro lab was his domain. His best friend, Kingston, stood beside him, pawing over the samples, looking very disappointed.

'It's just a pile of boring rock!' the eight-year-old moaned. He really wanted to be exploring the remote recesses of the colony or creating stories of imminent disasters and blood-sucking aliens.

'They're trace elements, for the plants,' Michael explained. 'If we can extract them from this stuff, we won't have to wait the usual ten months for supplies from Earth.'

But something else had caught Kingston's interest. 'A fossil!' he exclaimed, seizing an unusual lump of rock. 'An alien's eyeball!' Kingston's eyes widened. This was a real discovery. 'They're down there for sure. See, I told you! Big, black, scaly xenomorphs! And the deep-drilling program will disturb them. They'll come up through the tunnels at night and attack while we're asleep.'

Michael ignored him. Kingston had a rampant imagination and no-one paid much attention to his horrible scenarios of doom and gloom.

'I tell you, we're all going to end up as alien food,' Kingston warned, sneaking a berry from one of Michael's prized strawberry plants and popping it into his mouth.

'Don't!' Michael warned.

Too late. Kingston bit down on the fruit. His face contorted as an awful bitter taste exploded in his mouth. Shocked, he spat out the berry as if it was cyanide.

'I still haven't perfected them,' Michael added apologetically. 'The genetic structure. I *did* try to warn you.'

'What have I told you about poisoning small, inquisitive children, Michael?' joked a white-haired man appearing through the thick foliage and looking distractedly around him.

'I left them here somewhere,' the man muttered to himself as he rummaged around the bench top.

Professor Ingessol was one of the engineers who had built the colony on Io. Now in his sixties, he remained on Io as a scientific adviser, even though many of the adults viewed him as an eccentric crank.

Michael reached up to a shelf and casually produced a batch of info-files. He handed them to the grateful Professor who, as he turned to leave, noticed Michael's rock samples spread out over the bench top.

'Where did you get those?' he inquired.

'Down in G-7. For the plants.'

The tone in Ingessol's voice became uncharacteristically serious. 'Michael, I want you to stay out of the mines,' he warned solemnly. 'Promise me!'

Before Michael could respond, the flasks and

beakers on top of his work bench began to rattle and shake. Tremors from the drilling program sometimes rocked the colony, but Kingston looked around anxiously, suspecting an invasion of scaly xenomorphs.

'Please Michael, do as I say. It's not safe!' the Professor reiterated.

Michael nodded hesitantly, and as the tremor subsided, Ingessol hurried from the laboratory towards the colony's administration dome.

Kingston watched him disappear then turned to Michael. 'What did I tell you?! Xenomorphs!' he exclaimed excitedly, rushing away through the foliage to find more evidence of the aliens.

Michael packed up his samples and went to the other side of the lab to check for damage in the pressure chambers on the atmospheric purifier. As Io's surface was largely volcanic, the Professor had entrusted him with this task after any earth tremors, however minor.

He checked over the gauges and pipes connecting the towering machines to the algae tanks, but turned swiftly at the sound of a flask smashing to the floor behind him. Michael watched quietly as a hand reached beyond the broken flask towards one of his prized strawberry plants. 'Typical,' muttered Michael as he saw Gerard looking furtively around, then quickly pluck the red fruit from the plant. About to stuff a fistful of the fruit into his mouth, Gerard heard a voice behind him.

'You'll regret it!'

'I'm really quaking in my boots,' Gerard scoffed, turning to see Michael heading towards him.

The two boys had little time for each other. Michael thought Gerard hot-headed and Gerard was equally impatient with Michael's passion for hydroponics. Gerard would much prefer to be mucking in beside his father in the mines. Plants were for wimps! He sneered at Michael as he stuffed the berries into his mouth and chewed greedily. Then the terrible taste of the berries took full effect.

'I warned you,' Michael laughed, enjoying the sight.

Gerard spat the foul-tasting fruit across the floor. 'You're dead Faraday!' He lunged for Michael, but Michael was too quick for him. He raced through the foliage and out the main doors, Gerard in angry pursuit.

Michael clattered down the central stairwell, swung into an empty corridor, then turned a corner only to find the exit door locked. He looked about, searching for another way out. Trapped! He heard Gerard's slow and confident footsteps.

'You're dead meat, Faraday! There's no way out!' Gerard yelled gleefully.

As Gerard's footsteps echoed towards him, Michael heard a scraping noise from above. He looked up to see Kingston's face beaming down at him through an open air duct grate. Kingston beckoned him towards the opening, and Michael leapt up to the grate, swung his body through the gap and clambered through. Quickly and quietly, Kingston slid the grate back into place, just as Gerard appeared below.

Gerard sauntered into the empty corridor unaware of the two sets of eyes staring down at him. He looked around, confused by Michael's disappearance. 'You can run, Faraday, but you can't hide!' he yelled threateningly.

'What's with him?' Kingston whispered.

'Bad berries,' Michael replied. Kingston grinned knowingly as they watched Gerard turn away, defeated.

'You should have seen the look on his face,' Michael said with a grin as they clambered along the air duct to safer territory. 'I hope you know where you're going.'

'The tunnel rat knows everything, remember!' Kingston boasted. And it was true. Kingston knew the labyrinth of tunnels and air ducts like the back of his hand. Often left to his own devices, and naturally inquisitive, he had spent many hours exploring the myriad of tunnels and ducts that serviced the colony. What Kingston didn't know was hardly worth knowing.

As they scrambled along the duct, Kingston placed his finger to his lips. 'Sssh!' he whispered, pointing to a shaft of light beaming into the duct. 'Duffy's office.'

Michael's eyes widened. 'What!' he protested. 'Duffy'll murder us!' But Kingston wasn't to be stopped. He quietly crawled forward until he reached the grate and looked down into the office below.

George Duffy, the colony's chief administrator, sat behind his shiny ebony desk flossing his teeth meticulously. Professor Ingessol paced back and forth in front of him. 'Suspend the deep drilling. Please George. At least until the experts arrive,' Ingessol pleaded.

Duffy removed the floss from between his teeth and sucked on the dislodged food particles. 'That's impossible. You conveniently forget this is a commercial operation. I've got quotas to fill,' he replied coldly.

'But I tell you, we are too close to the lava chamber.'

Huddled around the grid, Kingston looked at Michael and swallowed uneasily. Lava chamber! Nobody had mentioned anything about mining near lava chambers before. This was hot news. They peered back through the air duct.

Ingessol tossed the set of info-files he had retrieved from the hydro lab on Duffy's spotless desk. 'There! There's your proof. You breach that lava chamber and heaven help us!' Ingessol said angrily.

'Stop! You hold it right there!' Duffy leaned forward menacingly in his chair. 'Do you seriously think that I'd continue the deep-drilling operation if it was going to risk the lives of anyone on this colony? Well, do you?'

Ingessol had no answer. Frustrated, he strode out of the office. 'Bureaucrats!' he scoffed as he disappeared into the corridor.

Duffy leaned back in his chair and smiled contentedly to himself—until another tremor startled him and he looked around in sudden fear.

'Let's get out of here!' Kingston whispered to Michael as the air duct began to vibrate. They tried to scramble away, but the duct lurched violently and straining under the combined weight of its two occupants, broke free from its couplings. Kingston yelped with fear as the duct, ripping from its fittings, tipped down like a slippery slide, spilling Kingston and Michael out onto Duffy's desk in a tangle of arms and legs.

Duffy leapt to his feet. 'What on earth do you think you're doing!' he demanded, the veins in his neck almost popping through his skin. 'Well!' he shouted, glaring at the two dust-covered explorers. Michael looked at Kingston, neither of them daring to speak for fear they might break into uncontrollable fits of laughter.

'This is not a children's playground! Those air ducts are out of bounds to the likes of you and I will not have you disobeying company rules! Understood?' Duffy glowered at the children waiting for a response. None came. 'I'm still waiting. What were you doing in there?' he persisted angrily.

'Checking for ... air?' Kingston finally muttered hesitantly, shooting Michael a cheeky wink. Michael bit down hard on his lip, trying not to giggle.

'Don't mess with me boy or you'll come off second best!' Duffy barked. Duffy resented the children's presence on Io. They created extra work, extra responsibilities. If he had his way, he would have the lot of them shipped back to Earth. 'Now, we'll see what your parents have to say about this!' he grumbled as he marched the two explorers out of his office.

After delivering Kingston to his mother, Duffy found

Sam, the colony's space tug pilot, in the departure bay preparing to collect the new arrivals from *Zargon 12*. 'Sam, someone is going to get hurt, seriously hurt, and I know who you'll blame then,' Duffy complained.

Sam listened patiently to Duffy, wondering secretly if his blood pressure would one day kill him. 'George, if Michael says he won't do it again, then that's the end of it,' he said calmly, turning to Michael for reassurance.

Michael shuffled awkwardly. 'Sorry Dad, it won't happen again.'

'I expect discipline,' Duffy added, wanting to have the last word.

'George, what do you want me to do? Stake him out on an ants' nest?' Sam quipped, his patience wearing thin.

Duffy's lip curled. 'Don't tempt me!' he sneered, still angry as he walked away.

Michael sighed, relieved to be let off so lightly. Since his mother had been called back to Earth to work on the company's deep-space program, Michael had enjoyed a close relationship with Sam. He was more like a friend than a father.

'What on earth were you up to? In an air duct, in Duffy's office of all places?' Sam asked. But before Michael could respond, he added, 'Second thoughts, I don't want to know.'

'Dad, what would happen, say, if the deep-drilling program struck the lava chamber?' Michael asked, recalling Ingessol's argument with Duffy.

Sam looked at Michael with surprise. 'What? Who put that idea in your head?'

'Professor Ingessol—'.

'Not again,' Sam said dismissively, all too familiar with Ingessol's crackpot theories. 'What was it last time? A comet about to crash into the colony? The viral decay of the atmospheric control computers? Now go on, hop it,' he said, opening the doors to the access tube that led to the space tug. 'Better clean up. Get ready for our visitors.'

'But I'm coming with you,' Michael protested.

'After your little stunt in Duffy's office! You've got to be joking,' Sam replied, hitting the controls to the access tube. The doors slid shut behind him.

Michael returned dejectedly to his quarters and climbed into a clean set of clothes. He set his picto-gram running and stared longingly at the 3D image of his mother, Celia. It had been nine months since she had left and the pictograms were his only contact with her now.

Her image flickered before him. 'It's not much fun here without you and Dad. Next year eh? And I've found this great beach. You'll love it. The light's flash-ing. Give your Dad a kiss for me ... '

'Not likely,' Michael quipped, as he pulled a fresh shirt over his head.

'And guess what, I've got a dog. And it's been raining. Just wait till you feel what that's like. Love you. Oh, Duffy, I called the dog, Duff ... ' The message ended abruptly and the pictogram vanished with a zap. Michael grinned at the thought of a dog called Duffy. Not many people on the colony liked the admin-istrator, his mother included.

Fully dressed, Michael stood in front of his mirror and checked his appearance. He had heard that the mining experts were bringing their daughter with them.

'Dressed to impress,' a voice smirked behind him.

Michael hadn't noticed Kingston enter his quarters. He stepped quickly away from the mirror.

'So what did you get?' Kingston asked with a grin.

'A warning. How about you? What'd your Mum say?'

'The usual. No time to think about it.'

Kingston's mother, Helen, was the colony's medical officer and her busy schedule meant that Kingston saw little of her. 'Someone had measles, or mumps or some other slimy life-threatening microbe,' he muttered, looking disappointed. 'There's always some excuse.'

'Think yourself lucky,' Michael said, trying to cheer him up.

Kingston shrugged as Michael checked himself in the mirror one final time. 'You ready?'

Kingston nodded and together they hurried out the door to greet the new arrivals.

As the battered space tug swung over the colony, veered sharply into the ravine and began its descent towards the landing platform, Kumiko sat rigidly in her seat, her jaw clenched tight, her hands gripping the arm rests firmly. She hated small space craft.

'Is she okay?' Sam inquired, noticing Kumiko's white knuckles.

'She'll be fine ... once she gets her feet on terra firma,' Tatsuya replied as Sam expertly manoeuvred the tug into the landing cradle. 'The boss will want to see you right away,' Sam told the new arrivals. 'He's waiting for you in the Jupiter Bar.'

Kumiko breathed in deeply with relief as Sam threw several switches on the control console in front of him and the tug's noisy thrusters droned to a welcome silence.

'Jupiter Bar? How quaint,' she sneered to herself, collecting her precious personal computer and scrambling from her seat, happy to see the last of the cramped cockpit. Tatsuya leaned over to Kumiko. 'Now we expect you to make an effort this time,' he said quietly but firmly, impatient with Kumiko's attitude to the colonies.

'Don't worry. I'll charm the socks off them,' Kumiko replied, muttering to herself—'If they wear any.'

'Scientists! I bet she's an egg head!' Kingston prattled as he and Michael raced towards the Jupiter Bar. They sped through the doors and almost slammed into Duffy hovering by the entrance.

'You're late,' Duffy snapped. Kingston and Michael shrugged a vague apology. 'I'm warning you, step out of line one more time, and you'll rue the day you were born!'

Before they could reply, Duffy turned and swept across the room to greet the new arrivals. 'Tatsuya, Akiko. Finally we meet. And this must be your daughter Kumiko,' he said pinching her on the cheek. Kumiko stiffened at the demeaning gesture and smiled icily.

'And no doubt a well-behaved young lady,' Duffy gushed smarmily. 'Welcome to Io.'

'I couldn't think of a nicer place to spend my holidays,' Kumiko responded with just the right amount of sarcasm.

'Right then,' Duffy said, summoning Michael and Kingston grandly with a broad sweep of his hand.

Deeming the introductions over, Duffy led the adults away for a briefing, while Kingston and Michael escorted Kumiko on a guided tour of the colony. 'You don't have to do this,' she said.

'It's the rule,' Kingston asserted. 'The last tourist who was left on their own opened the wrong door. Took three days to clean up the mess.'

'I'm not a tourist. I'm a conscript to this rock,' Kumiko responded bitterly and strode off down the corridor ahead of the two boys.

'Ice woman from hell!' Kingston muttered as they followed their charge towards the recreation centre. 'Maybe she's an android.'

In the recreation centre, Michael and Kumiko stood in front of a large viewing port, looking out over the other domes that made up the rest of the colony and its mining operations. 'The large dome, that's the ore separation plant. And over to the right, that's the furnaces and metal extraction plant,' Michael explained.

Behind them, Kingston manoeuvred his remote controlled ZIT, Zero Intelligence Transporter, across the room. It was his favourite toy, a birthday present from his mother. This sophisticated piece of electronics looked like a miniature lunar terrain vehicle but behaved like a crazed lap dog.

Kingston marched up to Kumiko and eyed her suspiciously. 'So, what do *you* know about the colony's deep-drilling program?' he demanded like a prosecuting attorney.

'What?'

'The mines. They're going to explode. That's why you're here, isn't it? We're all going to be turned into toast!'

Kumiko sighed petulantly. 'I'm here because my parents dragged me here.'

'You must know something! Come on, spill the beans,' Kingston persisted.

Kumiko thought for a moment. 'And what do *your* parents do?' she asked.

'My Mum's a doctor,' Kingston answered warily, not understanding the point to Kumiko's question.

'Right. So that makes you an expert in medicine does it?' Kumiko smirked victoriously at Michael who grinned back at her. 'What do you do for real fun on this dump?' she asked, feeling a little better.

Michael quickly volunteered a suggestion. 'We could go with Dad on the space tug. There's an ore carrier due for departure.'

'Get serious! I'm not going on that flying flea pit!'

'I'll show you the colony from the air. Dad lets me take the controls.'

'As if!' Kumiko said disbelievingly. There was no way she was going anywhere near the space tug, especially with an underage pilot.

'Not scared are you?'

Before Kumiko could respond, Kingston let out a loud wolf whistle as Gerard sauntered into the room. Decked out in sleeveless jacket and a pair of solar glare glasses, with his hair slicked back, he looked like an intergalactic rock musician.

'Who are you trying to impress?' Kingston demanded, eyeing Gerard's get-up.

'Drop dead worm,' Gerard sneered dismissively as he strode up to Kumiko to introduce himself.

'Hi. I'm Gerard,' he said suavely.

'The local neanderthal,' Michael quipped.

'Hey. Lay off my brother, you big lug,' another voice said protectively. Gerard hadn't noticed his eight-year-old sister, Anna, following him into the room.

'And who's this, your bodyguard?' Kumiko asked wryly.

Gerard squirmed with embarrassment. 'Anna, beat it,' he muttered out of the corner of his mouth. But Anna wasn't going anywhere. She sidled up to Kumiko and whispered loudly in her ear. 'He got dressed up just for you.'

Michael and Kingston cackled with pleasure as Gerard squirmed some more.

'This close worm,' Gerard threatened, holding up his thumb and forefinger to Kingston as if measuring the very short distance between life and death. Kingston gulped. 'You too, jungle boy!' he warned Michael before returning his attention to Kumiko.

'You bored with these idiots yet?' Gerard asked confidently. Kumiko grinned. She was ready for a challenge now and followed Gerard out of the room.

Michael looked at Kingston worriedly and they hurried after them. Duffy had left the new arrival in their charge and there was no way they wanted another run in with the irascible administrator. They'd be on extra chores for the rest of their lives!

Gerard led Kumiko to a sealed door with a 'no entry'

sign emblazoned on it. He waved his hand over an electronic keypad. With a rush of air, the entrance to the mining tunnel slid open.

'One of the old personnel entrances,' he explained to Kumiko. 'Anything you want to know, just ask. My Dad is the chief engineer,' he said with a hint of pride, then stepped through the entrance into the mine. Kumiko followed, but Michael, Kingston and Anna held back a little.

'This is not a good idea,' Michael warned, remembering his promise to Professor Ingessol.

'Come on. You guys were so keen to find out about the deep-drilling program. Here's your big chance,' Kumiko said cheekily.

'Michael, we're in enough trouble already,' Kingston whispered to Michael.

'Well I can't let her go off by herself.'

'She's not by herself. Muscle head's with her!' Kingston said, turning quickly to Anna to apologise. 'No offence.'

'None taken,' Anna replied.

Michael hovered near the entrance to the tunnel, unsure of what to do. Kumiko threw down the final challenge. 'Not scared are you?'

Gerard sniggered with pleasure and Michael, not wanting to back down in front of his rival, stepped inside the tunnel. 'Cover for us,' he said to Kingston.

'No way!' Kingston protested. 'Don't blame me if you get blown up into little squishy bits,' Kingston yelled as they disappeared down the tunnel, 'and don't expect us to rescue you!'

'That girl is definitely trouble,' Anna said as the door slid shut with an ominous thud.

The air inside the narrow tunnel was stale and warm and heavy with the pungent smell of sulphur dioxide. Rotten eggs. It was a smell that Kumiko could never get used to, no matter how many mines she visited.

They made their way down the tunnel, following the string of low voltage lights that dimly lit their path. As they crunched over the gravel floor, close to the craggy red-rock walls, Gerard kept up a commentary on the mining operation.

'Everything's automated, five extraction shafts, all of them operational. Lightweight metals mostly, used in computer tech and spacecraft ... ' Boring, thought Kumiko.

'What's that noise?' she asked uneasily as a series of far-off explosions boomed through the tunnels.

'It's the new deep-drilling site,' Gerard answered, amazed that she, the daughter of mining experts, knew nothing about the new processes. 'Boy, where are you from?' Gerard quipped, beckoning Kumiko to follow.

'Earth! Where I should be right now,' Kumiko snapped. She took a deep breath, and followed the boys, deeper into the red-stained tunnels.

They moved without speaking down the mine towards the thundering sound of the deep drilling. Abruptly, Kumiko stopped in her tracks, spooked by another tremor. Up ahead several pieces of the red rock superstructure tumbled ominously to the floor of the tunnel. Feeling suddenly claustrophobic, a shiver travelled down Kumiko's spine.

'Relax, it happens all the time,' Gerard said.

'We can go back if you like,' Michael shouted above the noise, hoping that Kumiko would stop pretending to be brave.

But Kumiko was not about to weaken. 'Let's just do it and get out of here!' she said stubbornly, stepping off down the tunnel.

It took them another 15 minutes to reach the deep-drilling site. They stumbled down the tunnel, finally arriving at a sealed chamber where the pounding from the drilling operation was deafening. A huge cylindrical dome rose up out of the floor of the tunnel, towering above them into a cavernous void carved into the rock roof.

'We came all this way for *that*?' Kumiko yelled, staring at the sealed chamber.

Gerard grinned. 'Mining technology like you've never seen,' he gloated. 'Prepare yourselves, best seats in the house.' He opened a large service vent in the side of the chamber and beckoned Michael and Kumiko forward.

As they leaned into the opening and looked down at the mining operation far below, a rush of air and fumes warmed their faces and stung their eyes. At the bottom of the deep chamber, giant automated machines roared loudly as they blasted their explosive drills through the moon's substrata.

Kumiko reeled back, suddenly overcome by vertigo and the pummelling sound. She leaned against the chamber to steady herself. 'Can we go now?' she gasped, desperate to return to the surface, away from the noise and the smells.

'But we only just got here,' Gerard protested, wobbling a little on his feet as another tremor struck the tunnel. Gerard saw the look of panic on Kumiko's face.

'It's the drills. Explosive heads,' he said trying to reassure her. But before he could finish, another tremor hit the mine. This time it was more severe and the ground shook violently, surprising even Gerard.

'That's it! I'm out of here!' Kumiko said as she turned on her heels and rushed back up the tunnel.

'Talk about a panic merchant,' Gerard called after her, trying to ignore the strong blast of gas that rushed up the tunnel and ruffled his hair. The stench was overwhelming.

'Pure sulphur dioxide! Gerard, we've got to get out of here! It'll poison the lot of us!' Michael yelled above the deafening roar of the mining machinery. As they began to run, another explosion blasted up the tunnel, the shock wave throwing the children to the ground. Kumiko screamed with fright as behind them, rocks began to tumble to the floor.

'Gerard! Get us out of here!' Michael yelled, dragging Kumiko to her feet. 'The whole place is going to come down!'

'You don't have to panic,' Gerard shouted at them, trying desperately to remain calm as they raced through the tunnel.

'Who's panicking?' Kumiko said, slowing up a little as the tremor died away. 'I don't want to be stuck in here for the rest of my life. Not with you two!'

In another part of the tunnel, Gerard's father Karl *was* sounding a little panicky as he conferred with Duffy about the tremors.

'We have to close it all down,' he warned as he strode down the tunnel to inspect the damage. 'At least until it's stabilised, until I can find out what's happened.'

'Then do it!' Duffy ordered, as if the idea was his own. 'And do it quietly. I don't want any fuss.' Karl looked at Duffy incredulously. The deep-drilling chamber might have exploded, half the mine might have collapsed, and Duffy didn't want any fuss.

Gerard led them further and further into the tunnels. 'Come on,' he said, 'I know a better way. It'll be quicker.'

'This *is* the quickest way,' Michael protested stubbornly.

'How would you know jungle boy,' Gerard sneered. 'You coming or what?'

Stopping at a rusted, sulphur-stained door, Gerard wrestled with its wheel lock, and after a struggle, opened it with a creak and a groan. Boldly he stepped through, into the darkness, while Michael and Kumiko followed more cautiously.

'Gerard! Are you out of your mind?' Kumiko asked, looking around the battered ancient tunnel.

'This place hasn't been used for years,' Michael agreed. 'Look at it!'

Gerard pulled his multi-mate from his pocket. He switched the multi-function hand tool to light mode and shone the beam up the tunnel. 'It's okay,' he said. 'It cuts back into the main tunnels further up. Trust me'

Kumiko and Michael followed reluctantly. The air was stale and hot on their skin. As they made their way tentatively up the tunnel, they passed a sealed emergency shelter. Gerard shone his light on the door. 'That's where they keep the dead bodies. After the accidents,' he said jokingly.

Kumiko glared at him. 'Just get us out of here!' she shouted as a deep rumbling sound echoed up the tunnel. Distant at first, it came closer and closer, and finally became a terrible roar. The ground began to shake under their feet, and rocks and dust showered from the roof of the tunnel. Small rocks fell first, then whole sections of the roof began to cave in.

'Run!' Michael yelled above the chaos.

'Where?' Kumiko shrieked as they stumbled through the darkness.

'Gerard! Where to?' Michael yelled. Gerard stood there, unsure. Michael grabbed him and shook him by the arm. 'Gerard! Decide! You'll kill us all!' he screamed, as another shock wave hit the tunnel. Behind them the walls started to collapse; above them the roof began to crack and tear.

'There!' Gerard yelled, pointing back along the tunnel to a beacon flashing above the emergency shelter.

They raced to the doorway and Kumiko began punching the air lock controls. The door stayed firmly shut. Kumiko tried again. Nothing.

'It won't budge,' she shouted.

Gerard quickly ripped open the control panel, revealing a red safety release lever. He savagely punched it with his fist and the emergency shelter door slowly opened.

'In!' he ordered as another tremor began to rumble up the tunnel towards them. 'Move it!' He pushed Kumiko and Michael through the opening as the tremor struck.

As they stumbled inside, Gerard slammed his fist against the door close mechanism and the door slid shut, just as the walls outside the chamber crashed down against the door, sealing it beneath tons of sulphur-laden rocks.

TRAPPED

T ucked away in a corner of the Jupiter Bar, Kingston and Anna were deeply involved in a
game of Astroblaze. In the centre of the circular
machine, lasers projected 3D images of a city landscape complete with flying space ships zipping
between the towering sky scrapers.

Kingston expertly manipulated the controls and his
spacecraft rocketed between the tall buildings,
banking and diving past obstacles, in pursuit of his
adversary. He deftly floated his hands over the machine's light sensor controls, and as a rogue 3D missile
loomed up at his craft, fired a blast of laser light. When
the missile evaporated in mid air, Kingston leapt into
the air victoriously.

'Yes! Surrender now or risk total annihilation!' he
cried.

'Don't push your luck,' Anna replied, patiently
waiting her turn to retaliate.

'Okay, you asked for it,' Kingston said with a sly
grin, then took the controls again, preparing for his
final attack. But just as he began to play, the table
started to wobble violently.

'You moved the table!' he accused Anna.

'I did not. It's just a tremor. Now do you want to play
or not,' Anna said indignantly.

But Kingston remained distracted. 'Professor Ingessol warned them. The deep drilling. We'll all be blown
to space dust!'

Anna sighed. Kingston was deeply boring when he
talked about the end of the world. But as she moved

to take over the controls, another tremor hit the colony, and the floor began to shake fiercely. Quickly, Kingston grabbed her by the arm, and dragged her to the centre of the room, away from the viewing port. He knew that if the plexi-windows cracked, they'd be sucked out into space.

'We've got to get out of here,' he yelled as a nearby stanchion crashed from the ceiling, missing them by inches.

'The others! They're in the mines!' Anna screamed. But Kingston wasn't listening. Realising his prized copy of Astroblaze was still in the 3D machine, he rushed back into the viewing dome to collect it.

'Kingston!' Anna screamed as warning lights began to flash, and the heavy security shield descended to seal off the windows.

Kingston ripped the game card from its slot and turned to see the security shield half way to the floor. He raced forward, took a flying leap and somersaulted under the descending shield as it crashed to the floor.

Rebounding to his feet, Kingston grabbed Anna by the arm. Together they rushed towards the main door of the Jupiter Bar, but before they could reach it, another tremor brought a section of the roof crashing down, blocking their way.

'Over here!' Kingston yelled, heading towards another exit. But Anna couldn't move—she was petrified. Kingston rushed back to collect her. Too late. The walls of the Jupiter bar began to crash down, imprisoning them in the falling rubble as the colony rocked from the force of the mines exploding deep below the surface.

Trapped inside the emergency shelter in the mining tunnels, Gerard, Kumiko and Michael scrambled to their feet and dusted themselves off as the last of the tremors subsided.

Kumiko rushed to the door and began to examine the control panel in the dim light.

'I hope you're satisfied, jerk,' Michael said, blaming Gerard for their predicament.

'Watch it smart mouth,' Gerard replied threateningly. 'And what do you think *you're* doing?' he snapped, spotting Kumiko tampering with the control panel.

'I don't know about you, but I plan to get out of here,' she replied defiantly.

Gerard moved across to the door, placing himself between Kumiko and the controls. 'Listen brains, you don't know what's out there. It could be lava,' he warned.

'If it was lava, the door would be red hot wouldn't it?' Kumiko replied, trying to reach past Gerard.

'I said leave it.' Gerard pushed her hand away from the controls. 'There could be gas. Sulphur dioxide, remember?'

'I'm not going to touch the stupid door. There's got to be a communication system down here somewhere.'

'You're wasting your time,' Gerard said, as he unclipped a small panel next to the door, revealing a tangle of frayed and broken wires.

Kumiko stared at the mess in disbelief. 'What is the point of an emergency shelter if you can't reach the outside world to tell them about your emergency!'

'These tunnels were abandoned years ago,' Gerard muttered. 'After they were mined out, everything was transferred to the new tunnel system.'

'Then what are we doing in here?' Michael exclaimed angrily. 'You led us down here knowing that they were abandoned tunnels.'

Kumiko glared at the two boys. 'That's just great!' she said, realising that they were on their own. 'So now what?'

'We wait until we're rescued. Stay put,' Gerard said. 'That's the rule.'

'Oh so *now* you're worried about rules,' Kumiko exclaimed.

'Don't you ever stop whingeing?' Gerard asked, tired of hearing what he should or shouldn't have done.

'Not when I'm about to die, no! We can't just sit here and wait. What if there's nobody left up there? What if they're all dead?'

As horrible as the thought might have been, Michael knew that Kumiko was right. They had no way of knowing what damage had been done by the tremor. They'd have to help themselves. He turned to Kumiko and pointed to the other end of the chamber. 'You take that end,' he said, and they began searching the shelter for a possible escape route.

The Jupiter Bar had been hard hit by the quake. The inner wall had partially collapsed, tables and chairs were upended and some of the ceiling had caved in. The room was in darkness except for the intermittent flashing of warning lights.

From out of the darkness, a tiny voice cried out for help.

After a moment, a voice replied. 'Anna,' Kingston spluttered.

'Are you still alive?' Anna asked.

'I'm not sure, how about you?'

'I think so.'

Slowly, from the jumble of tables and chairs in the centre of the room, Anna's hand emerged. She felt around the pile of rubble for Kingston.

Moments later, another hand emerged, followed by Kingston's head, his hair filled with dust and dirt. Kingston spat grit from his mouth in disgust.

The forlorn pair looked at each other, and when

Kingston held out his hand to Anna, she reached over and held onto him tightly. 'It's okay,' Kingston said bravely, 'We're going to be all right.' Anna smiled uneasily and the two friends sat silently, trapped in the rubble, unable to move.

A section of wall across the other side of the room crashed and shattered on the floor, sending dust whirling into the air. Kingston and Anna gripped each other even tighter as two light beams appeared from the gaping hole, slicing through the dust-filled air.

Kingston's eyes widened as the lights moved towards them. He sank back into the rubble. Images of big, black, scaly xenomorphs, creatures with rows of deadly fangs and mouths dripping with saliva rushed through his mind. Xenomorphs disturbed by the deep drilling, he thought!

'Don't move!' he whispered quietly to Anna. 'Aliens! Come to suck the blood out of us, drip by drip; drop by drop!' Kingston watched as the figures, wearing strange-looking suits, moved closer.

'Anyone there?' a voice rang out.

'Dad! Over here,' Anna shouted loudly, relieved to hear her father's voice. Karl and Sam rushed across the room and quickly began to clear away the rubble. 'We'll have you out of there in a minute,' Karl said, as he hauled Anna from the twisted mess of tables and chairs.

'Hey! Haven't you forgotten something?' Kingston protested from his tangled prison.

'Relax mate,' Sam replied. 'You're next.' Sam worked quickly and Kingston was soon freed.

'The others. Where are they?' Karl demanded. Kingston looked at Anna knowingly. If their friends weren't already in trouble, they were now! 'They went down the mines,' he mumbled.

'What?!' Sam exclaimed in horror. 'They could be trapped down there, they could be injured—anything!'

Karl reacted immediately. He scooped Anna up into

his arms and headed for the door. 'We'll have to organise a search team. Now!' he called to Sam and Kingston as they hurried after him. 'We've got to find them! Before the whole mine subsides!'

Michael and Kumiko continued their search of the emergency shelter. There had to be a way out. At one end, Michael prised open a battered looking storage bin. 'Here, take a look at this,' he said as he examined a collection of old ration containers.

'Compressed soya meal,' he said, reading from a label.

'Great. So now we can enjoy a three-course meal while we suffocate,' Kumiko replied sarcastically.

Gerard took a water container from Michael and opened its lid. He turned the container upside down onto his open hand and thick brown sludge oozed out. 'You want to drink that?'

Michael looked defeated. 'Come on. Out of the way,' Gerard said as he pushed past Michael. He flicked his multi-mate to light mode and started rummaging through the supplies. Hanging inside the bin were a collection of ropes, slings and protective hard hats.

'They must have used this place as a base, when they first surveyed the mines,' he guessed. As Michael moved closer to examine the gear, he felt, or at least he thought he did, a slight breeze on his face.

Snatching Gerard's multi-mate from him, he switched it to flame mode. Slowly, he moved the tool around the storage bin. Nothing. Then he moved it to one side and the small naked flame began to flicker. 'There!' he exclaimed. 'A draught! There's got to be an opening here somewhere.'

'Here, give me a hand,' he said to Gerard, and together they heaved the storage bin from the wall, revealing an air duct grid hewn into the rock face.

Gerard ripped the grate from its fitting. Picking up

the multi-mate, he switched it back to light mode, poked his head inside the shaft and shone the light upwards.

'It goes straight up,' he said, looking into the blackness, 'and straight down. Forever!' Gerard was in his element, excited by the challenge. He quickly collected rope and climbing gear from the storage bin.

'When I get to the top, I'll lower the rope,' he said, tying one end of the coil to his waist and slinging the rest over one shoulder.

Kumiko peered up and down at the blackness.

'You've got to be crazy! I can't climb that!' she exclaimed, terrified. 'This has got to be a nightmare!'

Gerard grinned cheekily to Michael. 'Wake her up when I get to the top,' he said, then clambered into the air shaft, spilling rocks and dust into the black void below.

Inside the shaft, pressing his body against the roughly hewn walls, Gerard inched his way upwards, carefully searching the rock face with his fingers for ledges and holes, anything that could give him a grip.

Painstakingly, he made his way up the narrow shaft, his heart pumping fear and adrenalin through his body. His fingers ached as he hauled himself upwards and sweat trickled down his forehead, stinging his eyes.

Not far above him, he could see that the shaft opened out into a larger cavity. Safety, he thought to himself. Just a few more metres. But as he reached for another foothold, the rock crumbled beneath him and Gerard felt his grip slipping. He gasped for air, desperately struggling to regain his footing. After an eternity of scratching and clawing, he managed to cling to the rock face like a spider. He hung there for a moment, pausing, his chest heaving, while he sucked air into his tight lungs.

From below he heard Michael's voice echoing up the shaft.

'Gerard! What's happening?

'It's all right. I'm fine,' he shouted back, slowly resuming his climb with renewed determination.

In the Jupiter Bar, order had been temporarily restored, with a makeshift medical facility set up among the rubble. Kingston and Anna sat propped on a table, while Helen gently applied a plaster to her son's forehead. 'There you go, good as new,' she said as she brushed Kingston's hair from his forehead affectionately. 'You're both very lucky.'

'Lucky!' Kingston replied indignantly. 'Half the roof caves in on top of us and we're lucky?'

Behind them, another stretcher was rushed into the room, bearing an injured colonist. 'Come on tough guy. I'm needed,' Helen said, and hurried to look after her patient. Sadly, Kingston watched her go. His mother was always needed, he thought to himself, not noticing Duffy, Sam and Karl bustling towards them.

'What were you lot doing down in the mines?' Duffy snarled in his ear, assuming Kingston and Anna were among the guilty culprits. They were children and, as far as Duffy was concerned, children were trouble! 'They're out of bounds!' he exclaimed.

'We weren't in the tunnels,' Kingston protested. 'We're innocent.'

'You know the rules,' Duffy growled.

Sam backed Kingston up. 'They weren't in the tunnels, George. It's the others,' he said, trying to remain calm. He leant down to Kingston and Anna and spoke softly. 'Now listen kids,' he said, 'Where was Michael going?'

Kingston looked at Anna, uncertain whether to volunteer the information. 'G-7,' he finally replied. 'They went to see the deep drilling.'

'Gerard took them,' Anna blurted out, not intending to get her brother in trouble.

'I'm going to kill that kid,' Karl muttered to himself. 'George, I'll need print-outs of the G-7 tunnel system. And Sam, you'd better find the blasting equipment.'

The three men hurried off. Kingston turned to Anna with a worried look. 'Blasting equipment? Haven't we had enough explosions? The whole mine could cave-in!'

Gerard could see the top of the shaft. Just a little bit further. Clawing his way, he slowly heaved himself out of the vertical shaft and collapsed into the small open chamber. He lay there for a moment trying to catch his breath. 'Beat that Faraday,' he muttered to himself. Then he clambered to his feet, took one end of the rope and secured it to his waist. He tossed the other end into the pitch black shaft. 'The rope. Coming down,' he yelled.

Michael watched as the rope slowly descended down the shaft, finally appearing at the open duct in the emergency shelter. He reached for the loose end and fed it around Kumiko's waist. 'Just do what Gerard says and you'll be fine,' he said trying to reassure her.

'So how come he's the expert all of a sudden?' Kumiko asked. Taking a deep breath to calm herself, she squeezed into the air shaft, hanging there for a moment, waiting for her eyes to adjust to the darkness. As the rock walls came into focus, she began inching herself awkwardly up the passageway. Climbing hand over hand up the rope, she pushed herself up with her feet, not daring to stop. Her hands burned from the coarse fibre of the rope and every muscle in her body screamed for her to stop.

'Are you all right?' she heard Michael call from below. Instinctively, Kumiko looked down the shaft to answer but had a sudden rush of vertigo. Quickly she lifted her head upwards, panting, unable to speak, trying to overcome her dizziness.

28

'Just don't look down,' Michael yelled.

'Then stop talking to me!' Kumiko gasped, trying to focus on her task. But as she slowly started climbing again, the shaft began to vibrate. Another earth tremor.

'Gerard!' she screamed, as her feet slipped from the rock face and she was left dangling from the rope, sliding slowly, relentlessly into the black void.

Kumiko's weight dragged Gerard towards the shaft opening. Holding on grimly to the rope, skating on his backside across the loose gravel, he slid uncontrollably towards the gaping hole. Desperately, he fought for a foothold on the floor of the cavern. He knew if he fell onto Kumiko, they would both fall—forever. Red-faced and fighting every inch of the way, Gerard finally managed to wedge himself against the rock face just inches from the vertical shaft. The rope jerked sharply, Gerard's face contorting as he strained to hold Kumiko's weight.

Kumiko's voice echoed out of the shaft. 'Get me out of here!'

'Press against the wall. Climb up with your feet,' Gerard replied, his voice quaking after his ordeal.

Kumiko tried desperately to follow Gerard's instructions. 'What am I? A trained gorilla!' she groaned, trying to contain her fear.

Michael's voice echoed up the shaft from below. 'You're doing fine,' he said reassuringly.

'Yeah? And who asked?!' Kumiko muttered to herself as she scrambled up the last few metres.

At the top of the shaft, Kumiko reached for Gerard's hand and he hauled her out of the shaft. She sprawled on the cavern floor like a sack of potatoes. She had made it. 'I gave up three weeks holiday, on Earth, on an island, on a beach—for this!' she gasped.

Inside the emergency shelter below, Michael turned away anxiously from the duct. He'd never been much good at physical things. That was Gerard's speciality. But the sight of yellow toxic gases billowing under the shelter door soon changed his mind. 'Get me out of here,' he shouted up the open shaft, as the stench of the sulphur dioxide filled his nostrils.

In the control room, the nerve centre of the colony, everyone was battling to bring the situation under control. Computer operators were struggling to maintain atmospheric pressure, technicians were trying to stabilise the few remaining intact domes, and rescue teams were ferrying injured personnel to the medical bay.

While the chaos raged around Kingston and Anna, waiting despondently for news of their friends, Professor Ingessol angrily confronted Duffy. 'I warned you,' he said. 'The deep drilling did this!' Duffy interrupted him: 'You've got no proof!' But Tatsuya, standing at the computer consoles, held out a new readout to Ingessol. 'Professor,' he said, 'The main access to the mines has collapsed. And we've got lava rising in the shafts!'

'What are they waiting for?' Kingston exclaimed to Anna. 'They could be dying down there!'

Behind them Karl and Sam hurried into the room. 'Professor! We need those print outs of the G-7 system,' Karl demanded. 'Without them we're blind.'

Ingessol looked hopefully towards Gerard's mother, Beth, the best of the colony's computer technicians. 'The data base is down. We're still trying. I've got atmospheric control, emergency lighting systems. Nothing else,' she replied anxiously.

'Communications to Earth? Can we get through?' Duffy asked.

'No chance. We're on our own,' Beth replied.

'I bet we could find them,' Kingston muttered to Anna.

'You stay put,' Beth warned, not wanting any more lost children.

Duffy leaned down towards the two children. 'Don't worry,' he said. 'If they're alive, we'll find them.' He patted Kingston on the head as he walked away.

'What a turkey!' Kingston exclaimed, as Duffy disappeared into the chaos.

'Sometimes,' Anna said thoughtfully as Professor Ingessol reappeared from another section of the room carrying a rolled-up collection of plasti-film. 'Original blueprints. G-7 included,' he announced, thrusting the diagrams at Karl. 'Sorry. It's the best I can do.'

Kingston and Anna watched closely as Karl unfurled the blueprints of the G-7 tunnel system. 'Here. We start from here,' Karl said to Sam and Tatsuya, pointing to the map. 'Sam, better find spare breathing gear, and first aid. We'll have to use the explosives. Blast through from here, G-6.'

Kingston turned to Anna. There's that word again, he thought.

Karl, Sam and Tatsuya hurried off to collect the necessary equipment, Kingston leaned over the blueprints and studied them carefully. 'There's got to be something we can do,' he said anxiously. 'What if they're not in G-7?'

In an empty mining tunnel of the old G-3 system, an air duct grate abruptly clattered to the rocky floor and Gerard dropped from the opening. Michael and Kumiko followed close behind.

Kumiko looked up and down the tunnel. 'Now which way Einstein?' she challenged Gerard.

'Give me a break,' he snarled, 'I just saved your neck.'

'Not yet you haven't,' Kumiko added, as she felt the ground beneath her beginning to vibrate.

Gerard felt it too. 'Come on, this way,' he said,

leading the others along the tunnel, the lights from their hard hats cutting a path through the dust-filled shaft. Gerard knew they had to be close now. They rushed up through the mine, moving as fast as they could in the semi-dark.

But rounding a corner in the tunnel, Gerard skidded to a halt. He thrust his arm out in front of Kumiko and Michael. 'Hold it!' he screamed, grasping Michael's shirtsleeve tightly.

'Now what?' Kumiko demanded. Gerard flopped back against the rock wall and pointed towards the floor. Kumiko looked down at Gerard's feet and saw the huge gaping hole. One of the down shafts had subsided, leaving a gaping crevice. Another step and the three of them would have disappeared into blackness.

'We're never going to get across there,' Michael exclaimed as he looked across the massive breach.

Kumiko looked back down the tunnel. 'We'll have to go back.'

'No. We're close. We've got to be close,' Gerard thought aloud. They couldn't give in now. He leant forwards and peered down into the black void below. The hole seemed to extend forever, right into the belly of the moon, flaring red intermittently far below with eerie rumbling sounds floating up towards them amid the smoke and gasses.

Gerard wiped the smoke from his eyes and looked across the gap. 'We go over. Across there,' he said, pointing to a narrow rock ledge that protruded from the tunnel wall and traversed the edge of the gap like a window ledge on the side of a skyscraper.

Kumiko looked at the ledge, then down into the void. She felt her stomach tighten and her head begin to spin. 'Are you totally deranged?' she objected. 'It's too narrow!'

Ignoring her, Gerard bent down and picked up a small stone. Concealing it in one of his hands, he held his clenched fists out to Michael.

'The rock goes first,' Gerard said, challenging Michael to make a choice. Michael hesitated. 'Go on, pick one wimp,' Gerard demanded.

Michael looked at the craggy ledge, then back at Gerard's fists. Hesitantly, he touched Gerard's left hand.

'What about me?' Kumiko asked, feeling a little annoyed that she'd been left out.

'I've only got two hands,' Gerard replied cheekily and slowly opened his left fist. It was empty. 'I guess I win,' he said as he opened his right fist to reveal the small stone. He tossed the rock into the void and listened. Nothing.

Gerard looked down into the crevice not really sure whether he had won or lost. Slowly, he climbed out onto the narrow ledge. Pressing his back up against the tunnel wall and inching his way along, he carefully tested his weight as he went. As he edged across the narrow pathway, a blast of hot air shot up and the ledge trembled beneath his feet. Gerard froze as the middle section of the ledge, a metre or two in length, collapsed and disappeared below.

Kumiko screamed with fright. 'Hang on Gerard,' she yelled above the loud rumbling.

'Hang onto what?' Gerard shouted back. Regaining his balance and standing on one side of the ledge, he stretched out with his foot, trying to reach the other side. 'Further, just a bit further,' Michael urged.

Gerard inched his foot further and further across the void. At last he felt his shoe make contact with the other side. But as he tried to transfer his weight, his foot slipped on the loose surface on the ledge.

'Gerard!' Kumiko screamed as he struggled to stay on the ledge.

'You'll have to come back,' Michael yelled.

'Quit telling me what to do, will you!' Gerard replied, finally steadying himself. He took a deep breath and again reached out with his foot. This time, stretching across the gap with a half lunge half jump, he hauled himself to the other side. He stood for a moment, hands on knees, settling his nerves, then turned back to the others with a confident grin.

'Piece of cake,' he grinned between his pounding heartbeats. 'Okay, she's next.'

Kumiko stared at the narrow ledge. '*She* does have a name,' she replied, fear rising within her.

'Sorry. Kumiko, you're next. Now hurry. That ledge isn't going to last too much longer.'

'Kumi. My father calls me Kumiko.' Stepping onto the ledge, Kumiko inched her way towards the gap, eyes straight ahead, not daring to look down. Again a blast of smoke-filled air surged up from the cavity below. Kumiko wedged her back hard up against the rock wall.

Michael reached out and took hold of her hand. 'What do you think you're doing?' Kumiko asked, pulling her hand free.

'For safety.'

'Well don't!' Kumiko edged her way across the ledge and stopped at the edge of the void. She looked down and felt the hot air rushing up through the crevice.

'Grab my hand,' Gerard yelled, reaching out towards her. As the ledge began to shake again, Kumiko stepped back. Instinctively, she grabbed Michael by the hand to help her balance, and he smiled.

'What's your problem?' Kumiko snapped, embarrassed she was now holding his hand so tightly.

'Nothing,' Michael said. 'Use me for balance. Reach out.' And using Michael as an anchor, she leaned out again for Gerard's hand.

'Just a bit further,' Michael yelled. 'Stretch!'

Kumiko reached for Gerard's outstretched hand, straining as far as she could without losing her balance, but remaining inches from his grasp. 'It's hopeless,' she said, 'You'll have to go without us.'

'No! I'm not leaving here without you,' Gerard replied stubbornly. He was not about to abandon them, having dragged them there in the first place.

'She's right,' Michael said. 'Get out of here!'

'No way!' Gerard looked back along the tunnel, hesitantly.

Michael was getting desperate: 'Gerard, you're wasting time. Go. Go now! Get help!'

As the rescue team prepared to blast its way through G-6, Kingston and Anna pawed over the blueprints of the mines. 'The old G-3 tunnel system, there, they join into G-7!' Kingston muttered as he traced his finger along the map. He knew the area, having spent many an hour exploring and investigating the shafts and air ducts, though it had been some time since he'd visited this part of the colony. 'Look. Here. The old system, the shelter. Maybe they went ... ' Kingston thought for a moment, searching his memory for detail, then looked up at Anna. 'There's a way out ... There! 'That's where they are,' he said, tapping his finger on the map. 'The tunnel rat strikes again!'

'Shouldn't we tell someone?' Anna asked as she looked around the empty room. Kingston removed a piece of bubble gum from his mouth and stuck it to the map. 'No need, no time' he said with a grin and together they sprinted from the room and made their way into the old tunnel system.

When they reached a section that had partially collapsed, Kingston stopped and examined the wreckage. He could see through a narrow opening that the tunnel up ahead was still intact. They scrambled on all fours through the dust and rubble and continued their search.

'You sure you know what you're doing?' Anna asked.

'Don't worry, I'll look after you.'

'And who's going to look after you?' Anna asked, as they headed further into the tunnel system. Kingston ignored the comment and hurried along the dim tunnel. 'Come on, they can't be too much further.'

Michael and Kumiko stood on one side of the void, a sense of stalemate in the air. Michael realised that they were not going to make it. Neither of them were as tall as Gerard. They didn't have his strength or his reach to make it across the gap in the ledge. 'Gerard! Will you get out of here! You can't wait any longer,' Michael exclaimed, realising Gerard was their only hope.

'All right, all right!' Gerard conceded.

Suddenly they heard a voice further up the tunnel. 'Michael! Gerard!'

Gerard wheeled around to see two lights moving towards him. Finally! Rescue! 'Down here!' he yelled excitedly. The lights moved closer, then from out of the darkness, Kingston and Anna appeared.

'It's the rodent,' Gerard yelled back to Michael and Kumiko.

'Kingston? Where are the others?' Michael asked.

'It's only us,' Anna yelled happily, pleased to see her friends were safe. 'We've come to save you.'

Kumiko stared across the void at her two rescuers. 'Great! A cavalry of two.'

Gerard sprang into action. 'Right, grab hold will you.' Offering his hand to Kingston, the three of them linked arms to form a human chain, and with Kingston and Anna acting as anchor, Gerard reached out to grab Kumiko's outstretched hand. Quickly, he hauled her across to safety.

'So what's next,' Kumiko said with relief. 'Abseiling the Himalayas?'

'Come on Faraday, you're next,' ordered Gerard.

'All right, don't rush me,' Michael said as he peered into the abyss below.

Gerard leaned out towards Michael, his body poised over the gap. As Michael edged closer to Gerard's hand, another tremor struck and a blast of hot air came rushing up through the hole. Michael's eyes burned from the smoke and gas.

'Don't look down, look straight ahead,' Gerard called to him. 'You'll have to jump. Aim for my hand.'

'Will you stop telling me what to do,' Michael said defensively.

Stepping back a little, he took a deep breath and lunged for Gerard's outstretched hand. For a moment, Michael thought he was falling down and away, through the suffocatingly hot air, until he felt Gerard's firm hand grab him and haul him to safety. The two of them sprawled onto the tunnel floor.

'Couldn't do it the easy way, could you?' Gerard smirked.

'Thanks muscle head,' Michael replied gratefully.

Kumiko turned to Kingston. 'Can you get us out of here?' Kingston needed no prompting. He was on his feet and leading the others quickly up the tunnel to safety as another loud rumble filled the air.

Michael looked back along the tunnel to see bits of rock subsiding into the void and collapsing over their tracks. He hoped that it would hold for just a little longer. They raced along the tunnel, Kingston and Anna leading the way, and finally clambered from an air duct into the entrance chamber to the tunnel system.

The children dropped to the floor, relieved to be safe, out of the dusty tunnels and away from the vile stench of sulphur dioxide. Michael looked across at Kumiko with an exhausted grin. 'Had enough excitement for one day?'

'Plenty,' Kumiko replied, returning the grin.

Gerard hugged Anna warmly, embarrassing both of

them, then slapped Kingston on the shoulder. 'Thanks rodent, you saved our necks,' he said gratefully.

'I wouldn't bet on it,' Kingston replied with a grimace as he turned to see Sam, Karl, Duffy and Tatsuya hurrying down the corridor towards them.

CHAPTER THREE

LIFE BOAT

F ortunately for the children, their parents were so relieved to find them alive, they were let off lightly. Duffy, however, was not so forgiving. He could always find time to reprimand the children, and he gave them a stern lecture as they made their way back to the living area.

Once the mines had been sealed, the colonists wasted no time systematically checking the remaining above-ground domes. The damage was extensive and they worked frantically to salvage stores and equipment, sealing off damaged areas as they went to prevent dangerous air leaks.

The industrial sector, the ore processing plant, the furnaces and metal extraction plant had been destroyed. A large underground fissure had split the foundations and ruptured the superstructure of their protective domes. Most of the living quarters were intact, but off limits to the children until thorough safety checks could be completed.

The children were told to remain in the Jupiter Bar. It had been converted into a centre of operations and colonists busily stored supplies, patched up those injured, monitored safety checks and collated damage reports.

Duffy's voice boomed out over the static-filled intercom. 'Attention all personnel,' he said. 'Now that the emergency situation has been stabilised, all efforts will be made to get the colony fully operational as soon as possible. Until then all personnel should confine themselves to designated safe areas.'

In one corner of the room, Kingston and Anna popped up from behind a pile of boxes, relieved to hear the crisis was under control, albeit tenuously. 'You sure this is all right?' Anna whispered nervously as they surveyed the chaos.

Kingston grinned cheekily at her. 'They're all busy, can you think of a better time?' Satisfied no-one was watching them, they darted across the room, ducking behind boxes, heading towards the food reconstitution machines. 'Uh-oh! Trouble!', Kingston said, hauling Anna down behind a bench to avoid Karl and Tatsuya.

'I want to know what that lava does, even before it does it,' Karl said, as Tatsuya began to set up a pressure sensor designed to measure shockwaves from seismic disturbances. He set the thin, metre-high cylinder on the ground, its base sealed by black metal. At the top, a clear plasti-tube encased a collection of circuits and lights, which flickered on and off.

'With this I can monitor any increase in pressure in the lava chamber,' Tatsuya said, flicking a switch on top of the sensor, which immediately began to pulse an intermittent signal.

As Karl and Tatsuya continued towards the exit, Kingston reappeared, raced across to the milkshake machine and dusted it off. 'Lime or chocolate?' he asked Anna.

'Both,' she said, hungrily.

Kingston beamed with delight as he spooned bright green lime concentrate into the milkshake maker. While it whirred vigorously, Anna stood by his side and added chocolate essence to the mixture.

'That's disgusting,' Kingston said.

'I know,' Anna agreed with a grin, checking the mixture. 'That's enough,' she said, as Duffy's voice crackled over the intercom, announcing new salvage team rosters.

As Duffy's voice died away, Kumiko hurried along a

deserted corridor, away from the Jupiter Bar. With Michael following reluctantly, she checked left and right, then crawled under a bright yellow safety barrier and headed towards the living quarters.

'Will you hurry up,' Kumiko snapped impatiently.

But Michael wasn't happy. The living quarters still hadn't been declared safe after the crisis and he knew they'd be in real trouble if they were caught, not to mention the danger they could be walking into. 'I don't know what's so important about a dumb computer,' he protested as they rushed down the corridor.

'It just is, all right,' Kumiko snapped. 'If you don't want to help. Fine. I'll get it myself.'

'But the safety checks ... ?'

'So who's going to know?' Kumiko replied, rounding a corner and slamming head long into Duffy.

'Who indeed?!' he sneered.

'Mr Duffy, how'd you get here?' Kumiko babbled, caught off guard.

Duffy glowered at them. 'Where you kids are concerned, I'm omnipresent!' he warned, herding them back towards the Jupiter Bar. 'Now explain yourselves. What were you doing down there?'

'I have to get to my quarters,' Kumiko replied.

'You stay put! The pair of you! What's the point of having rules if you totally disregard them?' Duffy said angrily. 'It's for your own safety!'

'But I have to get my computer,' Kumiko persisted.

'I don't give a flea's freckle about your computer!' Duffy shouted, before being distracted by the noises erupting from the milkshake maker on the other side of the Jupiter Bar. Wheeling around, he spotted Kingston and Anna fiddling with the machine. 'You pair! What do you think *you're* doing?'

Kingston immediately leant down and flicked the 'off' switch. Nothing. The machine refused to respond. Instead it began to shake and splutter. He tried the switch again, flicking it back and forth as the noise grew louder.

'I didn't touch it,' he protested to Duffy, throwing his hands in the air, trying to look innocent.

'We just tried to stop it,' Anna added.

'Yeah. It was a power surge.'

Storming across the room, Duffy jostled Kingston and Anna away from the gurgling machine. As he bent down to disconnect it, the machine gave one final loud groan. The inlet pipe exploded and Duffy was showered with the thick green-brown milky sludge. Kingston and Anna looked across to Kumiko and Michael, trying not to laugh as sludge dripped slowly down Duffy's startled face.

Duffy never liked to look foolish, especially in front of the children, but covered in green-brown sludge he couldn't avoid it. As he wiped the last of it from his face and hair, he glared at the guilty faces lined up before him. 'Now, perhaps one of you might like to enlighten me. Are you just stupid, or are you being deliberately disobedient?' he demanded angrily.

Kingston leant across to Michael. 'I'll take stupid,' he whispered cheekily from the corner of his mouth. His timing was poor.

'That's enough!' Duffy barked. 'You mob are nothing but a liability, a non-productive unit, a negative contribution. I will not be disobeyed. Is that clear?' He leaned forwards, waiting for a response.

The children shuffled uneasily. Duffy's outbursts were never enjoyable. 'Maybe if we could help instead of being locked away somewhere,' Kumiko suggested tentatively.

'Yeah. If we were helping, at least you would know where we are!' Kingston added enthusiastically, sensing that Kumiko was on to something.

Moments later, Kingston wondered how he could have been so wrong. Unhappily, he surveyed the mountain of medical supplies Duffy had ordered them to stack and itemise.

'If we were helping, at least you'd know where we are,' Michael imitated Kingston sarcastically, dumping a case of surgical dressing on makeshift shelving.

'It wasn't my fault,' Kingston protested, half-heartedly stacking bandages while Kumiko scribbled the details onto a plasti-sheet inventory.

'This would be a whole lot easier if I had my computer,' she suggested slyly.

'Don't even think about it,' Michael replied.

Kumiko, as usual, refused to listen. She slammed her checklist down and headed towards the door.

'She is so stubborn!' Michael muttered under his breath as Kumiko disappeared into the corridor. 'Cover for us,' he said to Kingston.

'That's not fair! Why is it always us having to cover for you?' he moaned, but Michael had already gone.

Kumiko hurried towards her living quarters, determined to retrieve her computer. Keeping a watchful eye out for Duffy, she made her way down the central stairwell, into a long corridor, dodging rubble and salvaged supplies that had been stacked haphazardly in the passageway. As she moved further into the restricted zone searching for a familiar landmark, she began to feel uneasy, spooked by the eerie quiet.

She finally spotted a familiar entrance-way. As she sprinted towards it, she noticed Duffy up ahead, patrolling the corridor, issuing commands to a passing salvage crew. She was cornered. Suddenly a hand reached out from an adjoining corridor and pulled her out of sight behind a pile of crates.

'I know what I'm doing,' Kumiko protested indignantly, as she ducked down next to Michael.

'So how come you're going the wrong way?' Michael replied. 'The living quarters are this way.' Kumiko squirmed awkwardly—she hated being wrong. 'Come on. We go straight there and straight back. And you do as I say,' Michael whispered, checking to see that Duffy was at a safe distance.

As they were about to sneak off, they were distracted by a second, more distressed voice, echoing down the corridor. Michael and Kumiko peered out from their hiding place to see Professor Ingessol rushing up the corridor to confront Duffy.

'George, your announcement. Now that the colony is stabilised. What are you talking about?' Ingessol asked incredulously.

'Exactly what I said.'

'But the emergency isn't over! The colony's finished!'

Duffy leaned menacingly towards Ingessol, lowering his voice. 'Now you listen to me,' he warned. 'I don't need you creating panic with your hare-brained predictions. I'll have this colony fully functional within the next 48 hours.'

'But we don't have 48 hours,' Ingessol argued. 'We must evacuate. Immediately! To KL5!'

Michael turned to Kumiko, mystified by the Professor's words. Space station KL5 hadn't been used in more than 20 years!

Once safely back in the Jupiter Bar, Michael explained KL5 to Kumiko.

'It was transported from earth, bit by bit, and pieced together in orbit above Io. It was used as a base. The engineers used it until the colony was finished. Then the thing was gutted—machinery, equipment, everything.'

'KL5's nothing but a derelict old hulk,' Gerard added, nonplussed by Ingessol's suggestion. 'The place is a floating junk yard!'

'Evacuate to a floating tin can or be incinerated! Some choice,' said Kingston.

'Relax! We won't be going anywhere. Ingessol's out of his mind,' Gerard snorted in disbelief.

'He built it. He should know what he's talking

about,' Michael argued. 'He must have some idea how to restore it.'

Gerard leaned back in his chair, shaking his head. 'All we have to do is sit tight. Wait to be rescued,' he said authoritatively.

'Rescued from where? Nobody knows we're in trouble,' Kumiko chipped in, dumbfounded by Gerard's oversight. 'Communications to Earth have been destroyed, and it'll be six months before the supply ship arrives. If Ingessol's right, none of us will survive that long. If the lava doesn't get us, we'll run out of supplies.'

'Great, so now we'll starve to death,' Kingston moaned, flopping down in a chair. 'That's it! We're history!'

The children continued to argue among themselves until a distant explosion produced an instant silence. Kumiko jumped up nervously. 'Relax. That's ours. They're setting off mining charges to redirect the lava flow,' Gerard said comfortingly.

'But if everything's so stable, why are they blowing up the lava?' Kumiko asked.

Gerard had no reply.

'Oh great! So now we're going to be fossilised. A hundred years from now, some miner will dig us up and shove us in a museum. Here lies Kingston Lewis: Lava man from hell!' Kingston exclaimed dramatically.

'Shut up rodent,' Gerard snapped, then turned to Michael. 'All right, if Ingessol's so smart, what are we supposed to live on up there? Space dust?'

Michael shrugged. He couldn't provide an answer, but he felt sure the Professor would know how to revive the old space station and make it habitable once again. He went in search of the Professor and found him wandering through the damaged hydroponics lab, sadly inspecting the broken light fittings, upturned plant beds and cracked algae tanks, their contents spilled on the floor.

45

'Not a pretty sight is it? I used to love this place,' he said forlornly to Michael. 'Reminded me of Earth.'

'Professor, just say for instance,' Michael said, trying to find the right words. 'Well, if we do have to evacuate, and if we did get to KL5 ... ?'

Surprised by the mention of KL5, Professor Ingessol wheeled around. 'Kumi and I, we overheard you and Duffy,' Michael apologised. 'Professor, what's going on? Nobody'll tell us anything.'

Ingessol placed a hand on Michael's shoulder. 'It's our only chance, Michael. Io is finished. We've punctured the lava chamber below the colony, and all that pressure has to go somewhere. The space station is our only hope.'

'But I thought the place was gutted. How would we survive?'

Ingessol pulled his white hair back from his face and began to pace back and forth, deep in thought. 'That's easy. Well maybe not easy, but I've thought it through. There are ways. We use our brains, we improvise, we invent. KL5 may be old but it's not useless.' The Professor stopped in his tracks and turned to Michael. 'We have to try Michael. We have to convince the others.'

Sadly, Michael looked around the devastated hydro lab. He desperately wanted to help the Professor but he knew Duffy and the other colonists would be quick to dismiss him as a crank. They would never agree to the plan. If only he could get his father to listen, it would be a start. Michael suddenly brightened. His father was the key. Perhaps there was something he could do, but he would need Kumiko's help. They had to get proof.

Michael found Kumiko in the Jupiter Bar and quickly outlined his idea. If they could find the latest figures from the pressure sensors, they might be able to convince his father to listen to Professor Ingessol.

'Duffy's office,' Kumiko grinned. 'We can access the data from his computer.'

While Michael went to locate his father, Kumiko enlisted the help of Gerard and Kingston. They'd keep watch outside Duffy's office, while she hacked into the computer.

Sliding behind Duffy's desk, Kumiko quickly and efficiently began keying commands into the computer console. As she worked, Gerard poked his head through the door. 'Will you hurry up! If Duffy catches us, we're dead,' he whispered anxiously.

'Don't interrupt. Just a few more minutes,' Kumiko said as she continued to collect data from the computer's memory banks. 'You just keep watch.'

Outside Duffy's office, Kingston paced about anxiously. 'We're going to get caught, I just know it,' he muttered to himself as Gerard reappeared. 'Do you have to be so obvious?' Gerard said, glancing about to see if anyone was coming. 'Why don't you just hold up a sign that says guilty?!'

'Yeah right. And you can have one that says idiot!' Kingston quipped.

'You're dead!' Gerard said, grabbing Kingston by the shirt front and hauling him threateningly to within an inch of his nose.

Kingston shook his head slightly. 'Uh-uh, we're both dead!' he croaked, staring across the room. Over Gerard's shoulder he could see Duffy returning to his office.

Kumiko retrieved the info-file from the computer and quickly turned the machine off, taking care that everything was returned to its rightful place. Getting up from Duffy's chair, she moved towards the door, then remembering the medical supply inventory, took it from her pocket and placed it on Duffy's desk.

Outside the office, Duffy cornered Gerard and Kingston. 'I smell guilt,' he sniffed in an accusing tone.

'It's not us,' Kingston said, trying to sound innocent but making Duffy more suspicious. Turning abruptly towards his office, he bumped into Kumiko at the door.

'And what do you think you're doing in there?' he demanded.

'Nothing. I mean, the inventory for the medical supplies. I left it on your desk,' Kumiko replied, surreptitiously sliding the info-file into her pocket.

Duffy glared at the children, certain that they were up to something. 'Make yourselves scarce. The lot of you. And stay out of my face!' he warned, before disappearing into his office.

'Did you have any trouble?' Michael asked, as they headed to the departure bay.

'Nothing we couldn't handle,' Kumiko replied confidently, stepping through the narrow access tube that connected to the space tug.

Sam was working in the tug's cockpit when Michael and Kumiko interrupted him. Kumiko set up her computer and slid in the info-file. 'The latest figures from the pressure sensors,' she said as she keyed commands into the computer. 'The pressure in the lava chamber, it's definitely increasing.'

'Dad, the Professor *could* be right. Don't you think you should hear him out?' Michael said, as Kumiko keyed through the latest figures collated by her father.

Sam gazed at the records that scrolled down the screen. 'Michael, I'm a pilot, not a scientist,' he replied, dazed by the configurations.

'You could at least take the Professor to KL5 and let him check it out. What have you got to lose?' Michael implored.

'I'm sure Duffy knows what he's doing,' Sam said, returning to his repairs on the space tug.

'Just like he did when he began the deep-drilling program. Professor Ingessol was right then, what if he's right now?'

Sam looked at his son for a moment then glanced at the computer screen one more time. 'So where's your Professor now?' he asked with a resigned smile.

Michael looked across to Kumiko and grinned. Success.

Wasting no time, the pair quickly found Professor Ingessol and rushed him to the space tug.

'I don't know how you managed it,' Ingessol said as they arrived at the access tube.

'Don't ask,' Michael replied, as Sam appeared through the tube and ushered Ingessol towards the tug. Michael and Kumiko followed but Sam turned to block their way. 'Where do you think you're going?' he asked.

'To KL5. We're coming with you,' Michael replied.

'Not this time, you're not.' Before Michael could protest, Sam disappeared through the access tube and into the space tug.

'It's not fair,' Kumiko complained. 'We do all the ground work and get left behind.' Quickly checking to see if anyone was watching, she moved furtively into the access tube. 'Come on,' she said, hurrying towards the tug door.

'We can't,' Michael exclaimed. 'Besides, you hate flying.'

'Not as much as I hate being treated like a kid.' Kumiko looked at Michael pleadingly. 'Aren't you even curious? Don't you want to see the place for yourself?'

'Of course! But I don't want to die in the process. Dad will murder us!'

'Then you stay! But I'm going,' Kumiko said stubbornly, as she marched off.

Inside the cramped cockpit, Sam flicked through the controls, preparing for take off. Ingessol was seated beside him, beaming. 'You won't regret this Sam,' he said, 'You're doing the right thing.'

'Let me be the judge about that. Duffy's going to implode when he hears this,' Sam said.

As the tug swung out over the colony and began

its journey to the derelict space station, Kingston and Anna led Gerard into the control room on Io. 'I can't find them anywhere. I tell you, they've gone to KL5!' Kingston babbled excitedly.

Gerard looked at him disbelievingly. 'Faraday? He wouldn't dare,' he snarled, peeved that if Michael had dared, *he'd* been left behind.

At the control centre's computer console, Beth turned to one of the technical assistants. 'Better get Duffy down here. Now!' she demanded urgently. 'We've got an unauthorised take off.'

'See. Told you,' Anna whispered to Gerard as they watched the assistant rush from the control room. 'They're on board the space tug.'

Sam expertly manoeuvred the tug towards KL5, when a warning light began to bleep ominously in front of him.

'What is it?' Ingessol asked with a worried look.

'The scanners. Something in the cargo pod,' Sam answered, flicking switches in front of him. On the control panel, a small video mesh flickered, revealing Michael and Kumiko.

'I don't believe this,' he muttered to Ingessol. 'I want to see you both in the cockpit. Now!' he barked through the intercom.

The stowaways unbuckled themselves, clambered apprehensively into the cockpit and stood, eyes downcast, while Sam reprimanded them for their blatant disobedience. 'This time, you've gone too far,' he said, glaring at Michael. 'I thought I could trust you.'

'It was my idea,' Kumiko said in his defence. 'Michael was dead against it.'

'Hmm, well, I'll deal with you later,' Sam said, returning to the controls, manoeuvring the tug towards the giant station.

Michael and Kumiko gazed at the station as it

loomed towards them. It was dark and foreboding—a giant, rambling collection of mismatched components, joined together at odd shapes and angles. At the top, was a huge, egg-shaped dome, trailing below to a long tail-like structure held together by a network of pipes and conduits.

'Time to activate the boarding tube,' Ingessol said, seeing KL5's docking port rise up beside him.

As the tug docked with the station, Sam flicked a series of switches to activate the boarding tube. No response. He ran through the sequence again. Still no response. The boarding tube remained stubbornly closed.

'Something's wrong,' Ingessol muttered aloud, 'When we shut the station down, we left this access point open. Somehow everything's been shut down.'

'Then how do we get inside?' Michael asked, turning to his father. 'It's sealed as tight as a drum.' Professor Ingessol thought to himself, searching for an answer.

'We've got to get to the control centre. The central computer. It's the only way to reactivate the power supply.' Again he went quiet, tapping his fingers rhythmically on the control panel. 'Rubbish,' he muttered quietly, then became more animated. 'Rubbish. Garbage!' he exclaimed. 'That's our answer.'

Sam looked confused, unable to find a connection. 'Sam, the waste disposal port. That's our way in,' Ingessol said. 'It's small, too small for you or I but—' he turned to look at Kumiko and Michael.

Sam immediately threw up his hands in protest.

'Sam, there are other lives at stake,' Ingessol pleaded.

Huddled together in the control room on Io, Kingston, Gerard and Anna anxiously waited for news and watched a red-faced Duffy lean into the transmitter, trying to raise the space tug.

Suddenly Karl, Tatsuya and Akiko burst into the control centre with news nobody wanted to hear. The crisis had worsened.

'The lava, it's heading straight for the colony!' Tatsuya shouted breathlessly as Duffy wheeled around from the transmitter. 'All the sensors give the same readings.'

'The charges didn't work. The fissure is still growing,' Karl continued, trying to get Duffy to see reason. 'We have to evacuate! This whole place is going to crack like an egg.'

Duffy stared at the colonists, assessing the situation, unsure what action to take. 'Ingessol was right,' Karl added forcefully. 'The space station, it's our only chance.'

Duffy spun around and leaned into the transmitter with sudden urgency. 'Professor! Sam! Come in space tug. It's vital you get aboard KL5!' he shouted.

'So now he panics!' Kingston whispered to Anna. 'When it's probably too late!'

With the space tug securely coupled to the waste disposal port on KL5, Sam acknowledged Duffy's message then turned to help Michael and Kumiko prepare for their trek inside the space station.

They climbed into pressure suits and donned helmets with miniature cameras mounted in their crowns. Ingessol quickly tested the cameras and the charge levels on the suits' power packs.

'Power's very low,' he muttered to Sam. 'Ten minutes, no more.'

'Right! At the first sign of trouble, I'll hit the recall button and you get back here. And no arguments,' Sam insisted as he activated the access tube door. It swung open to reveal the narrow tube that led into KL5's garbage disposal port.

Professor Ingessol handed Michael a multi-mate

with a map showing the way to the station's control room. 'Remember, you've got ten minutes. No more.' Michael looked down at his watch and nodded. Giving his father a last look, he heaved himself inside the narrow opening.

As Kumiko stepped up to the opening, Ingessol placed a supportive hand on her shoulder. 'Just follow my instructions and you'll be fine,' he said. 'Bring the central computer on line and it'll automatically initiate basic life-support systems.' Kumiko nodded and followed Michael through the opening. With an ominous clunk, Sam secured the hatchway after them.

Inside the access tube, Michael and Kumiko crawled belly down until they reached the garbage hatch. Michael reached out and heaved on the lever to activate the door. It refused to budge. Michael's voice crackled over Kumiko's headset. 'It's stuck,' he said as he heaved on the lever once more. This time it gave a little, and slowly, heavily, the hatchway creaked opened. Michael peered through, deep into the bowels of KL5.

'What can you see?' Kumiko asked.

Michael squinted at the space beyond. 'Nothing. It's pitch black in there.'

One after the other, they squeezed through the opening and entered KL5. They looked about them at the ghostly environment, their helmet lights barely piercing the black gloom. They were standing in what appeared to be a garbage compacting room, their lights creating ghoulish shadows as they caught the idle machinery that jutted out at all angles.

Following a walkway that angled its way around the machinery, they made their way through an open hatchway, into a small chamber beyond, and onto a set of stairs that led into the heart of the station. They moved down the stairs, silenced by the unfamiliar surroundings.

Kumiko shivered. Even through the pressure suit, she felt the icy chill of the frozen station. 'One hundred and twelve below,' she said, checking the temperature gauge on her pressure suit controls. 'Keep moving,' Michael replied, worrying that they'd already wasted too much time.

Arriving at the bottom of the stairs, they rounded a corner of the dark corridor, then came to an abrupt halt. Frosted metal blocked their way. Dead end! Michael quickly re-examined Ingessol's diagram. 'This has to be right,' he said with concern. They'd followed his instructions to the letter.

'We'll have to go back,' he said, realising that their ten minutes was diminishing quickly. He looked down at the timer on his power pack. 'Five minutes left,' he said. 'Half way. We've got no choice.'

'No!' Kumiko replied, pointing to a line of computer cables that ran back along the corridor. 'Maybe *they'll* lead us to the central control room.'

'It's too risky,' Michael said.

'But we have to try,' Kumiko insisted, and charged down the corridor, following the twists and turns of the cables.

At the end of the passageway they found a closed door, the cables disappearing through the wall above it. On the door was a symbol indicating entry was restricted. Kumiko looked at Michael, unsure how to proceed. Cautiously, Michael reached for the manual override lever but it wouldn't budge. Kumiko joined him and together they tried again, applying all their strength to the lever. It gave way and the door swung open slowly, a rush of air issuing from the chamber beyond. Michael checked his power pack. The pointer was dropping rapidly towards the red line and zero charge.

Anxiously, Sam and Professor Ingessol watched their video mesh as Michael and Kumiko moved through the large, desolate chamber.

'Three minutes,' Ingessol noted as he checked the time again.

'That map of yours had better be accurate,' Sam warned him. The Professor smiled weakly.

'How long since you've been inside that old relic?' Sam asked.

'Seven, maybe eight years,' Ingessol replied apologetically.

Sam looked at him incredulously. 'That's it! I'm recalling them,' he said and reached for the recall switch. But before he could activate it, a loud blast of static filled the speakers, and Michael and Kumiko disappeared from the screen.

Sam tried frantically to restore contact but Ingessol gently stopped him. 'It's no use Sam. The control room is electronically protected. The interference is coming from it. They're on their own now.' Sam slumped in despair.

Inside KL5's cavernous control room, Michael and Kumiko made their way to the main desk, searching for the central computer controls. Time was running out. Michael checked his time-piece and gestured to Kumiko. Only two minutes.

Kumiko nodded. She moved quickly to the main computer console and began searching through the electronic parts littering the desk.

As she found the necessary components and checked out the mainframe controls, Michael noticed a warning light on her helmet beginning to flash. Her power pack had reached critical levels. If they didn't head back, her suit would close down and she'd freeze to death. He grabbed her by the arm and tried to pull her towards the door. Kumiko shook her head, determined to stay.

She knew that even if they were to turn back now, they'd never make it to the space tug in time. Instead she had to access the mainframe, get the atmospheric generators working, and isolate the control room.

Immediately! If the power was restored, heat and air would be pumped into it first.

Kumiko looked at the console in front of her. Everything was as Ingessol had described it. In front of her were three exposed circuit boards protruding from the machine.

Quickly, she keyed commands into the main terminal. Then she slid the first of the circuit boards into place. Michael looked on anxiously, hoping that Kumiko knew what she was doing. He watched as she slid the second of the boards into its slot, then the third. She waited for a moment. No response. Nothing.

Kumiko turned back to the console and removed the third circuit board, keyed more commands into the computer console, then slammed the circuit board back into its slot. Still nothing. In desperation, she thumped the circuit with her fist. Almost magically, a single light flickered, then another, then another.

Michael looked over to Kumiko. She turned to him and smiled as the console in front of them came to life. Overhead, a bank of lights lit up the darkness. Deep within the bowels of the station, they heard the generators and air turbines begin to groan. They could feel the warm air being pumped into the room. Despite their clumsy suits, they both did a little jig of joy, leaping into the air and throwing their arms around each other.

Sam and the Professor watched with relief as the huge solar sails of the space station began to unfurl like gigantic butterfly wings, opening out to the solar system, soaking up its radiation and charging the station's power systems.

Anna and Kingston and everyone in the control room on Io cheered with delight as the video mesh started picking up images of Michael and Kumiko dancing and hugging each other.

Grinning from ear to ear, Kingston turned to Duffy. 'Told you they could do it,' he said cheekily. 'Now that's what I'd call a productive unit. A positive contribution. A force to be reckoned with. Don't you think?'

Duffy smiled weakly and squirmed as he looked back at the video mesh.

They could see Michael and Kumiko in KL5's control room, removing their helmets and breathing in the rush of warm air as it coursed through the room. It smelt stale, musky and dank, and reeked of old machinery, but to Michael just at that moment it was sweeter than he imagined any air on an Earth beach.

Kumiko grinned triumphantly and a much relieved Michael flopped down on a nearby seat. 'Piece of cake,' he sighed heavily.

Together they looked about the vast, mysterious control room, knowing for the time being at least the colony was out of danger. KL5 had come alive.

CHAPTER FOUR

IN THE NICK OF TIME

L ocked in orbit above the crumbling colony, space station KL5 floated in space, its solar sails spread wide. Under Professor Ingessol's instructions, a handful of technicians began the exhaustive procedure of making the giant satellite habitable.

Under Duffy's command, plans for evacuation of the unstable colony were also being put into action. The tug, its thrusters glowing red, did shuttle run after run, while the colonists brought boxes and crates filled with salvaged equipment and supplies to the departure bay, ready for shipping to the space station.

Helen rushed into the busy bay with Kingston and Anna in tow. 'But I don't want to go first,' Kingston protested loudly. 'Guinea pigs! That's what we are. Research rats! I want to stay with you.'

'It's too dangerous here,' Helen said decisively, then gestured to Kumiko who was packing scientific equipment into nearby crates.

'Kumi. She'll look after you.'

Kumiko nodded. 'Sure. I'll put them to work.'

'Yeah right. Slave labour,' Kingston moaned.

Helen bent down, gathered Kingston and Anna in her arms, gave them a parting hug then hurried from the room to prepare the medical facilities for transport.

In the hydroponics laboratory, Michael was busy gathering and packing equipment and plant stocks while Gerard stood at the doorway complaining to his father. If there was one thing Gerard hated, it was gardening and he was riled at being commandeered to rescue a bunch of boring plants.

'Gardening's for wimps,' he said. 'I want to help you in the mines.'

'Don't argue. Just pitch in and help Michael,' Karl insisted, turning to leave. 'For your old man, all right?' Gerard nodded resignedly and strode across to Michael.

'Well you got what you wanted Faraday, I've been reduced to a common gardener,' he snarled, as he bent down and brutally wrenched a berry plant from its bedding and tossed it into a box. 'Bunch of dumb, mouldy plants! Don't see the point.'

'We're going to need them to survive,' Michael said assertively. 'Professor Ingessol reckons ... '

Gerard cut him off. 'Yeah, yeah. The man's a living legend. I've heard it all before,' he said sarcastically. 'He'll probably kill us all!'

Ignoring Gerard's barb, Michael continued to carefully pack his plants and organic nutrients, ready for shipment. As quickly as he filled his containers, they were ferried off to the departure bay, where Kingston sat perched on a pile of crates, a deep frown furrowing his brow.

He and Anna were surveying the bustling activity as colonists came and went, dumping supplies, then setting off in search of more. 'I bet nobody remembers to collect our stuff,' he said, worried that his precious belongings would be sacrificed to the molten lava.

'What about Ronald? We can't just abandon him,' Anna muttered, concerned that she might never again see her favourite toy dinosaur.

'Right! I bet they forget ZIT!' Kingston agreed. He clambered down from the crates, accidentally bumping one of Tatsuya's lava pressure sensors.

'Kingston!' Kumiko yelled as the sensor clattered to the floor.

'It's only a dumb old pole,' Kingston said defensively.

'That dumb old pole tells us how much danger we're

in,' Kumiko explained, as she returned the sensor to its upright position.

Kingston stared after Kumiko incredulously. 'You need a pole to tell you that!' He turned to Anna. 'Come on. They won't even know we've gone,' he said, grabbing her by the hand and making a dash for the door.

While Kingston and Anna raced off towards the living quarters, Gerard and Michael were making their way to the departure bay. Pushing a trolley laden with plants and hydroponics equipment, they hurried down a deserted corridor. 'And you needn't think I'm going to spend the next six months babysitting a bunch of mouldy plants!' Gerard growled.

'Yeah right, brains! You'll be too busy inventing a matter transfer unit to beam us back to Earth!' Michael replied sarcastically, as Kumiko rushed around the corner.

'Kingston and Anna? Have you seen them?' she exclaimed, breathlessly.

Gerard turned on Kumiko at the mention of his sister's name. 'Anna? She should be with you!'

'It's not my fault! I only took my eyes off them for a second. You know what Kingston's like.'

Gerard did know what Kingston was like. 'Little rat! I'll murder him!' he muttered as Duffy's voice boomed out over the intercom ordering all personnel to make their way to the departure bay ready for evacuation.

'You'd better keep going,' Michael said. 'I'll search for the runaways.'

'She's *my* sister,' Gerard said, stopping Michael. 'You try their quarters. I'll meet you back in the departure bay!'

They set off in different directions, Kumiko hurrying after Michael. 'And where do you think you're going?' Michael asked.

'I lost them,' she said, determined not to be left behind.

'No. You'll only slow me down.'

'Yeah right. I forgot, I'm only a girl!' Kumiko replied as she took off down the corridor. 'You better keep up,' she yelled cheekily as she raced past Michael.

In a deserted section of the colony close to the living quarters, Kingston's ZIT peered around a corner. 'The coast is clear,' it announced in its cheeky high-pitched chatter, as it wheeled out into the corridor closely followed by Kingston and Anna. Under one arm, Anna clutched her favourite pillow and a large sack filled to the brim with precious bits and pieces, and under the other arm her favourite toy, Ronald the dinosaur.

'Can't you go any faster?' Kingston moaned as he struggled with his own belongings.

Anna dumped her sack onto the floor. 'Its too heavy,' she complained.

'Then ditch some of it. You're not going to need this flea-bitten thing!' Kingston said, snatching the toy dinosaur.

'Not Ronald!' Anna exclaimed indignantly, grabbing it back. 'I'm not leaving him!'

'Well hurry up. Before we're missed,' he said, shouldering Anna's sack for her. Then, hearing approaching footsteps, he quickly bustled Anna around a corner. 'Quick, it might be Duffy,' he whispered, and they sped off down the passageway, missing Michael and Kumiko by seconds.

'You sure this is the right way?' Kumiko asked, tensing, as another tremor rumbled underfoot.

Michael glared at her. 'I live here, don't I? I should know what I'm doing,' he said, steering her towards the living quarters.

As Duffy's voice crackled over the intercom announcing plans for the final evacuation, the space tug's reverse thrusters gave one final burst before setting down on Io's landing cradle. In the busy departure bay, the access tube doors opened with a hiss and Sam appeared, tired and dishevelled after long hours ferrying supplies and equipment to KL5.

'You better get your friends ready for boarding,' he called to Gerard across the cluttered room. 'You'll be on the next flight.'

Gerard looked about the room anxiously. Kingston and Anna were still nowhere to be seen. 'Come on, make it snappy,' Sam growled.

Gerard shuffled nervously. 'There's a bit of a problem,' he said, not wishing to get anyone into trouble.

Sam was in no mood for riddles. 'Gerard, where are they?' he demanded.

'They went looking for Kingston and Anna,' he replied uneasily. 'I don't know where they are.'

As Michael and Kumiko continued their search through the living quarters, tremors rocked the colony at shorter intervals. More and more debris littered the corridors and hampered their way.

'It's getting too dangerous!' Michael yelled, grabbing hold of Kumiko as a section of roofing crashed to the floor in front of them. 'We can't get through here. We've got to go back.'

'We can't just abandon them,' Kumiko protested. She tried to continue but Michael stopped her.

'We've looked everywhere. They're probably back in the departure bay,' he said hopefully.

'And if they're not?'

'Well Gerard's not totally stupid. He would have organised a search party by now.'

'You'd better be right.' Reluctantly they turned back. Just as they reached the doorway that led to the departure bay, another tremor struck. The door's controls sparked and spluttered—the electrical short jamming it shut.

'Now what?' Kumiko said.

Michael considered the options. One way, the wrecked door; the other way, rubble blocking their path. Looking around, he spied a nearby air duct. Where was the tunnel rat when you really needed him, he thought, reaching up and removing the grate.

As Kingston and Anna struggled their way towards the departure bay, ZIT turned the corner first and immediately screeched: 'Warning! Warning! Sam and Gerard closing fast!' Sensing serious trouble, Kingston snatched ZIT, and looked around for an escape route. As he turned to head off the other way, he saw Duffy and Tatsuya bearing down on them. They were cornered. Kingston gulped. 'Ronald, I think we're about to become extinct!'

Half an hour later, and still stinging from Duffy's reprimand, Kingston and Anna were loaded onto the space tug with Gerard.

'If anything happens to Kumi and Michael, it'll be your fault,' Gerard said gruffly as the space tug's thrusters roared and began its climb up to the space station. 'You broke every rule in the book!'

'We just wanted our stuff,' Anna said clutching Ronald and gazing sadly up at Gerard.

'Yeah, we didn't mean to get anyone into trouble,' Kingston added, although deep down he knew that Gerard was right.

Gerard eyed his two companions scathingly. 'All for the sake of a dumb dinosaur and a feral robot!'

Anna slid her hand into her bag of belongings and produced Gerard's multi-mate. 'I got this for you,' she said sheepishly, looking up at Gerard.

Gerard melted. He could never withstand the wide-eye treatment from his baby sister. 'Don't worry, they'll find them,' he said, wrapping his arm around Anna. 'Probably found them already.'

An air shaft grid flew from its fittings and clattered to

the floor below one of the few walls still intact in the Jupiter Bar.

'Come on,' a voice echoed. Out of the blackened duct, Michael's face appeared, dust covered and dirty.

Quickly, he clambered from the opening and turned to help Kumiko out of the duct. She slid awkwardly from the confined space and sprawled on the floor, resembling a bit of debris brought down by the tremors.

Michael helped her to her feet. She moved slowly, tired and exhausted by the battering she'd suffered over the past few days. Since arriving on Io, she seemed to have spent most of her waking hours either crawling, slithering, worming or falling through air ducts and tunnels, mine shafts and corridors. Enough was enough. She was tired of it!

'If I never see another air duct, it'll be too soon,' she complained.

'It's okay. We're nearly there,' Michael said reassuringly, scrambling across the piles of rubble in the room, dodging the stanchions that had collapsed and hung obliquely from the ceiling.

'I'm sorry, Michael, sorry for getting you into this.'

'You can apologise later. Now move it.' Michael steered Kumiko towards the lift in the corner that would take them up to the space tug departure bay and hopefully to safety.

Reaching the lift well, Michael slammed his hand on its control buttons. Nothing. Prising the doors open slightly, he peered through and saw, to his horror, the tangled and broken cables dangling in the shaft. The lift was dead. 'It's our only way out! We're not going to make it,' he muttered, slumping down against the adjacent wall.

Kumiko stared at him disbelievingly. 'There has to be another way!' she said, her eyes searching intently for an alternative escape route.

'We're finished,' Michael said miserably, staring

blankly ahead of him as the final evacuation siren rang out. 'We're never going to get out of here.'

Kumiko heard him but didn't respond. Her eyes were fixed on a pressure sensor that lay among the rubble, still blinking out its signal. She moved slowly towards it, an idea forming in her mind.

'Is there anywhere else the space tug can pick us up?' she asked, turning back to Michael.

'You don't understand, no-one knows where we are.'

'Is there?' Kumiko demanded.

Confused, Michael ran quickly through the layout of the colony in his head. He'd flown with his father many times in the space tug, even taking the controls on occasions, but they'd always set down at the landing bay, never anywhere else.

'There has to be somewhere,' Kumiko insisted. She couldn't believe that a mining colony would only have the one landing cradle.

There was one place, Michael recalled. He'd never used it but he'd heard the Professor mention it. 'The old transport platform,' he said. 'It was the original landing area when the colony was first built.'

'Can we get to it from here?' Kumiko asked, as she examined the pressure sensor.

Michael turned towards an entrance that led back into the colony. 'Through there. But you don't understand, no-one will know we've gone that way,' he said.

Kumiko wasn't listening. She thrust the pressure sensor into Michael's arms, then, checking that her computer was still safely attached to her belt, she hurried towards the door, a reluctant Michael following after her.

'I don't know if we can get through!' he yelled after her, but Kumiko continued down the wrecked passageway, intent on her mission. 'You want to get to KL5, don't you?'

On the derelict space station, a blackened door slid open and Beth directed Anna towards the old abandoned living quarters. Kingston trailed along behind, gazing excitedly at the vast labyrinth of corridors, passageways and tunnels just waiting to be explored.

'This is your room,' Beth announced to Anna, trying as best she could to sound positive as she ushered them inside a small, cramped room.

'This dump!' Anna exclaimed, as she looked around the junk-filled room. 'It's a mess!'

'So it needs a bit of fixing up,' Beth conceded. 'With a bit of work and imagination, it'll be just like home in no time at all.'

Anna wasn't convinced. After all they'd been through on Io, she had hoped for something more comfortable than such a dingy, pokey little cubicle.

'Just think, when Michael and Kumiko get here, you'll be able to show them what a great room you've got,' Beth added, trying hard to inspire Kingston and Anna before turning to leave.

'That's if we ever see them again,' Kingston muttered despondently as he sank down on a battered looking crate in the centre of the room. 'This is great, this is,' he babbled indignantly. 'We risk life and limb on Io, we survive all manner of disasters, we manage to escape within an inch of our lives, just in the nick of time and what's the first thing we get lumped with? We have to clean up our rooms! Life sucks!'

Anna nodded at the truth of it. 'It's all our fault,' Anna said forlornly to Kingston, who turned to Ronald the dinosaur sitting propped up on a nearby crate. 'No, it's all *your* fault,' he said to the bug-eyed reptile. 'If we didn't have to rescue you, none of this would have happened.'

They sat for a moment, gazing around the room, thinking of their friends, until Kingston jumped up and began cleaning and reorganising the boxes and crates. Best to keep active, he thought, encouraging Anna to do likewise.

Anna heaved on a large crate that was stacked against a wall. 'I miss them already.'

'Yeah, if only we knew what was going on,' Kingston said, adding his weight to the stubborn crate.

As they pushed the crate from the wall, Kingston's eyes widened—an air duct. He bent down and peered inside. 'Where did it go?' he wondered. 'Only one way to find out,' he said, crawling inside. Anna hesitated. 'Come on,' Kingston said, his voice echoing out of the duct and Anna, not wanting to be left behind, clambered in after him.

As they crawled through the duct towards the centre of the station, the duct rattled slightly, and they could hear the distant roar of the tug's thrusters as it blasted away from KL5.

The space tug slowly descended towards Io, its reverse thrusters finally easing it into the landing cradle. As its engines shut down, the access tube locked onto the platform's departure bay and Sam rushed from the tug to find Duffy, Karl, Tatsuya and Akiko huddled together. 'Have you found them?' he asked anxiously.

Duffy's face said it all. There'd been no sign of Michael or Kumiko.

'Well, what are you standing round for?' Sam snapped, as he rushed towards the doorway that led into the colony proper.

Duffy intercepted him. 'Sam, everywhere's falling apart. We can't get through. We have to evacuate!' As Duffy spoke, a distant rumble heralded a much louder, nearby explosion, much closer to the bay. The colonists ducked for cover as a section of the roof crashed down around them. Time was running out and Sam knew it. He wheeled around to Duffy. 'I can't just abandon them,' he warned, 'There must be some way of getting through.' Duffy's reply was interrupted by another explosion ripping through the colony.

In a dark corridor on the other side of the colony, an evacuation light, dangling by its wiring and swaying back and forth, continued to flash its warning. Nearby, an air duct hatch popped open in the roof and Michael and Kumiko lowered themselves to the floor.

Michael hesitated, looking left and right, searching for a familiar landmark.

'Which way?' Kumiko pleaded but Michael didn't answer. Nothing looked familiar in the flashing half light. Finally he turned to the left.

'I wish Kingston was here,' he muttered, as together they made their way down the darkened corridor. If anyone could get them to the old landing platform, he could. Kingston knew all the twists and turns of these corridors and tunnels.

The tunnel rat was at that very moment expanding his knowledge on KL5. Crawling through a very grimy air duct, he spotted a shaft of light ahead. He quickened his pace, beckoning to Anna, and crawled towards an opening a few metres ahead. Clambering through, they settled into a small service gallery high above the central control room, beaming proudly. It was the perfect hideout. They could see everything and no-one could see them. Together, they settled down to watch, hoping for news of Michael and Kumiko.

Below them, Beth sat at a work station, monitoring the pressure sensors on Io and recording the incoming data while Professor Ingessol hovered beside her, working frantically to bring KL5's outmoded computers fully on line.

Suddenly, Beth wheeled around from her console

and called urgently to Professor Ingessol. 'There's no response from the tug!'

'Keep trying,' Ingessol snapped. 'They must have docked by now. Maybe there's no-one on board.'

Up in the service gallery, Kingston turned to Anna. 'The space tug! Maybe it's been destroyed by an earth tremor, or maybe it's been swallowed up by molten lava, or maybe it's even exploded mid flight. If something's happened to that thing, we'll never see Michael and Kumiko again!'

'They'll find them,' Anna said, trying to reassure herself. 'They have to!' The young explorers huddled together, realising that time was running out for their friends.

Still surrounded by rubble and falling debris, Michael and Kumiko battled their way towards the old transport platform. The tremors were becoming increasingly volatile and whole sections of corridors were beginning to warp and crack.

As they sped down a semi-lit corridor, a large section of roof collapsed into a pile of twisted metal and plasti-shield, blocking their path. They heaved on the rubble and it gradually slid away, revealing a narrow passageway into the corridor beyond. They crawled through. When they reached the doorway to the old transport platform, Michael hastily punched the control buttons. The door refused to open. He quickly opened the manual override panel and heaved on the lever. The door slid partly open and they scrambled through.

The chamber inside appeared to be still intact. Emergency lights flooded the graveyard of machinery and mining equipment that over the years had been stored or discarded. At the front of the room, two dirty and clouded plexi-glass panels ran the height of the dome and looked out onto the old transport landing cradle. Now if only the tug could find them! While Michael cautiously walked the perimeter of the room, checking for potentially dangerous cracks or fractures, Kumiko went to work on the pressure sensor. Clearing a space in the centre, she began tweaking the sensor's controls. Michael watched her, uncertain what she was doing but impressed by her apparent skill and dogged determination.

'Are you going to tell me what this is all about?' he asked.

'It's a pressure sensor, right? It records the pressure of the lava below the moon's surface.'

'So?'

'And it sends out signals,' Kumiko continued.

Michael suddenly twigged. 'The monitors,' he blurted out. 'They'll see the new signals on their monitors.'

Kumiko paused in her work. 'Right! If my Dad sees new signal patterns coming from this area ... '

'Then we're saved!'

Kumiko smiled at him, trying to hide the many doubts that still haunted her. Saved, she thought—*if* the tug was still on Io, *if* Sam was still able to fly it and *if* the tug was able to touch down on the old transport platform.

Pushing her doubts to the back of her mind, Kumiko positioned the sensor and extended its small transmitting aerial.

'Kumi, you're a genius,' Michael exclaimed.

'Maybe—if my Dad still has his monitor. And if it's turned on. *And* if he sees it blinking.' More ifs, she thought!

'Don't be such a pessimist,' Michael said, convinced that their plan was a winner.

Kumiko leant down and checked the pressure sensor one final time. Everything seemed ready. Then, crossing her fingers, she flicked its switch and waited for the sonic pulse to sound. Nothing. Frantically, she tried the switch again, flicking the toggle back and forth.

'What have you done with it?' she said, turning on Michael.

'I didn't do anything! Honest!' he protested, as another seismic disturbance rumbled beneath the chamber, unsettling the pair of them. 'Can't you fix it? There's got to be something you can do.'

But Kumiko couldn't think of anything. She'd reached the limits of her expertise.

'There's no other way to signal them?' Michael asked hopefully. Kumiko shook her head. 'Not unless you and your father have some sort of telepathic thing going,' she said, forcing a smile.

Sam, however, was half-buried under a pile of debris brought down by the last explosion. He peered through a tiny opening. 'I can see through,' he said, clawing frantically at the collapsed roofing blocking the exit from the departure bay. Karl, Tatsuya and Akiko worked alongside him, trying to clear a path.

They were almost through. Sam heaved on a large slab of fallen moulding and it gave way to expose a larger opening to the corridor beyond. He scrambled up to the opening and called loudly down the corridor. 'Michael, Kumi ... Can you hear me?! Michael!'

'Sam, it's no use,' came Duffy's voice behind him. 'They could be anywhere.'

Ignoring Duffy, Sam clawed his way closer to the narrow opening. Then he smelt it. The putrid stench of sulphur dioxide. Gas was being forced up through the mining tunnels ahead of the lava. Sam reeled back from the opening, coughing and spluttering, trying to catch his breath.

Duffy placed a hand on Sam's shoulder, his voice heavy with responsibility. 'Sam, we've done all we can.'

'We don't go anywhere until I find my son!'

'I have to think of the others,' Duffy said. 'You're the

only one who can fly the tug. You want *them* on your conscience as well?' he persisted.

'Back off George, I know what my responsibilities are!' But Sam knew only too well that he had to comply. He couldn't risk the lives of his three colleagues. They would have to evacuate.

Unaware of the debate raging in the departure bay, Kumiko ripped a side panel off the tubular pressure sensor, hoping to find the fault. Perhaps it was something simple, something she'd overlooked. She flipped open the power source and examined the mass of circuits. Everything seemed intact.

'You sure you know what you're doing?' Michael asked.

'You want to try?' she replied as she yanked the power cell from the sensor and examined it closely.

'Tell me you've found the problem, Michael said hopefully.

'It's the power cell.'

'Great!' Michael said happily. 'Now tell me you can fix it.'

'It's a power cell. You can't fix it,' Kumiko replied bluntly.

Michael sank back on his heels. This time, they'd reached the end of the line. Kumiko thought for a moment, then unclipped her computer from her waist band. She opened the back to reveal its power pack. 'We can't fix it,' she mused. 'But maybe we can substitute it.'

'You sure it'll work?'

'No. Got any better ideas?'

Kumiko delicately connected the power pack to the pressure sensor. Satisfied that everything was in place, she looked up at Michael, then took a deep breath. 'Here goes nothing,' she muttered, carefully flicking the switch on the sensor.

Seconds ticked by; seconds that seemed like forever. And then at last, with a beep and a flicker, the sensor came to life, pulsing out its signal.

Michael threw his arms around Kumiko and hugged her affectionately. 'Brilliant! I knew it would work,' he lied. 'I love that computer!'

'You'd better pray that one of the monitors is still working,' Kumiko said ominously.

On the portable monitor in the departure bay, a new signal began to flicker insistently, but Duffy was already herding Tatsuya, Akiko and Karl into the access tube and on board the space tug.

Sam lingered by the entrance, hoping that some miracle would bring Michael and Kumiko rushing into the room. 'I'm sorry Sam,' Duffy said sympathetically, as he gestured towards their escape route. 'We go now or we don't go at all.'

As they turned to go, another violent tremor struck the colony. In the centre of the departure bay, a stanchion gave way from its wall mounts and crashed down, bringing with it huge sections of roofing.

Sam climbed heavily into the pilot's seat in the space tug and keyed commands into the communication panel. He looked up to the video mesh as it came to life and the Professor's worried face faded up on the screen.

'Sam, you must evacuate! Now! The whole colony is about to blow!'

But Sam was resolute. 'No. We wait! We wait until the last possible moment.'

'Sam, please,' Duffy pleaded. 'Think about it! What would Michael want you to do?'

Sam glared at Duffy incredulously. 'What do you reckon? He'd want me to wait!'

'I'm in charge. We have to lift off!' Duffy commanded.

Sam held Duffy's gaze for a moment then turned back to Tatsuya and Akiko who were huddled behind him. Sadly, Tatsuya nodded his permission. Turning back to the console, Sam thumped the controls and the cockpit filled with the roar of the thrusters.

'We're very sorry Sam,' Ingessol said, clearly distressed—Michael had been his closest companion on Io.

Suddenly Beth called to the Professor. 'I've got new readings from the pressure sensors!' she reported, as she studied another monitor in front of her. 'From a different section this time. It doesn't make sense! It wasn't there before.'

As the Professor leaned in to check the monitor, a voice yelled out from behind them. 'It's them, it has to be!' Kingston shouted as he and Anna raced from their hiding place into the control room. 'It's them!' Kingston babbled excitedly. 'Kumi showed me. The sensors. She knows all about them. She knows how they work. It has to be them!'

'Its a machine that goes *boing*,' Anna added emphatically.

'It's a signal,' Kingston continued. 'An SOS!'

Ingessol needed no convincing. He rushed to the communication panel.

'It's south. The old mining zone. I can't pinpoint it exactly,' he shouted to Sam.

Sam immediately punched new commands into the space tug's console. 'The old transport platform. Changing course now!' he told Ingessol, and the tug launched from the landing cradle and swung out over the colony towards the derelict platform.

Inside the chamber adjoining the platform, Kumiko and Michael sat staring hopefully at the pressure sensor, seemingly mesmerised by its blinking signal.

'If we get out of this, maybe we could be friends,' Kumiko said optimistically.

'If we get out of this, maybe I'll consider it,' Michael replied.

'Could be a short friendship,' Kumiko muttered as another seismic rumble shook the chamber, bringing down dust and rubble from above.

They both knew their chances of survival were

diminishing by the second. The room was beginning to disintegrate around them and smoke and gasses were pouring into the chamber from the adjacent corridor.

'Some holiday this has been,' Kumiko spluttered.

'Don't worry, it'll soon be over,' Michael said glumly.

Without warning the chamber shook violently, throwing Michael and Kumiko to the floor. Kumiko shrieked as a roof support gave way and collapsed nearby, sending a cloud of dust swirling into the air and dragging electrical cables from their fittings. The lighting flickered and sparked, and as Michael dragged Kumiko to her feet away from the live cables, a section of the chamber wall split with a loud explosive crack.

'The outer wall,' Michael yelled, watching horrified as dust and smoke was sucked through the crack into the weak, poisonous atmosphere of Io beyond. Their time had run out. If they weren't crushed to death by falling debris, they'd suffocate as the remaining air was sucked out of the chamber.

Michael stared across at the plexi-glass panels, waiting for them to crack and explode. Suddenly, he rushed across to the panels, leaping across fallen rubble, and pressed his face against the glass. 'The tug!' he yelled, pointing to the thrusters in the distance glowing red.

'They're leaving! They're going without us!' Kumiko yelled.

'No! It's descending. Look!' he replied ecstatically as the tug swung down towards them.

Michael rushed to the air lock that led out to the landing platform. Kumiko raced to join him and they saw the tug's landing lights sweep into view as it approached the old landing cradle. They began yelling for help, pounding on the door. Only moments later, they heard the crashing of rubble being cleared from the air-lock doorway.

As Sam's muffled voice called to them, Michael and

Kumiko clawed frantically at the door with their fingers. It was jammed. Michael quickly grabbed a piece of broken stanchion and slammed it into the corner of the air lock. Using it as a lever, he threw his weight against it. Still the door refused to budge. Kumiko joined him and together they made one last desperate lunge. The door began to move.

Sam and Tatsuya rushed inside the chamber, throwing their arms around Michael and Kumiko in relief.

'Come on, we're not out of this yet,' Sam warned, leading them all down the access tube. They quickly climbed inside and Sam hit the door controls, sealing in the tug as the colony started to explode around them.

Inside the cockpit, Tatsuya held Kumiko close to him. 'We thought we'd lost you,' Akiko said, hugging her tightly, her voice cracking.

Sam punched the controls in front of him and the thrusters roared to life. 'We'd better get you to your new home,' he said to Michael, leaning on the power controls as an explosion ripped through the old landing bay. The tug lurched violently from side to side as Sam struggled to regain equilibrium. They just cleared the platform as another explosion wrenched the landing cradle, and blasted their way towards KL5.

Looking down at Kumiko's white knuckles, Michael reached across to her and gently prised her fingers from the chair's arm rest. 'It's okay,' he said happily. 'We're clear. We made it.'

On the video mesh in front of them, Kingston's face appeared, beaming from ear to ear. Michael leaned over Duffy's shoulder and faced the transmitter.

'Hey Kingston,' he called to his young friend, 'Dad tells me we owe you one.' Kingston grinned cheekily back at him. 'Hear that? He owes me one! I've got witnesses, Michael.'

'I think we're going to regret that,' Michael said with a wry grin, settling back next to Kumiko.

As the tug blasted further and further away from Io, the fissure in the substrata finally cracked open on the moon colony. Molten lava gushed through the mining tunnels destroying everything in its path.

Michael and Kumiko looked back to see the colony finally explode in a ball of fire and lava. Io was gone. Exhausted, Michael sank back into his seat, an overwhelming sadness welling up inside him. His home of 13 years was no more.

CHAPTER FIVE

BLAST OFF

S afely aboard KL5, the colonists began the onerous task of making the derelict hulk their home. It was a nerve-racking time for everyone, living in make-shift quarters, working long hours, and struggling to marry salvaged equipment from Io to the outmoded, dismantled remains of KL5.

While Professor Ingessol battled to restore life support systems, Duffy set up his headquarters in the control room, the heart of the station, where an arc of consoles provided access to the central computer. On the forward wall, a large video mesh inclined towards the floor, giving the computer technicians a view of space and its vast star field beyond. It was here, in the control room, that Duffy kept an ever watchful eye on proceedings, overseeing repairs, organising rosters, and ensuring the children were kept under tight control.

An atmosphere of uncertainty coloured life on KL5. Many of the colonists believed their efforts were futile. With the possibility of rescue almost negligible, their chances of survival seemed bleak.

Doing their best to ignore the gloomy predictions, the children had completely restored the food preparation area, as ordered by Duffy, and converted the room into a makeshift recreation centre, where they regularly met and related the latest station gossip.

'Hey, have you heard Ingessol's latest brilliant idea?' Gerard asked excitedly as Michael placed a thin green wafer of dried algae into the food reconstitution machine.

'No, what?' Michael replied, keenly interested.

'Nor have I. I just wondered if he had any idea of how he was going to get us out of this mess,' Gerard scoffed, slurping the last of his reconstituted green algae sludge.

'Oh good joke Gerard. That's a real knee slapper, that is!' Kingston mocked, carefully unwrapping a piece of chocolate that he'd been saving.

Gerard glared at him, then wrenched the chocolate from Kingston's hands. 'Don't get smart with me rodent!'

'Hey, give that back,' said Kingston, and moving quickly, grabbed Gerard's multi-mate as revenge. 'If you eat it, I'll ... '

'You'll what rodent?' said Gerard, snatching up ZIT's remote control and beginning to speed the hapless vehicle around the room.

'Hand it over rodent, or I trash the ZIT!' he threatened.

'No! You nicked my chocolate!' Kingston protested ineffectually.

'Cough up or I launch the feral robot into hyper-space!' Kingston watched with alarm as Gerard increased speed on the remote control and ZIT accelerated around the room, screeching wildly.

'All right. All right!' he yelled and Gerard backed off on the controls. Kingston eyed Gerard warily. 'Trade,' he said, tentatively offering Gerard his multi-mate.

Without warning, Gerard made a grab for the device but Kingston was too quick for him. He tossed the tool to Michael who was near the food reconstitution machine.

Michael quickly opened the machine and tossed the multi-mate inside.

'I'm warning you Faraday, hand it over!' Gerard threatened.

But Michael ignored him. He knew he had Gerard over a barrel. 'Give it to him or else *melt down*,' he said threatening to activate the machine.

'Do it!' Kingston urged. 'Push the button! Zap it!'

'No!' Gerard conceded as Michael reached for the controls. 'Stop! All right. Trade.'

Gerard placed ZIT's remote control on the table in front of him and stepped back slightly. Michael hesitated, then removed the multi-mate from the food machine and placed it at the other end of the table. The two boys eyed each other warily, neither one completely trusting the other. Stand off.

Lightning fast, Gerard lunged for the multi-mate, grabbed both it and the remote, and raced towards the door.

'You double crosser!' Kingston shrieked as Gerard sprinted from the room.

'You won't get away with this,' Michael yelled, giving chase. They sprinted down the corridor, trading insults, yelling and laughing.

In the control room of KL5, Professor Ingessol, looking tired and dishevelled, hovered over one of the computer consoles, trying to couple together components of KL5's central computer system and salvaged equipment from Io.

Duffy loomed over his shoulder. 'You may have built this bucket of bolts, but that doesn't put you in charge,' he said authoritatively. 'I will not allow you to risk the lives of everyone on board.'

'I tell you George, there's no alternative. Open your mind, think of the consequences,' Ingessol pleaded.

'I have!' Duffy exclaimed angrily. 'And I'm putting a stop to this madness right now! KL5 is a space station. It's not meant to fly!'

Frustrated, Professor Ingessol wheeled around on Duffy, but before he could continue the argument, Gerard suddenly burst into the room, hotly pursued by Michael and Kingston. Duffy spun around to see what all the commotion was about. 'You lot! What do you think you're playing at?' he demanded angrily.

The boys fought to catch their breath. Duffy was clearly in a bad mood and none of them wanted to tangle with him. 'Explain yourselves!' he insisted.

Michael, Gerard and Kingston squirmed, not knowing what to say. 'They've come to help me,' Ingessol interjected, taking the boys by surprise.

Duffy looked at Ingessol askance. 'Then I want them out of here. All of them. Right now!' he ordered, suspecting he had been duped.

'I saved you three from the wrath of Duffy for a purpose,' Ingessol said, as he led them out of the room. Collecting Anna and Kumiko on the way, he told them there was important work to be done, and everybody had to help. 'Anything but gardening,' Gerard said jokingly. Ingessol ignored him, being deliberately mysterious as he led them down to one of the lower levels of the station.

With a flourish, Professor Ingessol finally flung open a large heavy door that led into a musty, abandoned hydroponics laboratory. 'Gardening! I knew it! I hate gardening!' Gerard complained as Professor Ingessol ushered them inside.

Michael surveyed the neglected lab, his technical interest overwhelmed by despair. The plant beds were empty, algae tanks overflowed with thick murky sludge, light frames hung disconnected from the power source and the atmospheric purifier stood partly dismantled. 'It's a wreck. We'll never get it working. It's impossible,' he said dejectedly.

'Difficult maybe, but not impossible. Most of the original equipment was taken to Io,' Professor Ingessol explained. 'But if we clean out the tanks, repair the lights, reconnect the purifiers, get the algae to bloom—'

'Move the sun a little to the left,' Gerard added.

'It'll give us a couple of months breathing space,' Professor Ingessol said, trying to evoke some enthusiasm.

Gerard turned to the Professor. Something wasn't quite right. 'A couple of months?' he repeated. 'But Duffy said it could take *ten* months before we're rescued.'

'Yes. That's if we sit here and wait,' Ingessol replied enthusiastically.

'Oh yeah, right. Hey I know, let's save ourselves,' Gerard scoffed. 'Let's fly KL5 to Earth!'

Ingessol beamed with delight. He made a buzzer sound as if Gerard were a contestant in a quiz. 'Bzzzt! Correct! Give that boy a dinosaur,' he said, grabbing Ronald the dinosaur from Anna and thrusting it into Gerard's arms.

'Fly KL5? And what do we do for engines?' asked Michael, dumbfounded by Ingessol's revelation.

'The space tug. We couple it to KL5 and *pshong!*' Ingessol replied, gesturing as if his hand was jetting off into space. 'You're in charge here, Michael,' he added and before his stunned audience could respond, he disappeared through the door and was on his way back to the control room.

'He's mental!' Gerard exclaimed, as Michael rushed out the door after him.

'Professor, you're not serious?' he yelled after Ingessol. 'Are you?'

Ingessol looked at Michael, who saw by the look on his face that he was. Deadly serious. The Professor sighed deeply. 'Michael, I've got enough sceptics as it is,' he said quietly. 'If we're to survive, we need that hydro lab.'

'But it's a wreck! You saw it.'

'That's why I'm putting you in charge. Nobody else has the expertise. I know you can do it. It's the same principle as the one on Io,' Ingessol said, placing a hand on Michael's shoulder. 'And you've got four willing volunteers in there.' Ingessol shot Michael a grin then strode off towards the control room.

Two of the willing volunteers peered into one of the

algae tanks. Bits and pieces of discarded rubbish floated on top of the thick sludge. It looked just like a pool of toxic waste.

Anna screwed up her nose. 'I'm not touching that!'

Kingston agreed and began to stagger around the room clutching his chest. 'The attack of the toxic slime. First come the spasms, then you turn green, and finally, you go stark raving bonkers,' he choked dramatically.

Gerard was in no mood for Kingston's jokes. He reached forward and clipped him under the ear.

'Ow! What'd you do that for?'

'Because you're an idiot!'

Indignantly, Kingston returned to the algae tank and hoisted Ronald the dinosaur up to view the foul sludge. 'Look Ronald, the beginning of civilisation as *you* know it.'

'Yeah, take a good look Ronald,' Gerard sneered pointedly as Michael returned to the lab. 'It could be the end of civilisation as *we* know it!'

Collecting his thoughts, Michael wandered silently through the mess, the others watching him expectantly.

'So is he crazy or what?' Gerard asked, finally breaking the silence. Michael ignored the barb and much to Gerard's irritation, began to organise them into a repair crew. Michael realised that Ingessol was right. Even if Duffy and the other colonists didn't accept his daring plan, they'd still need the hydro lab if they were to survive.

The children worked tirelessly cleaning up the lab, section by section. They began by restoring the plant beds and reconnecting the lighting grid. Even Gerard chipped in, reluctantly helping to repair the plumbing system, while Michael reassembled the connections to the atmospheric purifier. Kumiko, Kingston and Anna cleaned out the algae tanks, pumped water into them, and added live algae spores ready for blooming.

They scrounged and borrowed materials, improvising where necessary, and after weeks of hard work, the hydro lab finally began to take shape. As each day passed, they waited anxiously for news of Ingessol's daring plan to fly KL5 to Earth. But still no decision had been reached.

One morning, Kumiko rushed in to tell them that the colonists were meeting to decide the future of the station. The children downed tools, scrambled out of the lab and sprinted along the system of corridors and passageways that led to the control room.

As they arrived at the control room, Duffy stepped in front of them, blocking their entrance. 'And where do you think you're going?' he sneered officiously.

'Nowhere,' Kingston replied, trying to look innocent, standing on tiptoes, peering past Duffy into the control room.

'Correct,' Duffy said smugly and closed the door in his face.

Kumiko turned to the others. 'That's not fair! We've got a right to know what's going on,' she protested.

Sauntering away from the door, Kingston smiled cheekily at the others. 'What?' Michael asked, sensing he was up to something.

'First, tell me I'm a genius,' Kingston teased.

'No. You're an idiot!' Gerard snapped, reaching out to cuff his ear but missing as Kingston ducked.

'Wrong! You lose. Next please,' he said playfully. Faced with another Kingston game, Gerard decided to take direct action. He grabbed him by the shirt front threateningly. Kingston grimaced and quickly rethought his position.

'I know a way in!' he exclaimed, trying to wriggle free. 'The tunnel rat has struck again!' Gerard eyed him suspiciously, but he released his grip, and Kingston led them to the hatchway that connected to the service gallery high up in the control room.

'Kingston you're fantastic,' Kumiko said as she

peered out over the control room. The other children huddled beside her, secretly watching the colonists below as they discussed Ingessol's plan to fly KL5 to Earth.

The mood of the meeting was tense. Duffy was on his feet, pacing about, trying to assert his position. 'At the outside, help should be here in ten months,' he argued.

'Should be?' Helen interjected. 'In ten months! And what if we don't get the air purifiers working? And what about food? And medical supplies? No, we can't be sure. It's too much of a gamble.'

'Gamble!' Duffy exclaimed. 'And haring across the solar system in a derelict space station? What do you call that?'

'Stupidity, I'd say,' Gerard whispered to the others as the meeting continued.

'It's our only chance,' Ingessol argued. 'We couple the tug to KL5 and we use it to break orbit. We fly the station to Earth.'

'This is insane!' Duffy exploded.

Gerard agreed. 'He's going to kill us all!'

'We patch the space tug's ignition controls through to KL5's control room, into the central computers. 'But,' Ingessol admitted, 'there is *one* small snag.'

'Terrific! We can add it to the long list of giant impossibilities,' Duffy added sarcastically, throwing his hands in the air.

Ignoring Duffy, Ingessol made his final point with quiet force. 'We *must* rendezvous with the last ore carrier that left Io, to replenish our fuel. And after studying the alignment of the planets, our only window of opportunity is within the next 48 hours. We must go now, or not at all.' Ingessol looked around the group of attentive faces. 'The question is, do we stay and die, or do we go?'

Michael leant forwards waiting for the reply. The adults looked at one another, considering Ingessol's proposal. 'We go. Go on, say it! We go,' Michael urged in a low whisper.

'You go. I'm staying!' Gerard replied.

Moments later the meeting was over. The children managed to scramble out of the service hatchway and into the corridor just as the control room doors were being flung open. The colonists emerged, abuzz with excitement, and dispersed to their respective work stations. Duffy stormed through the doors with a dark gloomy look on his face.

Kingston bounced up to him. 'How'd it go Mr Duffy?' he asked jovially.

Duffy turned and glared at him. 'You, shut up.'

But Kingston never knew when to quit. 'So do we go, or do we stay?'

'Which part of the word don't you understand?' Duffy sneered. 'Is it the *shut* or is it the *up*?' Kingston gulped and backed off. Duffy eyed the children for a moment and then turned on his heels and stormed off. 'So much for secret ballots,' Kingston said, as they watched Duffy disappear down the corridor. 'I'd say we're going, wouldn't you? He's got loser written all over him!'

Professor Ingessol finally emerged from the control room. He'd won, but now he had the enormous task of connecting the space tug to the station and preparing the computer systems for blast off. He beckoned to Kumiko to follow him.

'You've got a good understanding of computers and I'll need all the help I can get if we're going to make the deadline. And I'll need your computer,' he added as an afterthought.

Kumiko was thrilled by the opportunity. No more algae, she thought happily to herself, then turned to Michael and shrugged an apology. 'Sorry, duty calls,' she said, and left the others to return to their work in the hydro lab.

'Just think, when we get to Earth, we'll be hailed as heroes!' Kingston chattered away excitedly as Ingessol and Kumiko disappeared into the control room.

Gerard didn't share Kingston's confidence.

'Dream on bubble head! One puny space tug trying to push this dump across the solar system. You're all mental! The whole station'll disintegrate, that's what'll happen,' he said, as they made their way back to the hydro lab.

Later that night and unable to sleep, Michael sat in his quarters sadly replaying his last pictogram from his mother. It had been 12 months since he had seen her and although he trusted the Professor, he wondered if Gerard was right. Maybe Ingessol's plan was too risky. Perhaps he might never see his mother again, he worried. Sam quietly entered the room behind him.

Michael quickly turned the pictogram off and removed the disk. 'Just sorting out some old stuff,' he said, feeling a little embarrassed.

'So how's the lab going?' Sam asked, sitting down next to Michael.

'We're getting there.'

'So why the long face?'

Michael shrugged. 'Dad, what if the professor's wrong? What if we never see Mum again?' he said, looking down at the pictogram disk.

Sam put his arm around Michael. 'This isn't like you,' he said. 'We'll see her again. You just get the hydro lab working.'

'But won't you need me to help with the space tug?' Michael asked.

'Not this time. The hydro lab is just as important. No matter what happens, we're going to need it. Okay?' Michael smiled shakily. He could hear the uncertainty in his father's voice. He too was worried.

Alone in the viewing bubble, Kumiko sat staring blankly out into space, a frown wrinkling her brow.

The tiny chamber had become her favourite retreat, a quiet place to think and meditate, and look at the stars dotting the surrounding space.

As she gazed thoughtfully out at Jupiter, Michael entered noiselessly and sat down beside her. 'Couldn't sleep,' she said, almost as an apology.

'Me neither. Looks pretty hostile down there,' Michael added as he gazed out at the huge planet.

They sat together for a while staring out into space, content to share the view quietly. Finally Michael broke the silence. 'What does rain feel like?' he asked, remembering his mother talking about it on her pictogram.

Kumiko looked at him quizzically, surprised by his question. 'I can't believe you've never been to Earth.'

'Well I haven't. What's wrong with that?' Michael said defensively.

'Nothing. It's just, well, I've never met anyone like you.'

'So what does it feel like? I mean, I've experienced it in virtual reality programs, but that isn't really the same, is it?' Michael persisted.

Kumiko thought for a moment. She didn't really know how to describe the sensation. It was something that she took for granted.

'Well I guess it's like being in the shower. Only you're outside. I don't know.'

'I've never even seen a tree. Or a beach,' Michael added sadly. 'Next year they said. I was supposed to join my Mum next year.'

'Well look on the bright side. It might be sooner than you think,' she said with a smile, trying to lighten the mood.

'Yeah, and maybe Gerard's right. Maybe the space tug won't be enough. And maybe I can't get the hydroponics working.'

Kumiko turned to Michael and saw his concern. 'You'll do it,' she said, secretly worried herself.

The following day, the adults prepared to launch the station from Jupiter's orbit, while Michael and Gerard continued with their duties in the lab. By now the algae tanks had been restored, the algae replenished, and most of the broken water piping running between each tank and plant bed replaced, although in make-shift fashion.

The pair then turned their attention to the atmospheric purifier, trying to secure pipes between the purifier and the algae tanks.

'The other way, turn it the other way,' Gerard exclaimed to Michael, who was struggling to release a water valve on the purifier with a wrench.

'You want to do it?' Michael snapped back, thrusting the wrench at Gerard.

'Sure. Let an expert at it,' Gerard mocked, snatching the tool as Kumiko rushed into the room.

'Thought you might like to know, the tug, they're about to couple it to the station,' she said breathlessly. 'Sam's in the tug right now.'

Gerard looked enviously in the direction of the space tug. 'That's where I should be. Out in the thick of things. Not wading around up to my neck in algae,' he said disconsolately, applying his weight to the stubborn valve.

'Come on. Hurry up. You'll miss it,' Kumiko urged, then rushed from the lab towards the docking bay.

'Right. I'm out of here,' Gerard said as he finally released the valve and made off after Kumiko.

'Gerard! I need you here,' Michael yelled. But it was no use. Gerard had already disappeared.

In the space tug, Sam carefully manoeuvred the tiny vessel closer to the giant station. He leant in towards the communicator. 'Engaging reverse thruster, port side only, 180 degree rotation,' he said, expertly manipulating the controls.

The thrusters roared and the tiny vessel moved closer to the station's cargo bay. As it moved nearer and nearer, two manipulating claws—used to place containers on the ore carriers—began to open, ready to lock onto the station's superstructure.

Pressing their faces to the viewing port, Gerard, Kumiko, Kingston and Anna huddled together, peering out at the tug as it moved closer to the station, its claws wide apart. Michael appeared in the doorway looking tired and dirty, and eased his way in beside Kumiko, forcing Kingston aside.

Complaining bitterly, and not wanting to miss a single moment, Kingston promptly clambered up onto a crate to get a better view. 'That's what I'm going to be when I grow up,' he exclaimed excitedly. 'A space tug pilot. Kingston Lewis: *Space Ace!*'

'If this doesn't work, genius, you won't have to worry about a career. You won't even see your next birthday!' Gerard growled under his breath, watching nervously as the tug finally connected with the station, locking onto the superstructure with a loud reverberating clang.

The children silently watched as the red glow of the tug's thrusters died away. The excitement over, they realised that with the tug finally in place, the perilous moment of blast off would soon be a reality. In three hours, the tug's thrusters would be re-ignited, and they would know for certain if they would survive Ingessol's daring plan.

'I guess that's it then,' Kingston announced from the gloom, and he and Anna raced to the service gallery above the control room to watch preparations for blast off while Kumiko returned to assist Professor Ingessol with the central computers.

Michael took one last look at the space tug, gripping onto the giant hull of the station. It looked tiny by comparison, and at that moment, its task seemed impossible. Michael could feel the knot forming in the pit of his stomach as he made his way back to the hydro lab, Gerard following grudgingly behind.

By now the lab was almost complete. Michael and Gerard had managed to scrounge enough materials and equipment from various parts of the station to make the necessary connections from the algae tanks to the atmospheric purifier. All that remained was some minor plumbing and final checking.

Michael was tackling one of the last valves on the purifier when a loud clanging noise behind him stopped him in his tracks. Gerard was hammering a stubborn piece of pipe with a large wrench.

'You're going to split it!' Michael complained.

'Look I'm helping aren't I? Quit your whingeing,' Gerard snapped. He was growing very tired of working in the lab and even more tired of Michael telling him what to do.

Just as Michael was about to snap back, Kingston rushed into the lab. 'Gerard,' he called, 'Karl wants you down at the docking room, on the double. Something about the tug's thrusters.'

Gerard grinned at Michael. Finally he was rid of him *and* the hydro lab. 'Just when I was getting attached to all this algae,' he quipped sarcastically. Tossing his wrench to Michael, he sprinted from the lab. Kingston was quick to follow. He knew if he hung around, he'd end up with a job or two. 'Sorry Michael,' he said as he left. 'Got to see a girl about a dinosaur.'

From their secret vantage point in the service gallery, Kingston and Anna watched nervously as the colonists below made last minute preparations for the launch from Jupiter's orbit. Kumiko was in her element, sitting next to Professor Ingessol behind one of the computer terminals.

'Kumi? Launch window, how long please?' Ingessol asked, as he carefully studied a computer generated diagram of their escape route.

Kumiko checked the readout on the video mesh in

front of her. 'Fifteen minutes,' she replied and Professor Ingessol began to key commands into his computer console. Suddenly he became alarmed, rekeying the commands and checking the image. Something was very wrong.

'Sam, we've lost control of the tug's thrusters,' he reported over the communicator. 'It's not the computers here. Our ignition systems check out. It must be in the tug. If we don't have those thrusters, we won't have enough power to pull out of gravity.'

Duffy glared at Ingessol. He'd had enough. This was just the excuse he needed. 'Right. That's it! We have to postpone. There's no alternative,' he insisted, striding across to Beth, ordering her to shut down the ignition sequence.

Kingston turned disappointedly to Anna. 'Looks like we won't be going after all,' he said. 'They'll never fix it in time.'

'Of course they'll fix it,' Anna scoffed, trying to reassure him. 'Gerard's with them. He can fix anything!'

In the space tug's cargo pod, Gerard was reaching inside the tiny service hatch. He felt for the manual thruster control hydraulics and checked that the pressure hoses were still intact.

'They're fine,' he reported to his father, wiping thick grease from his arm. Karl quickly sealed the service hatch while Gerard clambered through to the cockpit to convey the news to Sam.

'Professor, we'll fire it from here. We can do it manually,' Sam said to Ingessol. 'Gerard, better buckle yourself in. It's going to get a bit rough in here.'

Gerard quickly climbed into the seat next to Sam as he prepared to fire the tug's thrusters. As Gerard snapped the belt buckle shut, Duffy's face appeared on the video mesh in front of them. 'We can't risk it! Stop this madness!' he demanded. 'I will not be responsible.'

With five minutes remaining, there was no time to argue. 'George will you get off the air,' Sam exclaimed.

'Retract solar sails,' Ingessol commanded. 'And I'll need readouts on escape velocity.'

'Sails retracting,' Akiko advised, as the giant wings hanging over KL5 began to fold back into the body of the station.

Kumiko eyed her video mesh. 'Sails locked into position,' she reported then turned to the service gallery to see Kingston and Anna peering down at them. She crossed her fingers for luck, and Kingston and Anna did likewise with a wave.

'Three minutes,' Ingessol reported to Sam. 'On your toes everyone. We don't need any more surprises.'

The big moment had arrived. Michael checked the row of safety fuses on the atmospheric purifier. Everything appeared to be in order. He looked around him and happily surveyed the makeshift laboratory. Weeks of hard work were about to pay off. He drew a deep breath, reached for the switches and, flicking each of them on, watched for any sign of life. Nothing. The archaic machine didn't respond.

'Setting manual thrusters,' Sam yelled as he locked the tug's ignition switches onto stand by. Gerard turned towards the cargo pod and called to Karl who was securing the final thruster control into position.

'Dad! get out of there,' he yelled, 'ignition's commencing.' Years of surviving on spare parts, repairs and makeshift replacements had made the tug unpredictable at best.

Karl returned quickly to the cockpit. As he strapped himself in beside Sam and Gerard, Ingessol counted down the remaining seconds. 'Good luck Sam. Five, four, three, two ... '

Sam opened the ignition lock covers. He hit the ignition buttons and the shudder of the thrusters filled the cockpit, growing louder by the second.

The noise permeated throughout the station and up in the service gallery, Kingston and Anna huddled together as the air ducts and cable housings around the gallery began to vibrate wildly. As the noise increased, Anna tightened her grip on Ronald the dinosaur, almost causing his eyeballs to pop from their sockets.

Below them, Ingessol looked about anxiously as bits and pieces of machinery began to shake and rattle. 'Come on you piece of junk,' he muttered. 'Fifty per cent escape velocity,' Tatsuya reported as the giant station began to move slowly towards Jupiter.

In the space tug, Gerard gripped the sides of his seat as Sam increased power. The thrusters roared to capacity, sucking fuel from the reserve, straining to push the station forwards. 'I wanted to be in the thick of it, not up to my neck in it!' Gerard exclaimed, through gritted teeth.

'Acceleration ninety per cent,' Tatsuya reported to Ingessol. Kumiko looked up at the large video mesh above her. Jupiter loomed up towards them. 'Ninety two per cent and holding.'

Duffy rushed at Ingessol. 'We're not going to make it,' he shouted. 'You'll kill us all!'

'Throw everything at it Sam,' Ingessol yelled over the communicator.

'No! You'll cook the thrusters. You'll blow the tug to smithereens!' Duffy warned as Sam slid the thruster's power controls to their limit.

Michael steadied himself as the vibrations rattled through the hydro lab. The knot tightened in his stomach. 'Ninety three per cent,' Tatsuya's voice crackled over the intercom. 'Come on! What's another seven per cent!' Michael said determinedly, throwing open the control panels to the purifier and checking the safety fuses. Everything appeared to be in order. He threw the switches one more time as Tatsuya's voice crackled again. 'Ninety five ... '

'Come on you heap of junk!' Michael exclaimed, thumping the purifier with Gerard's wrench. To his surprise, the purifier came to life. Water began pumping through the machine, coursing through the algae tanks and plant beds. Michael leapt for joy. The hydro lab was operational. It'd better be worth it, he thought, listening for another report.

'Ninety seven per cent,' Tatsuya yelled to Ingessol. 'Ninety eight ... '

'Ninety nine ... Escape velocity,' Tatsuya reported loudly across the control room. Slowly, KL5 began to round the huge planet, using Jupiter's gravity against itself, picking up momentum, and swinging around and beyond the fierce giant in a slingshot action. As the colonists looked at the large video mesh above them, the images of turbulent Jupiter begin to recede behind them.

Kingston threw his arm around Anna and Ronald and hugged them tightly. 'We're going home,' he yelled above the loud cheering below them. 'We're going to Earth.'

While celebrations broke out in the control room, Michael slid down the side of the purifier, collapsing exhausted on the floor. He proudly surveyed the lab as lights blinked, machinery hummed, and invisibly, algae and oxygen began to flow. 'Nothing to it,' he muttered, as KL5 sailed beyond Jupiter, out into deep space.

CHAPTER SIX

FORBIDDEN REALITY

Safely beyond Jupiter's gravity, the colonists spent the next precious days assessing the station for damage caused during blast off. Fortunately, apart from some over-burning in the thrusters causing the tug's ignition systems to fuse, and ongoing problems with the central computers, damage was minimal. The derelict old hulk had held together.

As the weeks passed and the giant space station journeyed towards its destination, life on board the station gradually settled into a daily routine, with the colonists busily prepared for a fuel-saving, fly-by manoeuvre around Saturn. Duffy organised work schedules, Ingessol and Beth toiled to remove the bugs from the outmoded and unpredictable computers, Sam dismantled the space tug thrusters for repair while Karl tried to reconstruct the solar sail hydraulics. Their work required them to be resourceful. Spare parts were scarce, if not non-existent, and the colonists had to make do and invent and improvise where necessary, as they battled to maintain the station.

Gradually, the remaining handful of engineers carefully and methodically began checking the lower levels of the station, eventually declaring most of them safe, although Duffy still insisted that certain remote areas were off limits, particularly to the children.

With everyone in the space station busy, Duffy and Professor Ingessol had scheduled daily chores for each of the children.

Michael had been given the responsibility of maintaining the hydro lab. He spent his time grafting plants and inspecting the atmospheric purifiers. Kumiko assisted in the control room behind the computer consoles, while Gerard worked with his father servicing the power generators and helping out with essential mechanical repairs whenever needed. In their spare time, and whenever they could dodge Duffy's persistent surveillance, they explored the rest of the station. It was such a busy time during these first few weeks that nobody remembered it was Kingston's birthday.

Kingston couldn't believe the oversight. Even his mother had forgotten. Total disaster! He sat slouched and forlorn in the medical bay, determined to trigger Helen's memory. 'Aaaah,' he droned while Helen held a spatula to his tongue and examined the back of his throat.

'Nope,' she said, 'No fatal diseases in there.' She removed the spatula, then felt the glands under his throat. Normal. 'Any headaches?' she asked, gently brushing the hair from his forehead.

Kingston shrugged and looked even more miserable. 'Too much excitement I think.'

'You sure you haven't overlooked something?' Kingston squeaked in a croaky voice, looking hopefully at his mother.

'Don't think so,' she said. Just to make sure, Helen placed a thermometer in his mouth to check his temperature.

Kingston frowned. 'Something really important maybe?' he mumbled.

'Just sit still,' Helen said, collecting a tray of instruments and returning them to the room next door.

'Like what day it is,' Kingston muttered miserably to himself. While his mother was out of the room, he removed the thermometer from his mouth, took Gerard's multi-mate from his pocket, switched to flame mode and waved it gently under the bulb.

While Kingston was busy organising his illness,

Karl was in serious trouble. As he was trying to fix one of the power generators inside the machinery bay, the turbine suddenly activated and began to spray him with a cloud of gas. Sam immediately came to his aid, and sent Gerard in search of help.

In the control room, Beth was keying commands into her computer console. A frown crossed her face. 'Professor, the computer's downloading,' she reported to Ingessol. 'The whole system is going crazy. And I'm getting fire alerts! Level seven. The power generators.'

Duffy wheeled around to Ingessol. 'Contain it. Seal it off,' he ordered.

But before Ingessol could do anything, Gerard burst into the room and breathlessly yelled to Beth. 'No! Dad's in there. We need help. Gas leak! Call Helen!'

'Get him up here. Straight away!' Helen said, slamming the communicator back into its cradle. She rushed into the examination bay where Kingston sat innocently with the thermometer back in his mouth.

'Better make yourself scarce,' she said, quickly removing the thermometer and bustling Kingston from the room. 'I've got a crisis.'

'But what about my crisis? I could be dying,' he protested.

Obligingly, Helen quickly glanced at the temperature. 'Fifty degrees? I think we're too late,' she said throwing Kingston a suspicious look.

'What? What did I do?' Kingston protested, trying to look innocent.

'I don't have time for this,' she said, noticing the multi-mate and tossing it to him. 'Please Kingston. We'll talk later.'

'You never spend time with me any more. I bet Dad wouldn't forget if he were here,' Kingston grumbled, remembering his younger days on earth and the happy times he had spent with his father.

Helen saw the sad look on Kingston's face but before she could say anything, Sam, Duffy and Gerard rushed

Karl into the examination bay. 'Come on mate, out of the way,' Sam said as he bustled Kingston from the doorway. 'He copped a blast of gas in the face. The turbines went crazy. I don't know what happened.'

Deep in the lower levels of KL5, in a section that Duffy had deemed off-limits, Kumiko continued to key commands into a dust-covered terminal.

In the centre of the chamber, above two unusual looking chairs each with switches and electronic gadgets set in the arm rests, a pair of spherical-shaped, plexi-glass visors descended with a drone from the ceiling. Kumiko had seen similar machines on earth. These were older and less sophisticated, but still enticing nonetheless. When the visors were in place, she slid an info-file into the terminal, keyed in another command, and watched as images of a thick green forest spread across the visors.

Smiling to herself, Kumiko quickly removed the file and switched the terminal off. Casting one last look at the central apparatus, she slid her hand over the light switches and the chamber went dark.

Professor Ingessol swung open the control panel on the atmospheric purifier. 'You haven't noticed anything strange? No faults or hiccups?' he asked Michael, casting an expert eye over the gauges and safety switches.

'Valves need a bit of a thump now and then. But nothing out of the ordinary,' Michael replied, a little puzzled by Ingessol's behaviour.

'Everything seems okay. But just be careful anyway. I don't want a repeat of this morning's incident,' Ingessol warned as he checked the pressure valves.

'Is Karl going to be okay?' Michael asked.

'It seems so. Fire retardant, shock, that's all. The

computer went crazy. It thought there was a fire. So ... shhht! Some sort of phantom signals. A nasty, inexplicable bug in the system.' Ingessol shook his head, unable to explain the craziness. 'And we have to find it. The Saturn fly-by is critical. I don't want to navigate with a computer that's got a mind of its own.'

Kingston had come to the same conclusion as he scowled at the unappetising food wafer, then placed it in the recon machine. 'Today of all days. Fate, that's what it is!' he muttered to himself. 'A rogue computer. It's trying to take over. First Karl, then slowly the rest of us. One by one, we'll all be gassed.' He was so preoccupied with predicting disaster, he didn't notice Kumiko enter the room.

'Have you seen Michael?' she asked breathlessly.

Kingston ignored the question. 'Cyanide, I bet it was cyanide. The central computer, it's trying to gas us with cyanide,' he groaned.

'If it was cyanide, we'd all be dead!'

'Diluted cyanide then,' Kingston replied. 'Struck down in my prime. Not that anyone cares. I don't suppose *you* know what day it is?' he muttered, looking hopefully at Kumiko.

'It's the day after yesterday, when you asked me if I knew what day tomorrow was. Now have you seen Michael?'

Kingston looked annoyed. 'Why the sudden interest in Michael? I'm having a crisis here. Doesn't anybody care?'

Kumiko gave up with a sigh. She wasn't in the mood for Kingston's dramatics and rushed from the room, passing Gerard on the way out.

'All right rodent! Where is it?' Gerard said threateningly, clapping a hand on Kingston's shoulder. 'Hand it over or you'll regret you were ever born.'

Reaching into his pocket, Kingston retrieved Gerard's multi-mate and thrust it at him. 'Here have the stupid thing! I hate this place! I wish I was on Earth,' he exclaimed, rushing from the room, surprising Gerard by his outburst.

'Too easy,' Gerard thought to himself. 'What's up with him?' As Gerard pocketed his multi-mate, the food recon machine opened with a ping. 'What on earth is that?!' he exclaimed, peering down at the bubbling mass of repulsive brown sludge. 'What is it with this dump?'

Scrambling over a pile of boxes, Kingston settled into a seat at the front of the viewing bubble. He sat there silently staring out at the ringed planet, Saturn, far off in the distance, wishing it was Earth.

'What are you doing hiding in here?' Anna asked, peering over the pile of boxes. 'I've been looking for you. You want to play a game of Astroblaze?'

Kingston shook his head as Anna settled down beside him. 'Trust us to take the long way home,' he mumbled miserably, still gazing out at Saturn. 'If Duffy's so smart, how come we're going the wrong way? We're never going to get to Earth at this rate.'

'Kingston, what's the matter?' Anna asked, mystified by his morose behaviour.

'If you have to ask, then there's no point explaining,' he replied cryptically, climbing down from the seat, and abandoning Anna.

Deep within the bowels of KL5, Kumiko was steering Michael down a deserted corridor. 'So where are we going?' Michael asked, intrigued by Kumiko's secrecy.

'You'll see. At first I wasn't sure what it was. And then I didn't think it would work.'

'Didn't know if what would work?'

Kumiko glanced at Michael mysteriously, then hearing the scuffling of feet behind them, she wheeled around to see Kingston scampering after them. 'And where do you think you're going?' she asked.

'With you,' Kingston replied sheepishly.

'Oh no you're not!'

Kingston looked at Michael for support but none was forthcoming. 'Don't look at me,' he said.

'But you're supposed to be my friend,' Kingston complained bitterly. He glared at Michael for a second, then feeling betrayed, rushed off in the other direction.

Kumiko shrugged. 'Truly weird,' she said, then directed Michael to the end of the corridor. Forcing him to close his eyes, she led him into the eerie chamber.

'You can open them,' she said, running her hand over the light switches. As the room lit up, Michael stood staring at the strange looking apparatus in front of him. Two chairs, like pilot's seats, were raised on pedestals, with wires and coiled cables rising up to the plexi-glass domes suspended above them. Other cables ran from the arm rests to a computer console and a large video mesh to one side. It appeared to be some sort of bizarre cockpit.

'Virtual reality,' Michael heard Kumiko say behind him.

'Get out of here!' he exclaimed disbelievingly.

'You ever seen anything like it before?'

Michael shook his head. 'They had VR machines on Io for environment training. But nothing like these. These must be off the ark!'

Kumiko moved over to the machine and lifted one of the clear canopies. 'It's got everything. Full sensory illusion. Sound, touch, sight, even smell.'

Michael was fascinated by the machines. He moved around them, carefully inspecting the equipment. 'Kumi, I'm not really sure about this,' he said, as Kumiko rifled through the collection of info-files at the control module.

'Here's your big chance to go to Earth,' she said, holding up a file. 'You want to know what rain feels like, don't you?!'

Kumiko cheekily waved the file in front of Michael,

trying to tempt him. 'How do we know it works?' he asked, still uncertain.

'I've already tested it. Now what's it to be?' she said, ignoring Michael's look of surprise, and sorting through the files. 'Body surfing, flying, forests, lunar isolation training. Boring. Forget that!' she scoffed, tossing the training file to one side.

'Forests,' Michael finally said, overcoming his apprehension.

'Okay, forests it is,' Kumiko grinned and slid the file into the control module then threw several switches. The machine began to hum, and as it began to load the program, the overhead lights flickered to a dull half light.

Straining to see in the flickering light, Gerard carefully examined the rehydration unit in the food recon machine before sliding it back into place with a thump. 'What's it to be this time?' he joked to himself, checking the computer connections, and pressing the control buttons. The machine whirred normally for a second but, as the overhead lights flashed brightly, it gave an abrupt rattle and went dead.

'Come on, you antiquated piece of junk!' he muttered, thumping the machine with his fist, as Anna appeared behind him.

'Gerard, have you seen Kingston? He's disappeared again.'

'Little rodent's probably off sulking somewhere,' Gerard answered, more interested in his food than in Kingston's well being.

'Gerard! Have you?' Anna persisted.

'Look, he's probably skulking around in one of his air ducts. Give me a break, will you. Bloke's trying to eat,' he replied, cautiously opening the recon machine to discover thick sludge splattered over the interior.

Gerard was right. In a gloomy corridor on level 6, an air duct grid popped from its fitting and Kingston's grimy face appeared. He looked around, then squeezed himself through the opening and moved slowly towards the chamber where he could see Michael and Kumiko. He knew they were up to something and he intended to find out what. He was tired of being left out. As he moved cautiously inside the chamber, his eyes widened.

Kumiko and Michael were strapped into the virtual reality chairs. Cautiously, Kingston sneaked across the rear of the room and ducked down behind the VR control module.

'Relax. It won't hurt a bit,' Kumiko said to Michael as they prepared to enter the program. She placed a soft metallic helmet over her head and Michael did likewise.

'They pick up your thought patterns,' she explained. 'You have to think yourself inside the program.'

'I'm really not sure about this,' Michael said nervously.

'Don't be such a wimp.'

'But I can't see a thing,' Michael protested.

'You will.'

Kumiko's hand moved over the arm rest of her couch and punched a collection of switches. From above, the plexi-glass dome lowered to surround them. As Kumiko flicked another switch, an image of a forest, cool and green, appeared on their visors and the adjacent video mesh.

Michael's head jerked back for a moment, unsure of what was going on. The image distorted obliquely and then after a moment, as Michael settled, corrected itself.

'It's fantastic,' he exclaimed.

'You're only seeing it at the moment, wait until you're actually inside it,' Kumiko explained. 'Follow me,' she said and then began concentrating for all she was worth, thinking herself inside the program.

As she concentrated, the image of the forest again started to distort. Tall trees bent askew and colours flashed negative, positive, red and then green. After a moment, the image restored itself and this time Michael could see Kumiko standing amid the trees.

'Concentrate,' he heard her say through his head piece.

'I am concentrating.' Michael closed his eyes and thought of nothing but the forest and immediately found himself inside it. He had never been in the open air before without a pressure suit and instinctively, he began gulping for breath as the forest contorted around him. It was as if it were alive. The ground suddenly rose up around him, peaked then dropped away abruptly. Trees pitched back and forth, stretching and looming grotesquely towards him, as deep distorted electronic howls blasted through his headpiece.

'Kumi,' he yelled in a panic. 'Something's wrong!'

'Just relax. You have to control it! Just breathe normally.'

'Where's the switch for this thing?' Michael screamed, still gagging for air.

'In your head. Mind switch! Concentrate.'

Climbing out from behind the humming control console, Kingston peered up at the video mesh to see images of Michael and Kumiko standing in the forest. It didn't make any sense. They were sitting in the apparatus, yet on the screens they were standing in the forest.

Suddenly the image distorted again and a loud drone wailed over the speakers. Kingston quickly ducked down again, out of sight, as Michael disappeared from the program. 'What are you trying to do, kill me?' he yelled at Kumiko, who was still inside the program.

'Isn't it wild?'

'No. I could have been zapped. A thousand volts right to the brain!'

'But it's not real,' Kumiko reminded Michael via his head-piece.

'That's easy for you to say.'

'Just relax. You have to be calm to control the images. All you have to do is think yourself in and think yourself out.'

Kingston sat listening to the instructions, a smile passing from ear to ear, and watched as Michael once more appeared on the viewing screens. Kingston looked enviously up at the forest, feeling strangely melancholic. He wanted to be on Earth, safe and happy, far away from the space station and its dangers.

Standing in the forest, Michael slowly opened his eyes. This time he was in control. 'It's unbelievable!' he exclaimed as he looked around at the forest's beauty. 'How far does it go? Kumi?' But there was no reply. 'Come on! Stop messing around!' Michael yelled, feeling a little scared. 'Kumi? Where are you?'

'You'll have to find me,' he heard Kumiko reply from further in the forest. Relieved to hear her voice, Michael soon relaxed and began wandering cheerfully through the trees. He had never seen such amazing plant life. Feeling strangely euphoric, he reached out and touched the greenery, the leaves cool and clean in his hands.

'It's fantastic. I can even smell it,' he yelled, then set off after Kumiko, moving deeper inside the program.

Inside the control room, Beth looked at her computer console with alarm. 'The central computer's dumping its memory again,' she exclaimed to Ingessol, who was examining the readout on the video mesh in front of him.

'It's the same thing. Exactly. That same phantom signal,' Ingessol reported to Duffy, who hovered nearby waiting for an explanation. 'Something's hacking into the system.'

'I want a location before we have another disaster on our hands,' Duffy barked across the room.

'I'm trying, I'm trying,' Ingessol replied curtly as he keyed commands into Beth's console. 'Something's sucking the life out of this thing.'

Anna leaned over her mother's shoulder. Looking a little frightened, she turned to Gerard. 'Maybe Kingston was right. It's a rogue computer—and it's going to get us all, one by one,' she whispered.

'Well let's hope it gets him first,' Gerard sniggered as Professor Ingessol swung around to Duffy. 'Level six! It's sourced from level six,' he yelled and Duffy immediately turned on his heels and rushed from the room.

Moving deeper and deeper into the virtual reality program, Michael and Kumiko followed a narrow track through towering trees, flanked by ancient-looking tree ferns with fronds that threw a canopy over their path. Finding a stream, they followed it until it opened out into a clear pool. They stopped for a moment to catch their breath. 'You ever been to a real forest?' Michael asked.

'My parents took me once. Our last trip to Earth.' Kumiko checked her watch. 'We'd better head back.'

'Not yet. I want to go further,' Michael said, setting off again.

Suddenly Kumiko's head jerked back slightly. Her own image of the forest distorted momentarily, the glassy surface of the pool appearing to shatter. She looked around anxiously, uncertain of what had caused the visual jolt. 'I think we'd better get out of here,' she said.

But Michael wouldn't be dissuaded. He moved deeper into the forest. 'Don't be such a wimp. Let's see how far we can go,' he called back over his shoulder.

'There's something wrong. Image distortion. Didn't you see it?'

'You've got to control it, remember,' Michael said stubbornly, reminding Kumiko of her own instructions and moving further into the forest.

'Michael! No!' Kumiko yelled after him. 'We've gone too far. I don't think the computer has enough memory. The program is breaking up!'

'Don't be such a panic merchant,' Michael replied and Kumiko followed after him, trying to convince him to mind switch from their artificial surroundings.

Kingston stood by the computer console watching Kumiko chase after Michael, straining to hear what they were saying. The sound had become heavy with static and all he could make out were muffled voices. As he listened, he heard footsteps coming from outside, rushing towards the chamber. He ducked down out of sight, just as Duffy burst into the room.

Carefully, he peered out from his hiding place as Duffy moved slowly towards the VR apparatus, watching on the screen as Michael and Kumiko sprinted through the forest.

'Ten more minutes,' Michael pleaded with Kumiko.

Again Kumiko's head jerked back a little, as the forest in front of her seemed to split violently apart into a black void beyond.

'We go now,' she said anxiously.

'What are you so afraid of?' Michael asked, turning to Kumiko. But she was gone, her image disappearing from the forest. Overhead he heard her crackling voice surround him.

'Michael I think you'd better get out here. I'm not fooling around.'

Reluctantly, Michael began to concentrate but as he did, the images around him seemed to go crazy. Suddenly the ground seemed to open beneath him and he felt himself falling into blackness, his stomach rising into his mouth. Fighting back his panic, Michael concentrated as hard as he could and finally he felt himself pass through the mind switch back to reality.

'I think we'd better do the beach next time,' he said to Kumiko as he stood up.

'There won't be a next time,' a voice growled behind him. He wheeled around to see Duffy glowering at him. 'Out! The pair of you! This little escapade of yours has endangered the entire station and everyone on it.'

'It's just a program,' Kumiko said disbelievingly, as Duffy emphatically shut the machine down and ushered them from the room, slamming the door behind them.

'Need I remind you,' he sneered, 'that the computer on this station is old, not to mention unreliable! We're currently surviving on half the power we need. You start up a program as complicated as that and of course it's going to have an effect!'

'But it was just a bit of fun,' Michael murmured.

'Don't push me boy. It's a training device—not a toy,' Duffy said, securing the locking device on the chamber door. 'This room remains locked until I can have that thing dismantled. You understand?'

Michael and Kumiko nodded, defeated.

'And not a word to your little friends.'

Inside the dark chamber, Kingston clambered from behind the computer console. Looking back at the machinery, a strange smile crossed his face, then he clambered into the air duct, away from the chamber.

Anna was enjoying a wonderful dream about food, lots of it and not a dollop of recon sludge in sight, when Kingston woke her up. 'But I don't want to explore,' she groaned, still half asleep.

Kingston begged her and together they crept down the central stairwell and along the dark corridor that led to the virtual reality chamber.

As Kingston explained what they had to do to see a forest, Anna hesitated. 'I don't think we should be here doing this,' she said. 'No-one will ever know,' Kingston replied, helping her into the apparatus.

Beth was nearing the end of her long shift behind the computer console. The rest of the room was quiet, apart from the humming of the computers and rattling of air vents. She was half asleep when she noticed a flicker on her video mesh, and the overhead screen starting to flash and fuse. Worse, on her own screen, she saw the computer start to download its programs once more.

Kingston and Anna walked slowly through the forest, taking in their new surroundings. Kingston was awe-struck. He'd never seen such dense forest or tall trees, even on Earth. He'd been raised in the city in an apartment, and the only trees he'd seen were in parks and gardens. Everything seemed larger than life, even the bracken ferns and the vines and creepers that wrestled their way up the thick tree trunks.

Kingston gazed about, triumphant, but Anna looked anxiously around the unfamiliar landscape. It was getting dark, and sights and sounds bombarded her mind. She pleaded with Kingston to leave, but he ignored her.

'This would be a great spot for a tree house,' he joked, as he looked up an enormous tree towering above him. 'We could have a ladder made out of vines, catch our own food. And the best thing of all, no parents!'

But Anna wasn't listening. A shrill bird sound screeched from a nearby bush, causing her to jump. 'Kingston this isn't funny any more. What's the matter with you?'

'Nothing,' he replied, deliberately turning away from her, and wandering through the trees towards a nearby lake.

Not wanting to be left alone, Anna quickly followed along behind. 'You've been acting weird all day,' she said, glancing about anxiously. 'You're supposed to be my friend, remember?'

Finally Kingston conceded. 'Promise you won't tell? Cross your heart and hope to be blown into little squishy bits,' he insisted.

Anna crossed her heart with a quick gesture. 'I promise.'

'She forgot my birthday.'

'What? Today's your birthday?' Anna asked innocently.

Kingston nodded miserably. 'And my own mother? She forgets!'

'Well why didn't you say so?'

As Anna looked at the lake in the gathering gloom, a visual jolt rocked her eyes and she saw a large wave suddenly rise up and roll towards her. She let out a scream, then as quickly as it appeared, it disappeared again. Startled, she pleaded with Kingston. 'I want to go,' she said. 'I don't like it here!'

'No! I'm not going. I'm staying.'

'But you can't stay here forever,' Anna said to him.

'Just watch me,' Kingston said stubbornly, turning his back on her.

Anna had had enough. She disappeared from the program, leaving Kingston alone in the night air. 'So who needs you! I don't need anybody!' Kingston called out after her, a hint of uncertainty creeping into his voice.

Gerard was fast asleep when Anna rushed into his room. 'Gerard! Wake up,' she said, shaking him as hard as she could.

'He's in the machine. The computer's got him. You've got to get him out,' Anna pleaded.

'What are you babbling about?' Gerard replied groggily, still half asleep.

Anna quickly explained what had happened. Gerard

climbed from his bed and threw on a set of clothes. 'All right. Calm down. You'd better get Michael and Kumiko before the little rodent does some damage.'

In the control room, Beth, Professor Ingessol and Duffy studied the video mesh as the computer system downloaded its memory. 'Have you got a fix on it?' Duffy asked.

'Same as before. Level six,' Beth finally answered. Duffy turned towards the door. 'They're going to wish they were never born,' he muttered to himself, disappearing towards the lower levels.

As the children rushed to the VR chamber, they planned their next move. 'We've got to get him out of there before Duffy finds out,' Michael said, taking charge of the situation. He turned to Anna. 'You'd better get Helen, just in case.'

'I interrupted a perfectly good dream because of that little rodent,' Gerard complained, as Anna took off towards the medical bay. 'Why didn't he just tell us it was his birthday. Stubborn little rat!'

'His life's not going to be worth living if Duffy finds him first,' Michael warned, steering Gerard down the central stairwell and onto level five.

Duffy reached the virtual reality chamber before them. Entering the room, he moved towards the apparatus where Kingston's body sat perched in one of the chairs while his mind was elsewhere.

On the screen in front of him, Duffy could see Kingston moving further and further into the forest. 'Kingston! I want you out of there this instant!' he ordered.

Kingston didn't, couldn't, hear him, and Duffy looked at the humming machine unsure what to do. Lights flickered as Kingston moved deeper into the forest, and Duffy's hand passed over various switches and buttons, until finally it hovered over one that looked like a master control. He reached for the switch.

'Stop! Don't! You can't just turn it off,' Kumiko

shouted breathlessly, rushing across to him. 'It's not safe.'

'You'll fry his brain,' Michael added, dragging Duffy's hand away from the control switch.

Duffy angrily wrenched his hand away from Michael. 'I told you lot to stay away from here,' he barked. 'You disobeyed a direct order!'

'But Kingston didn't know!' Michael argued.

'I don't care! I won't have him endangering the station,' Duffy said, as he reached for the switch.

'No! You could really hurt him.' Kumiko was insistent. 'You want to take that risk?'

Duffy hesitated. Perhaps she was right.

'Someone'll have to go in there to talk him out. It's the safest way,' Kumiko suggested. 'You'll have to do it Michael.'

Michael looked anxiously up at the screen. The overhead lights began to flicker as the central computer continued to download to make room for the VR program.

'We don't have a lot of time,' Kumiko warned, as Gerard glanced up at the flickering lights.

'Yeah, move it. You're the only one he trusts,' he added.

Michael quickly climbed into the apparatus next to Kingston. Kumiko lowered the plexi-glass visor over him, and the screens around the visor immediately lit up with images of the forest. 'Wish me luck,' Michael said as he began to concentrate on the mind switch.

Duffy watched nervously as the flickering of the overhead lights intensified, and the VR computer continued to drain more power from the station's central computer system.

'This is madness,' he said. 'I'm pulling the plug on it right now.'

Before he could act, Helen and Anna appeared at the doorway. 'George! No! Please. It's too dangerous,' Helen warned. 'They could both suffer psychic shock.'

Duffy reluctantly bowed to Helen's expertise. 'I accept no responsibility,' he warned, turning to the screen. 'Five minutes. No more!'

Michael wandered uneasily through the dark forest. It appeared different this time. It wasn't just the darkness, somehow it seemed alive. He could hear strange sounds around him, shadows appeared to move, and the wind whispered through the trees like a thousand voices. Steeling himself, he trekked further into the forest, but the further he went, and the more anxious he felt, the more menacing his surroundings became. He called out to Kingston but there was no response. 'Kingston! Answer me. Stop fooling around.'

'What are you doing here?' Kingston asked, his voice floating around Michael. Turning he saw Kingston sitting forlornly on a large rock gazing out at the lake.

'I was going to ask you the same question. Are you going to tell me what's going on?'

'As if you'd care,' Kingston muttered, getting to his feet and moving further into the forest.

'Kingston please! We have to go back,' Michael pleaded.

'No way. I'm staying. Me here and them up there,' he said gesturing to the sky above him.

'You don't understand. It's too dangerous. The central computer is downloading.'

'Says who? I don't trust you any more. I'm not going back. I've run away from home!' he said in a petulant tone.

'You can't run away. Not here. It's not real,' Michael added, trying to get Kingston to see reason.

'So that means you're not real either. You're a fake.'

'Yes. No. I mean I'm just a computer representation. Kingston please. We're really sorry we forgot your birthday.'

'Anna! I knew she'd blab. You can't trust anyone any more.'

'She's worried about you. We all are, okay?'

114

Kingston walked further into the forest. 'If my Dad were still alive, I bet he wouldn't forget,' he said sadly.

'Kingston can we go please? Before our brains get fried,' Michael pleaded desperately.

'Every time I want something, my Mum's always too busy. The only way I can get any attention is if I've got the measles,' Kingston said.

'You can't blame your Mum. She's got everyone to look after.'

Duffy turned to Helen. 'The further they go in, the more danger they put the station in,' he warned ominously, watching the computer control module as it continued to search for additional memory space. 'They're placing us all at risk. I can't let it continue.' Duffy turned once more to the master controls.

'George no! These things were banned because they're dangerous. Addictive. They feed on your own mind set. You can't just rip them out of there,' Helen pleaded, trying to get Duffy to see reason.

Inside the program, Michael sat down next to Kingston. 'I'm sure your Mum really loves you. Deep down. You can't just pack up and leave. We need you.'

'Nobody would ever notice. I'm not important up there.'

'Of course you are. We couldn't survive without the tunnel rat. No offence. You know that.'

Kingston turned to Michael and looked at him hopefully. 'You're just saying that,' he said.

'Who else is going to guide us through the air ducts. And find short cuts. And trick Duffy.'

Kingston brightened at the thought of himself being indispensable. He grinned at Michael, 'And beat you at Astroblaze!'

'And do really stupid things,' Michael laughed.

'Duffy's really going to flip, isn't he?' Kingston worried.

'Probably. But we'll look after you. Promise,' Michael replied as he saw his image of the forest distort violently. The lake suddenly disappeared into a deep black gorge and shadows rose out of the gloom, taking on strange life forms. The computer was running out of memory. 'They're not real,' Michael muttered to himself over and over as the shadows swooped up at him. Grabbing Kingston by the arm, he leapt to his feet. 'We have to go. Now!' he shouted.

'Come on Michael. You can do it,' Kumiko urged, when without warning, the lights in the chamber failed altogether, and an eerie red emergency light kicked on. In the distance a siren rang out and the station's air purifiers began to shut down. On the screen in front of them, Kumiko watched in horror as the images of Michael and Kingston began to shake and shimmer. 'What's happening?' she asked, as their images fused into the background.

Duffy had had enough. The station was shutting itself down. He turned to the control console and reached for the master switches. 'Please Mr Duffy. Just one more minute. He's my friend,' Anna pleaded. She looked up at Duffy with her large and innocent eyes and he weakened. 'One more minute,' he said gruffly.

In the forest, Michael offered Kingston his hand. 'Friends?' he asked. 'I guess so,' Kingston grinned and gave him their secret handshake as a loud crack of thunder volleyed overhead. 'Right! I'm out of here,' Kingston yelled above the noise.

Inside the chamber, Kumiko looked up at the control screens on the VR machine, then to her relief, saw Michael's image stabilise, then disappear as he mind switched. Kingston followed slowly and hesitantly.

As Michael and Kingston stepped out of the machine, Duffy immediately threw the switches on the VR control console while Helen flung her arms around Kingston. 'I was worried sick,' she said, relieved that he was safe and well. 'I'm really sorry about your birthday.'

'Yeah, good one rodent. You nearly exterminated the lot of us! What a birthday!' Gerard joked.

'Happy birthday,' Kumiko added warmly, joining in the huddle. 'Sorry we forgot.'

'That's okay,' Kingston said, soaking up all the attention. 'You can make it up to me,' he said cheekily.

Suddenly Duffy's voice boomed out in the chamber. 'I want this place sealed off. Permanently. Until I have that machine demolished. And you lot haven't heard the last of this,' he warned ominously as the children hurriedly left the chamber.

CHAPTER SEVEN

FIGHTING FIT

George Duffy was a man of his word. The next day, he ordered the dismantling of the virtual reality machine. While the rest of the colonists began reprogramming the central computer, preparing for the crucial fly-by mission around Saturn, the children returned to their respective chores.

Nothing further had been said about their adventures in the virtual reality machine which, given Duffy's warning, was a surprise to each of them. Michael had expected to be punished severely but instead, he'd been told to resume his duties in the hydro lab.

He had been given the task of harvesting algae. Food supplies were running low and if they were to survive the long journey, they would have to supplement their diet with processed algae.

'Are we really going to have to eat that stuff,' Kingston muttered as he watched Michael decant the thick green sludge into plastic bags.

Nearby Gerard had downed tools and lay sunning himself under one of the hydro lamps, lazily carving his initials into his multi-mate. 'Watching algae grow. Riveting stuff,' he said to Michael. 'A bloke's going to go mental.'

'Look on the bright side,' Kingston interjected, 'You won't have far to go!'

'Knock it off rodent!' Gerard warned.

'If you'd stop your whingeing and get on with it, maybe we could help with the fly-by,' Michael added, keen to finish with the hydro lab so that he could watch the manoeuvre.

'As if Duffy'd agree to that. Not after your last little stunt!' Gerard muttered, adjusting a shiny reflector onto his face.

'He's probably forgotten all about it,' Kingston said hopefully. 'Maybe he's too busy.'

'As if,' Gerard replied, clearly unconvinced. 'He's probably got some filthy job saved up, ready to spring on us. And when he does, you're dead rodent.'

'Come on Gerard, lighten up! It's not every day you get to see Saturn!' Kingston said excitedly.

'Big deal! Seen one planet, seen them all.'

Kingston decided to ignore Gerard, and scooping up a container of algae, returned to help Michael. 'I don't get it,' Kingston said to Michael. 'Why Saturn, it's the wrong way, isn't it?'

'Watch and learn genius,' Michael said as he reached for a length of rubber that lay nearby on the floor. 'KL5 doesn't have enough fuel to get to earth, so we have to catch the ore carrier to raid its fuel, right?'

Kingston nodded. That part was easy.

'So, imagine Gerard is the ore carrier.'

'Makes sense, he's got rocks in his head,' Kingston quipped cheekily. Gerard glared at him. 'This close worm,' he said, holding up his thumb and forefinger, as if measuring the short distance between life and death.

Continuing his demonstration, Michael picked up an algae-filled bag. 'And this is KL5,' he said, placing the bag in the looped end of the rubber strap and beginning to swing it in a circle above his head.

'We fly towards Saturn. Then using gravity, we pick up speed, faster and faster. Then at the precise moment, we fire the thrusters and we rocket off towards the ore carrier and—'

Michael let go of one end of the rubber strap. The bag of algae sailed through the air, across the room, and splattered all over Gerard.

'You're for it now Einstein!' Gerard shouted

angrily, leaping to his feet, his clothes dripping.

Kingston looked at the split bag with a long face. 'Bad omen,' he thought to himself as Gerard picked up another bag of algae and hurled it at Michael. Quick on his feet, Michael managed to duck and the missile sailed past him and splattered on the wall next to the door just as Duffy entered, spraying him with the thick green sludge.

Duffy turned purple with rage. 'Come with me! The lot of you,' he ordered, and escorted the boys to the recreation room where Kumiko and Anna were waiting.

Standing at the head of the table, Duffy addressed the children in his typically officious way. 'Now that I have your complete and undivided attention, it is my unhappy duty to inform you all—' he began, smirking to himself, '—that after your misguided venture into the virtual reality program, and in accordance with long-term space flight requirements, each of you is to undergo a complete and thorough medical assessment.'

Kumiko's face dropped. She hated medicals. 'It's humiliating,' she whispered to Michael, 'being poked and prodded like some lab experiment.'

Gerard sank back in his seat and sneered across the table at Kingston. 'I knew he wouldn't forget,' he muttered.

'Your co-operation is expected, and I don't want any further trouble from any of you while we prepare for the Saturn fly-by,' Duffy continued. 'And one more thing. Oral intake will be limited three hours before your allotted assessment time. In the meantime, you can get on with your assigned duties.' Feeling pleased with himself, Duffy smiled sardonically at the children and strode out of the room.

Gerard leapt to his feet. 'Better hope they've got a special test for wimps,' he said cheekily to Michael.

'Drop dead!' Michael snarled as they returned to the hydro lab.

'He's just doing this to get even,' Kumiko complained bitterly. 'They might as well stick us in a cage and give us a little wheel to run around on.'

'Relax Kumi, there's nothing to worry about. Not if you're fit, and you look pretty fit to me,' Gerard said suavely.

'Stop grovelling Gerard,' Michael interjected, turning to the atmospheric purifiers to check the pressure valves. 'You're so obvious. As if Kumi has any interest in a neanderthal like you.'

Kumiko sighed in exasperation. 'But what happens if we fail?' she asked, trying to ignore the boys' banter.

'Physical torture for three weeks. Special diet. Special exercise,' Gerard replied as he tackled a difficult valve on the purifier. 'Duffy's special kind of hell!' he added, taking a swing at the valve and striking it hard with the end of his wrench.

'Gerard!' Michael exclaimed, worried the valve might split. 'Can't you use your brain for once.'

'What are you whingeing about, I fixed it didn't I?' Gerard replied provocatively, as the valve gave way and the pressure slowly subsided inside the filtration chamber.

Michael glared at Gerard. Being confined to close quarters on the space station, with little chance to escape one another, had exacerbated their natural dislike. For the remainder of the day, while he completed his work in the lab, Michael did his best to ignore Gerard's ongoing jibes.

The next morning Kingston bounded out of bed and raced off to his scheduled medical while the others made their way to the rec room for breakfast. Duffy had already begun food rationing on the station and normal meals were supplemented with algae.

'How are we expected to stay healthy on that?' Kumiko complained, poking at a bowl of algae soup.

'Can't let it go to waste,' Gerard said greedily.

As Kumiko pushed the bowl across the table, Kingston bounded into the room and struck an athletic-looking pose. 'Behold,' he announced proudly. 'You see before you a perfect physical specimen!'

Gerard wasn't impressed. 'All I can see is a scrawny little rodent,' he laughed, then turned to Kumiko. 'See! If he can pass, anyone can. Well, almost anyone.' Gerard shot Michael a sly glance.

'You'd better hope they don't throw in an intelligence test,' Michael retorted.

Kingston laughed. 'Yeah! Or a brain scan!'

'Right! That's it! I've had enough of your lip Faraday. You too rodent! You name it. I'm fitter, faster, and I've got more going on up here,' Gerard said, tapping his forehead.

'Prove it then,' Kumiko said, surprising all three boys. She'd grown tired of their constant bickering and now, she decided, was the time to put a stop to it. 'You think you can beat each other. Prove it. A race.' She gave Michael and Gerard a challenging look. 'Or maybe you're all talk,' she added, throwing down the gauntlet.

Michael and Gerard eyed one another. They knew that if they tried to back out now, they'd both suffer a serious loss of face. They had no option but to accept Kumiko's challenge.

Oblivious to the drama, Anna was cleaning patches of grease from Ronald the dinosaur when Kingston rushed into her quarters with the exciting news.

'There's going to be a race!' he babbled. 'Between Gerard and Michael!'

'And who's bright idea was that?' Anna asked.

'Kumi's. She's designing an obstacle course.'

'Michael won't stand a chance,' Anna replied as she polished Ronald's bulging glassy eyes. 'Gerard'll wipe the floor with him.'

But Kingston wasn't so sure. 'Maybe, maybe not,' he

said with a sly grin. 'It's not *just* a race. They have to use their brain as well.'

Plonking Ronald to one side, Anna sank back onto her bed. 'That could be a problem,' she said, knowing that thinking wasn't one of Gerard's strengths.

While Kumiko began planning the obstacle course, Kingston took it upon himself to act as Michael's personal trainer for the big event. Collecting bits and pieces of junk and old equipment, he secretly constructed a makeshift gymnasium in one of the old machinery bays.

'I don't know why I ever let you talk me into this,' Michael said as he surveyed the equipment. 'It's a stupid idea. I should just withdraw.'

'Are you kidding!' Kingston exclaimed. 'Gerard will never let you live it down. You'll be labelled a wimp forever. And what's Kumi going to think?'

Kingston had hit a raw nerve. Although Michael wasn't about to admit it, what Kumiko thought of him was very important. 'Kumi and her big mouth. Why do I feel like I've been conned? Surely she knows I can't win. The guy's a muscle head.'

'Oh great attitude! You have to believe in yourself. Believe you can win!' Kingston exclaimed as Michael half heartedly tried to lift a makeshift set of heavy weights. 'Or maybe hope that Gerard will lose,' he muttered under his breath, as Michael struggled with the weights.

Gerard lay flat out on his bed, filled with confidence about the victory that was to follow. 'I can beat Faraday with one hand tied behind my back,' he gloated, as Anna paced back and forth. 'Kumi's going to see what a total loser the guy really is!'

'It's not just a race,' Anna warned, trying to convince Gerard to prepare himself. 'What if there's tricky bits. What if you have to think?'

Gerard looked blankly at Anna.

'You know,' she said, 'Thinking. The activity that goes on between your ears.'

'What is there to think about? It's a race. You start, you run, you finish. And in *my* case, I win!' he laughed confidently.

Anna shook her head in frustration. She knew that to win, Gerard would have to kick his brain into gear, any gear. She tried another tack. 'If a man's brother is his nephew's cousin, what relationship is his mother to his second cousin?' she asked.

Gerard thought for a moment, then slumped back onto his bed. 'How should I know!'

'Think! It's good practice.'

'The only training I need to do is how to gloat. For when I annihilate Faraday!' Gerard replied. 'So what's the answer?'

Anna rolled her eyes in disbelief. 'Her next-door neighbour,' she said wryly, and marched out of the room in disgust.

Red-faced and dripping with perspiration, Michael heaved his chin painfully up to a horizontal piece of pipe while Kingston stood beside him urging him. 'That's great! You're doing really well! Five! Sixxxx!'

'You already said six,' Michael said, dangling from the pipe.

'Come on, put some effort into it.'

'I am!' Michael grunted, slowly hauling himself up to the crossbar again.

'You're not breathing. You've got to breathe,' Kingston said, striding around like a zealous football coach.

'How can I breathe and do chin-ups at the same time?' Michael gasped.

Kingston slapped his fist into his hand. 'Never say die. Think about winning. Think about Gerard *losing*. Think about Kumi *seeing* Gerard lose.'

That was exactly the encouragement Michael

needed. The thought of Kumiko watching as he sprinted down the home straight while Gerard swallowed his dust, spurred him on with new-found energy.

'That's more like it. Seven ... eight ... nine.' Michael heaved himself towards the bar one more time, but could go no further. He collapsed, gasping for air.

Kingston sighed despairingly. 'I think we'd better hope Kumiko designs a course that requires a lot of the brain and not so much of the brawn.'

Kumiko sat at her computer keying in commands, planning out the obstacle course. On a wire frame diagram of KL5, she began tracing a dotted red line over the route, beginning at the hydro lab then crossing to the central stairwell. The stairs ran the entire height of KL5, branching off at each level, providing access to the innumerable rooms and chambers on each.

Several of the lower levels remained empty or had been used for storage of supplies and equipment, but were safe nonetheless, although Duffy had deemed many of them off limits to the children.

The control room was located at the top of the station, handy to the solar converters and power generators, and the computer mainframe was housed in adjacent rooms. The hydro lab and atmospheric generators were on the next floor down, then the living quarters, the recreation room and below that, the space tug's docking bay and connecting access tube.

Kumiko wanted to make the race as demanding as possible—a clever test of mental and physical aptitude. Working late into the night, she mapped out a course that ran from the top to the bottom of the station, ducking and weaving through hatchways and service ducts. Keying in the final instructions, she leant back and stretched. 'Fools rush in,' she muttered with a wry smile.

The next morning, Gerard and Michael lined up to collect their food rations. 'Better get a double helping wimp. You're going to need it,' Gerard said as he slid his food wafer into the recon machine.

'Maybe you should stick your head in there,' Michael replied, gesturing to the machine. 'You could reconstitute that peanut of yours for a brain!'

Nearby, Anna and Kingston sat listening to the boys' bickering. 'I'm starting to think this race is a stupid idea,' Kingston whispered. 'It's turning them against one another. They're worse than ever!'

'If Gerard's head gets any bigger, it'll explode,' Anna agreed.

Watching the boys taunting one another, Kingston and Anna decided that it was up to them to do something about it—no matter who won the race, life on board KL5 would be totally unbearable. Kumiko would have to stop the race. After scoffing their food, they rushed off to find her.

'These are two very serious faces,' Kumiko said, glancing from Kingston to Anna.

'We want you to call it off,' Anna said.

'Yeah. It's getting out of hand. They're starting to fight like crazy.'

'They always fight,' Kumiko said dismissively. 'That's what the race is for. It'll put an end to it once and for all. But if either one of them wants to pull out, fine. I'm not forcing them to take part.'

'So if we get either one to pull out, then you'll drop the whole idea?' Anna asked.

'Sure. If either one of them is big enough,' Kumiko replied, confident that neither of them would back down. Too much was at stake.

Kingston finally located Michael in the machinery bay doing push-ups in a pool of sweat. 'We think you should call it off,' he announced.

Taken by surprise, Michael collapsed onto the floor. 'What? Concede to that thug? You're the same as the rest of them. You don't think I can win, do you?'

'It's a stupid idea. So what if you pull out?'

'I wouldn't give Gerard the satisfaction,' Michael said and continued his push-ups with renewed enthusiasm.

Inside his quarters, Gerard had cleared a space on his messy floor and was doing a set of sit-ups while Anna kneeled on his bed looking down at him.

'So what if you win? What does that prove?' she said to him.

'It proves I won't have to put up with that wimp and his smart-mouthed comments. And I *am* going to win. The only question is, by how much.'

'You're just being a macho dork! I think you should withdraw,' Anna said determinedly.

'So much for family loyalty,' Gerard said as he continued his sit-ups effortlessly. 'Forty-eight, forty-nine,' he counted to himself.

The day of the race arrived and the children gathered in the hydro lab for the start. 'It's a test of stamina, skill and endurance,' Kumiko announced as Michael and Gerard studied closely the course outline on her computer.

As they committed the course to memory, Gerard smirked at Michael, who tried not to look apprehensive.

'You ready champ?' Kingston asked, massaging Michael's shoulders.

'Don't worry rodent. He'll be following me all the way,' Gerard said, with infinite self-confidence.

'Thirty minutes, that's all you get,' Kumiko said as the boys lined up on the starting line. 'Are you ready?'

The boys glared at one another, then nodded to Kumiko.

'On your marks ... Set ... Go!'

Kumiko's snappy order took the boys by surprise. They bolted for the door and disappeared into the adjoining corridor, Gerard in the lead. Kingston and Anna rushed to the door to see them head down the corridor.

'Go Michael!' Kingston yelled.

'Go—!' Anna yelled, not sure who to barrack for.

Kumiko smiled smugly to herself as she joined Kingston and Anna at the door. 'What a pair of idiots,' she said, surprising Kingston and Anna.

Nearby, Duffy and Ingessol marched down a corridor, hurrying towards the control room. 'There's been a blip in the air seals,' Ingessol said, examining a computer readout. 'We've definitely had a drop in air mass.'

'I don't want to know about blips. I want to know what caused it,' Duffy said. 'And I want to know before we commence the fly-by. If we are losing air, it will affect our weight-to-mass ratio. Not to mention the immediate danger to those of us who breathe the stuff!'

'All right, George. No need for sarcasm. We'll find it.'

'See that you do. We've got three hours before the launch program,' said Duffy, just as Gerard and Michael sped around the corner and almost slammed straight into them.

'This isn't a race track. Walk!' yelled Duffy.

'Sorry,' Gerard said as he sprinted past them. 'Just getting fit. For the medical.'

'Those kids should be locked up!' Duffy muttered as both boys disappeared down the corridor, Gerard still in the lead.

As Gerard began to climb the central stairwell, he heard Michael's footsteps clattering on the metal stairs below him. He quickened his pace, taking the stairs two at a time.

Michael reached the second landing on level two,

and pausing momentarily to catch his breath, he heard Gerard's voice echo down the stairwell. 'Give up wimp. You haven't got a chance!'

'There's a long way to go yet,' Michael yelled over Gerard's laughter and continued up the stairs, his legs already feeling like jelly. He forced himself on, and despite his aching calf muscles, finally reached the exit door from the stairs. He punched the controls, the door slid open and he raced full speed down a gloomy corridor. There was no sign of Gerard. He continued down the corridor, then skidded to a halt at an open service hatchway.

Michael had reached the next major obstacle in the race, a ventilation shaft that serviced the upper levels of KL5. He shivered as he looked up into the towering shaft, then saw Gerard moving quickly, already halfway up.

'How's it feel? Coming second?' Gerard called back at him.

'That's one way of looking at it,' Michael replied as he heaved himself up the ageing ladder. 'On the other hand, wherever you go, I'm going to be hard on your heels. Waiting for that one mistake. And sooner or later—'

Gerard ignored the threat. He stopped for a second to catch his breath and looked down the shaft to see Michael edging closer.

But Michael was beginning to tire, and suddenly the rung he was standing on gave way. As he lost his footing and the broken rung tumbled down the shaft, clattering on the metal structure below, Michael scrambled frantically to haul himself up to the next rung.

Gerard looked down to see Michael fighting to hold on. 'You all right?' he yelled.

'Fine!' Michael replied, reaching up to the next rung.

'Good! I'll see you back at the lab!' Gerard laughed, then opened the air duct onto level three.

'Just one mistake, Gerard, that's all it takes,' Michael gasped, as he continued his climb, secretly regretting the whole race.

Gerard clambered out of the air duct and sprinted off down the unfamiliar corridor, grinning to himself. 'In the bag,' he thought as he raced towards the airlock network in the corridor up ahead.

Located in the forward hull of the station, and originally used to transfer cargo containers and personnel from docking space craft, the airlocks had remained idle and unserviced for years. Following normal procedure, Gerard checked the safety indicators on the outside. The light was green and he punched the control switch.

As the bulkhead door from corridor to airlock slowly slid open, Gerard suddenly had his breath snatched away by a powerful rush of air. Remorselessly, the violent gust dragged him into the airlock, battering his body against the wall inside, and dragging him towards the partially open outer door. Through the narrow breach in the outer airlock door, he could see the infinite blackness of space.

Michael was already rushing down the corridor towards Gerard and the airlock when he felt the sucking force. Startled, he managed to grab hold of a stanchion by the doorway, the escaping air threatening to drag him into the airlock as well.

Inside, he saw Gerard lying wedged against the malfunctioning open outer door. Michael knew that if he didn't act quickly, Gerard would be dragged out into space or he would suffocate. Either way, Gerard would die.

Battling against the torrent of disappearing air, Michael eased himself inside the airlock. Holding firmly onto the safety rails that lined the walls, he reached for the controls to the outer door. No response. He looked around frantically for a way out, and right next to the outer door he saw a compression compartment.

Michael took a deep breath, then slammed the controls for the bulkhead that led back into the corridor. The door slid closed behind him and the rush of air ceased. Holding his breath in the growing vacuum, he dragged Gerard's limp body into the compression compartment. He punched the controls, hoping that they still worked. To his relief, the compartment door slid shut, and heaving on the air release lever, Michael slumped beside Gerard, gasping as the compartment filled with air from an interior pressure valve.

Michael quickly laid Gerard out on the floor and after a second, he began to cough and splutter. 'I thought I was dead,' Gerard gasped, sucking air into his lungs. 'The indicator, it was green, I'm sure it was green!'

'Are you all right?' Michael said, trying to sit Gerard upright.

'Of course I'm not all right. I could have been sucked out into space,' he replied, peering through the plexiglass partition at the open outer airlock door.

Staring up at the image of nearby Saturn on the large video mesh, Duffy was nervously drumming his fingers on the back of Ingessol's computer console. 'Ignition sequence programmed and ready,' Ingessol reported, keying commands into the central computer. 'Fly-by to commence in 90 minutes.'

As the Professor locked into the computer the ignition sequence that would blast KL5 out of Saturn's gravity towards Earth, Beth looked up from her computer console. 'Professor! It's that same blip,' she reported. 'We've lost air again,' she said, returning to her console, trying to locate the source of the leak.

'Find it!' Duffy ordered. 'I want to know what's happening to our air supply.'

Inside the compression compartment, Gerard staggered to his feet. 'You should have left me there,' he said to Michael 'Save yourself. That's the rule.'

'I wouldn't want you on my conscience,' Michael replied as he looked around for an escape route.

'I would have won. You know that, don't you.'

Michael didn't bother to reply. Two yellow pressure suits were hanging inside the compartment. He lifted one of the suits down and examined it carefully. 'I don't know how much air these things have got,' he said, checking the pressure gauges set into the suit's belt, then passing it to Gerard.

Michael reached for the other suit, and he and Gerard climbed into them. Pulling on a pair of traction boots, Michael opened the door that led back into the airlock. They moved slowly and awkwardly towards the bulkhead door. Behind them, the outer door of the airlock gaped menacingly open.

Michael reached for the bulkhead controls. 'Hang on,' he said, gripping the safety rail. 'Get ready for a blast of air.'

Gerard nodded that he was ready and Michael pressed the controls. Nothing. The door remained firmly shut. Gerard leant forwards and thumped the switch with his gloved hand. Still nothing. They were trapped.

'The difference in air pressure. The security locks must have engaged,' Gerard said.

'Then I guess we wait,' Michael said, turning back towards the compression compartment. 'Someone will come looking for us sooner or later.'

Gerard glanced back at the open outer airlock door and the blackness of space beyond. 'And what if it's Anna or Kingston? If they try to open that door, who knows what'll happen. What if the outside safety indicator is still *green*?' he said worriedly.

Kingston and Anna were gazing anxiously down the empty corridor wondering what had happened to Michael and Gerard. An hour had passed and still there was no sign of them. 'Maybe they're in trouble,' Anna worried.

'Either that, or they're plotting their revenge together. To get even with you know who,' Kingston replied and pointedly shot a glance at Kumiko.

'Those two couldn't do anything together,' Kumiko said defensively, as she looked uneasily towards the door. 'Quit worrying, they'll be back soon.'

Anna wasn't convinced. 'Come on. We're going to find them,' she said to Kingston, and together they rushed off to retrace Gerard and Michael's route.

Trapped inside the airlock, Michael was fingering through the collection of wires and circuits. 'You know anything about these,' he said turning to Gerard.

'Thump it! If it works, I do. If it doesn't, I don't,' Gerard replied, stepping towards the outer door of the airlock and gazing into space. 'We *could* go through another air lock,' he said slowly, an idea forming in his mind.

Michael turned back to Gerard questioningly.

'The next level. We climb outside and up to the next level.'

'Are you out of your mind?' Michael exclaimed.

'Can you think of another way?'

Michael felt his heart begin to race. He knew that Gerard was right but the thought of leaving the safety of the station and going on a space walk filled him with fear. 'Have you ever done it before?' he asked uneasily as he looked out into space, beads of sweat already forming on his brow.

Gerard shook his head. He reached for a length of coiled rope that hung inside the compression compartment and secured one end to his belt. 'Where I go, you go,' he said, clipping the other end onto Michael's waist.

Together they heaved on the outer door to the

133

airlock, forcing it all the way open. It disappeared into the abutting wall with a clunk and they stood for a moment staring out at the vastness of space. Distant stars sparkled like diamonds against the black, and nearby, the great ringed planet of Saturn hung magically suspended, circled by cloudy bands of red and orange. 'What a view,' Gerard exclaimed, filled with exhilaration.

'Unreal,' Michael whispered, overwhelmed by the sight.

'You ready?' Gerard asked, looking above him at the superstructure.

Michael nodded and together they clambered outside the airlock, and began climbing up the station wall towards the next floor.

Beth and Ingessol continued to track the source of the air loss. 'If there was a malfunction, there's no sign of it now,' Beth reported, looking up from her console.

'Double-check everything,' Ingessol instructed, keeping a watchful eye on the fly-by program. 'Saturn's gravity is really tugging at us now. Fifty minutes to firing.'

'We're going to have to postpone,' Duffy said, hovering nearby and gazing up at the video mesh. 'If the computer is malfunctioning, we can't risk it.'

'There *is* no second chance George,' Ingessol warned as Kumiko entered and gazed around the room, hoping to find Gerard and Michael.

Suddenly, Beth wheeled around from her computer console. 'Got it!' she announced loudly. 'Level three, outer doors. Airlock breach.'

Kumiko felt her stomach knot with panic. That was where she had sent the boys on their race and that's where Kingston and Anna were headed at that very moment. She turned to Duffy. 'They could be in danger!' she said. 'It was a race, that's all, something must have gone wrong.'

'What are you babbling about, young lady?' Duffy asked impatiently.

'Gerard and Michael. They were on level three,' she replied.

Kumiko didn't have to say any more. Duffy turned on his heels and called to Sam. 'You'd better get down there. Level three. The airlock systems. They may be in trouble.'

Outlined by the blackness of space, Gerard and Michael climbed slowly up the side of the station towards the airlock door above them. Gerard stopped for a moment to catch his breath. 'It's harder than I thought,' he said, as Michael clambered up next to him.

'Don't turn wimp on me now,' Michael replied, and continued towards the airlock.

Gerard followed suit, climbing strongly upwards. 'This is one obstacle Kumi didn't count on,' he said, as he heaved himself up onto a stanchion next to the airlock. Through his headpiece, he heard Michael's breathing getting heavier.

'Are you all right?' he called back to him.

'Fine. Just out of breath. My air seems thin,' Michael replied.

'Well stop talking.'

'Then stop asking me questions. Just hurry up. Before Kingston tries to play hero.'

But at that very moment, the hero was emerging from the ventilation shaft on level three. He crawled out of the opening, and reaching back for Anna, they made their way along the corridor towards the airlock system. 'Kind of spooky, isn't it? Maybe they got eaten by aliens,' Kingston muttered.

Anna shuddered at the thought. 'Kumi should have

her head read sending them down here,' she said as
they moved uneasily down the dark corridor.

Gerard was the first to reach the upper-level airlock.
He heaved on the control lever, and its outer door slid
noiselessly open.

Further down the superstructure, Michael stretched
out for the next rung. Gasping for air, he looked down
to see the warning light beginning to flash on his pressure suit. His air supply was all but exhausted.

'Michael, come on. We're in,' Gerard yelled as he
hauled himself into the airlock. He lay on the floor of
the lock to catch his breath, and called again to
Michael. There was no response. He moved quickly to
the door to check on him.

Several metres below, he saw Michael's lifeless form
hunched over the superstructure. Gerard desperately
heaved on the safety line but it was stuck, wedged
between two crossbeams below him. He quickly
uncoupled the rope from his belt, and securing the end
to the airlock door, he reached down and wrenched it
free. Using all his strength, he heaved on the rope and
dragged Michael into the airlock, slamming his hand
against the door controls. The door slid shut and the
compartment filled with air as Michael slumped limply
to the floor.

Kingston and Anna had reached the bulkhead door to
the malfunctioning airlock. They checked the safety
indicator light. Again it was green and Anna unsus-
pectingly reached for the door entry controls. Suddenly, Kingston grabbed her hand. 'How do we know
what's behind there?' he said.

'We'll never know if you don't let me push the
button,' Anna replied matter-of-factly, and again
reached for the controls.

As her finger rested on the control, a warning voice echoed up the corridor behind them. They swung around to see Sam rushing towards them. 'Don't open it!' he yelled. 'The outer door is open!'

Kingston went pale. The thought of what would have happened if they had opened the door made him feel sick—sucked out into space, floating eternally through the solar system, gathering space dust, forever!

'We could have been alien food!' he shrieked, horrified by his own imagination. Then the realisation struck him. Had Gerard and Michael made the same mistake?

Gerard struggled to remove the headpiece from Michael's pressure suit, then reached for the communication panel and pressed the intercom button. It was working. 'I need help! Level four airlock,' he yelled breathlessly, before turning back to attend to Michael. As he laid him out flat, Michael began to cough and splutter.

'Are you all right?'

'It's okay. I'm fine. Thanks,' Michael said, between coughing fits, gradually regaining his strength.

'You scared the life out of me!' Gerard said, his heart still racing.

'Yeah. Let's not do that again in a hurry,' Michael said, as they clambered out of their pressure suits. He looked across at Gerard and a grin crossed his face. They'd both had their fill of obstacle courses.

'Now comes the difficult bit,' Gerard said, reaching for the bulkhead controls. Michael looked across at him anxiously.

'How are we going to explain this to Duffy?' Gerard added with a wry smile.

Half an hour later, Kingston was marvelling at Michael and Gerard's adventure. 'How lucky can you get. A space walk. You against the elements. Man against nature! So what was it like?'

Michael and Gerard looked at one another, then began to boast about their exploits.

'Incredibly dangerous,' Michael said.

'Awesomely hazardous,' Gerard continued.

'But we came, we saw, we conquered!' Michael said, puffing out his chest.

Kingston was highly impressed. 'Wow!' he exclaimed. 'But what about Duffy? I bet he's really going to give it to you!'

'Fear not,' Michael said with a glint in his eye. 'In view of your brave and precipitate action in alerting security to the danger posed by the malfunctioning airlock—' he said, doing a Duffy.

Gerard took over. '—the indiscretion causing you to be in the vicinity of the danger area will be overlooked.'

'In short, we're off the hook,' Michael concluded as Kumiko and Anna entered the room. 'So what's your problem,' Michael asked, noticing that Kumiko looked particularly miserable.

'She failed the medical,' Anna blurted out.

Kumiko glared at the boys indignantly. 'I failed. Big deal. It's just a nutritional imbalance,' she said, trying to make light of the situation.

Gerard and Michael looked at one another and burst out laughing. 'Just desserts!' Michael exclaimed as the intercom crackled with news of the imminent fly-by of Saturn.

As they rushed into the control room, they heard Beth count down the final sequence. 'Power source locked and primed. Cross your fingers everyone! Five seconds, four, three, two, one ... '

Ingessol looked up at the large video mesh and punched the ignition keys. 'Come on you old dinosaur,' he muttered. 'Don't let me down.'

Seconds ticked by and then a thundering roar

filled the control room as the space tug's thrusters came to life, propelling the station forwards. Equipment began to rattle and shake as the ungainly space station began to accelerate, gathering the necessary speed to finally steer away from the giant planet and escape its gravity.

The children sat perched on a bench at the rear of the room, their eyes glued to the video mesh as the images of Saturn grew larger and larger, looming ominously out at them.

When they were so close it seemed they would crash, the space tug's engines gave their final power surge and blasted them past the huge planet, its gravitational pull moving the station in a curving orbit at ever increasing speed. Accelerating quickly, they sped around the swirling rings of red and orange, and headed into the blackness beyond. They were on course for Earth!

'Well done everyone,' Duffy shouted as the celebrations died down. 'You'll be pleased to know, you'll be reverting back to normal shifts. You'll be able to relax for a while,' he added with an uncharactistic smile.

'At least until the asteroid belt,' Ingessol muttered, taking Duffy by surprise.

He wheeled around on Ingessol. 'We're going through the asteroid belt?' he demanded. 'Why wasn't I informed?'

'And if I had? Would you have agreed to the fly-by?' Ingessol replied. 'George, it's the only way we're going to catch the ore carrier.'

At the back of the room, Kingston flopped back in his seat and gulped nervously. Nobody had mentioned anything about asteroids before. He hated asteroids!

ASTEROIDS

K L5 was placed on full alert as it approached the vast asteroid belt that obstructed their path to Earth. Professor Ingessol had worked for weeks, charting a course through the floating minefield, and calculating co-ordinates to intersect with the ore carrier on its path to Earth. He knew it was a risky venture, but necessary if they were to rendezvous with the carrier and replenish their dwindling fuel reserves.

The prospect of crashing into a rogue asteroid filled Kingston with doom and gloom. 'Asteroids! Vermin of the skies. Sitting ducks, that's what we are!' he prattled, as Anna led him towards a dark and eerie chamber situated low down in the forward section of the massive station.

'Stop exaggerating,' Anna said, tired of Kingston's predictions of imminent disaster.

'You'll see. When you're hurtling out into space clinging onto a lump of rock!' Kingston insisted.

Anna was far more interested in her own discovery. She pressed the door controls, and led Kingston into the chamber. His eyes widened with excitement as they moved further into the room, wandering through the shadowy rows of crates that were stacked to the ceiling. At the front of the room they found a large window that looked out into space and gave them a perfect view of the vast, rapidly approaching asteroid belt.

'It's fantastic,' Kingston exclaimed, climbing up onto one of the benches in front of the window.

'And I found it,' Anna announced, proud of her discovery and plonking herself next to Kingston. 'They must have had a giant telescope in here. To study the stars.'

'Searching for strange beings from outer space, more like it,' Kingston replied with a shudder, the thought of slimy aliens sending a cold chill down his spine.

As they gazed into space, neither of them was aware of the strange figure spying on them from the shadows, further back in the chamber.

'Now you have to promise not to tell anyone. It's our secret,' Anna said to Kingston.

'As if I'm going to tell? We're not even supposed to be down here,' Kingston said, glancing about uneasily. 'Duffy'd murder us if he found out.' Kingston shuddered, then feeling an eerie presence nearby, he wheeled around and stared back into the shadows.

'What are you so jumpy about?' Anna asked, seeing the strange look on Kingston's face.

'Me? Jumpy? Why should I be jumpy? Just because we're about to be blown into little squishy bits by some rogue asteroid! And that's if Duffy doesn't get us first,' Kingston replied nervously, as he searched the shadows between the stacks of crates for any sign of movement. He was sure they were being watched.

Then, he saw it. A strange, alien-looking creature lurching out of the shadows, staggering towards him. It had piercing red lights for eyes, thick black leathery skin, plastic tubing running the length of its arms and legs, and bits of computer circuitry protruding from its chest.

Kingston watched helplessly as the creature swayed towards him. He desperately tried to call out, but no words came out of his mouth, just incoherent squeaks.

He reached across to Anna who remained engrossed in her view of the asteroids. 'This can be our very special window to the stars,' she prattled excitedly.

'And if you tell anyone, you're dead meat.'

'Dead meat!' Kingston wheezed, tugging on Anna's shirtsleeve.

Anna turned to Kingston and saw the look of sheer terror on his face. Then she saw it too. The creature! Lumbering slowly and awkwardly towards them, its arms reaching out menacingly.

'Aliens!' Kingston shrieked. His worse nightmare had come true. He leapt to his feet and grabbed Anna by the hand, the pair racing towards the door as fast as their legs would carry them. The creature lurched in their direction, trying to cut them off, but Kingston and Anna were too agile. They ducked from its grasp and sprinted from the chamber.

As they raced, squealing and yelling down the corridor, Duffy was anxiously pacing about the control room, while Professor Ingessol and Kumiko tracked the path of the nearest asteroid. 'I want the whole crew on stand by,' Duffy ordered. 'Until we get through the asteroid belt. If we get through it,' he added pointedly.

'If we're to rendezvous with the ore carrier, it is our only option,' Ingessol replied calmly. 'And we need that fuel.'

'It's insanity,' Duffy sneered contemptuously.

'George, if you don't stop worrying, it won't be an asteroid that finishes you off, it'll be an ulcer,' Professor Ingessol said, smiling at Kumiko.

'There's nothing wrong with my health,' Duffy said indignantly. 'I'm in the peak of physical condition.'

Duffy puffed out his chest as Kingston and Anna burst through the doors, white with fear. 'Run for your lives!' Kingston shrieked. 'Mr Duffy, it's down there!'

'We saw it!' Anna exclaimed, gasping to catch her breath.

Duffy wheeled around to see what all the commotion was about. Children. Always children, he thought to himself. He was getting very tired of them and their practical jokes. 'What's the meaning of this? How dare you burst in here like that!' he barked.

'You've got to do something. We went to watch for asteroids—' Kingston tried to explain.

'And it attacked us. A huge, ugly, horrible—'

'Alien!' Kingston finally blurted out. He stood there puffing and panting, glancing expectantly at the group of dumbfounded adults, waiting for someone to take action against the hostile creature.

Stepping out of the shadows of the secret chamber, Kingston's alien reached up and removed its head-piece, revealing a laughing, cheerful Gerard. He flopped down on a crate and wiped the sweat from his face. 'Their feet didn't even touch the ground,' he cackled, as Michael emerged from behind a row of crates.

'You don't think we went too far?'

'Get serious. You want to relieve the boredom on this dump, don't you? Gerard replied. 'Stop your worrying. It'll give the rodent something to boast about. His very own alien!'

'So how do you know about this place?'

'Come off it. She's my sister. She couldn't keep a secret if her life depended on it. Once she gets that weird look in her eye, I know she's up to something. So I followed her. Child's play,' Gerard laughed.

Anna paced nervously about the recreation room while Kingston sat solemnly in a chair, pondering their imminent demise. After shouting at them for telling stories, Duffy had ordered them out of the control room. 'They'll be sorry, when it starts picking them off, one by one,' Kingston said miserably. 'Just when they think it's safe to go to sleep, it'll suck their brains out through their eye sockets!'

'Kumi, you believe us, don't you?' Anna asked as Kumiko retrieved a plate of food from the recon machine. Kumiko looked at them quizzically. She knew there had to be a logical explanation for what they'd seen.

Before she could reply, Gerard and Michael came bouncing into the room. Kingston almost gabbled in his desire to tell them about the alien.

'It had horrible, red, piercing eyes—Honest!' Kingston exclaimed.

'And a computer for a brain. We're not imagining things Gerard. It's true! You've got to believe us!' said Anna as Gerard gave a little snicker. It was all he could do to keep a straight face.

'Perhaps if you had some proof,' he said innocently, giving Michael a conspiratorial glance.

'Yeah right, proof,' Michael joined in. 'A tooth, a toenail perhaps.' They couldn't control themselves any longer, and burst out laughing.

'It's not funny. We saw it,' Kingston said loudly. 'It had tubes, pumping its acid blood around the outside of its slimy body!'

'Acid blood?' Michael repeated, snickering to himself.

'Yeah! And just when we're about to be attacked by a mob of marauding asteroids, when the station is in confusion, it'll strike! We're obviously dealing with a creature of great intelligence!'

'I seriously doubt it,' Kumiko thought aloud, eyeing Gerard and Michael suspiciously. She knew they were up to something.

Back in the living quarters, Anna flopped angrily down on her bed while Kingston paced about the room. Both were annoyed that nobody believed them. 'They'll be laughing on the other side of their faces,' she muttered.

'They won't even have a face! Not when it sneaks up and attacks them in the middle of the night!' Kingston said savagely.

144

Anna suddenly bolted upright. 'Gerard's right. We need proof.'

'Oh no you don't,' Kingston exclaimed, one step ahead of her. 'I'm not going back down there again. I hate aliens!'

Anna thought for a moment. 'Maybe we don't have to,' she said shrewdly, as she reached for ZIT's remote control. 'We can send ZIT down there. It's got an in-built camera. We'll be able to see everything it sees,' she said, pointing to the tiny screen on the remote control.

'Brilliant!' Kingston exclaimed, and seizing the remote, he began operating its controls, sending ZIT speeding towards the observation chamber.

'We could be down here for hours,' Michael said, glancing around the gloomy chamber, as he assisted Gerard back into the home-made alien suit.

'Trust me. She's my sister, remember,' Gerard mumbled through the headpiece. He knew curiosity would get the better of Anna and Kingston, and sooner or later they'd return to investigate and get their proof. 'It must be driving them crazy. It's the perfect torture,' Gerard laughed. 'And we'll be waiting for them.'

As Gerard zipped the front of the suit, they heard a noise at the front of the chamber. 'Like rats into a trap,' he whispered, ducking down out of sight and flicking a switch to illuminate the alien's red eyes.

At the front of the chamber, Kumiko tiptoed through the rows of crates and boxes. She took a couple of steps, stopped and listened. Nothing. She continued further into the chamber, unaware of Kingston's ZIT speeding along behind her, transmitting images from its tiny eye camera.

Abruptly, Gerard's alien creature lurched out of the shadows and lunged towards her.

Anna shrieked. On ZIT's remote control screen, she

could see the creature charging at Kumiko. 'It's going to get her!' she shouted.

Kingston leapt to his feet and grabbed Anna by the hand. 'We have to save her!' he yelled as they raced towards the control room.

The alien creature moved threateningly towards Kumiko, the beams of light from its eyes momentarily blinding her. Kumiko stood unperturbed, folding her arms defiantly. 'All right,' she said calmly. 'Your little game is over.'

'Had you going for a while, didn't we?' Michael laughed, as he emerged from his hiding place behind a stack of crates.

'You guys are so juvenile,' Kumiko said, poking at the ridiculous looking creature. Bits and pieces of discarded computer circuitry had been stuck haphazardly to a battered old pressure suit. Plastic tubing filled with algae ran down the outside of its arms and legs, and it had two small hydro lamps inserted into the headpiece with red plasti-film stuck to each lens. 'As if anyone would believe that!' she added, prodding at a piece of black conduit that hung like a trunk from its mouth.

'The rodent did. I've never seen him move so fast,' Gerard replied.

'Well it's not funny. You really frightened them. They're just little kids,' she protested to Michael, hoping he would see reason.

'But Michael wasn't listening. Something had caught his attention. 'I think we've got visitors,' he whispered to Gerard, who pounced down and seized the spying ZIT.

Anna and Kingston meanwhile were charging into the control room yelling excitedly. 'It's going to get Kumi! The creature!' Anna shrieked.

'Look, we can prove it!' Kingston offered his remote control to Duffy. But as he did, he saw the alien lift his precious toy towards its open mouth, saw the image distort and suddenly die. Kingston stared at the blank screen in horror. 'It ate it! It swallowed ZIT!' he exclaimed.

'Right after it ate Kumi,' Anna chipped in.

Duffy had had enough of their ridiculous babbling. He snatched the remote control from Kingston, tossed it on his work station, and ordered Kingston and Anna from the room.

Gerard held ZIT in one hand and its power pack in the other. 'No power, no proof!' he said triumphantly.

'This has gone far enough,' Kumiko said. 'If you don't tell them, I will!'

'Don't be such a killjoy! We're just trying to relieve the boredom.'

'Maybe she's right. We'd better tell them,' Michael conceded.

'You happy now?' Gerard sneered.

But Kumiko didn't answer. She was staring blankly past the boys, out of the viewing windows at the front of the chamber and into the star-studded space beyond.

'Kumi, what is it?' Michael asked, seeing the look of horror on her face. Before she could reply, a deafening siren rang out and the intercom crackled an inaudible warning.

Gerard stumbled around, looking for the source of the emergency. 'Now what's wrong with this tub?' he yelled over the din, turning to Kumiko.

Silently, Kumiko pointed towards the window. Michael and Gerard spun around to see an asteroid hurtling directly towards them. Instinctively, they braced themselves for the inevitable collision, clutching onto each other as the giant projectile tumbled through space towards the station. As it disappeared from their view, sailing above them, the children relaxed momentarily. But as they moved slowly towards the plexi-panels for a clearer view, they felt a tremendous crash reverberate through the chamber as the asteroid ploughed into the station, tearing a large hole in one of the solar sails.

Anna let out a loud scream as she and Kingston were thrown to the floor inside the control room. The whole station was rocked by the collision. Alarms rang out, confusion was everywhere.

'The solar sails! Retract the sails!' Ingessol shouted over the noise. Beth swung back to her console and furiously keyed commands into the computer. As she looked up to the video mesh, she saw another asteroid bearing down on them. 'It's got a friend!' she yelled. 'Five hundred metres!'

Kingston looked up at the screen. 'Maybe they're not asteroids. The alien! We're being attacked by the mother ship,' he screamed as the asteroid glanced off the lower section of the station and hurtled into space.

'We're losing air,' Beth reported through the chaos. 'It's breached the hull. Levels five and six. Forward sectors.'

'Seal it off! Hit the compression doors!' Duffy ordered. 'Isolate the damaged area.'

The last asteroid had come dangerously close to the observation chamber. Michael picked himself up off the floor, then helped Kumiko to her feet as warning lights began to flash above the bulkhead leading into the chamber. 'We've got to get out of here,' he yelled above the emergency siren. Steering Kumiko towards the exit, he shouted at Gerard to get up and run.

Still draped in the alien suit, Gerard clambered awkwardly to his feet. 'I can't run!' he moaned, the weight of the suit restricting his movement. Michael and Kumiko rushed back to help him. 'If it wasn't for that stupid suit,' Kumiko yelled.

They dragged Gerard to the exit but before they could reach it, the compression door slammed shut, sealing them inside the chamber. Overhead, they heard the power generator slow, then the lights flicked off.

'What do you think has happened?' Gerard asked, as seconds later, the emergency lighting flickered on.

'We're flying through an asteroid belt! What do you think it was? A pink elephant?' Kumiko replied angrily.

Michael opened a panel next to the door and tried the emergency override switch. The door refused to open. The central computer had sealed their section and they were trapped.

Kumiko glared at the two boys. 'Now what brains? Think you can invent something to get us out of here?'

Inside the control room, the adults worked quickly and efficiently to stabilise the station. 'I want the damaged section kept sealed,' Duffy ordered. 'At least until we get a full report.'

Beth put her arm around Kingston and Anna. 'Better head to your quarters,' she said warmly. 'Better still, find Michael and Gerard. You'll be safe with them.' Kingston nodded grudgingly, and they made their way to Michael's quarters.

They found the room empty. As they were about to head off to the recreation room, Anna discovered a hand-drawn diagram of the alien lying on Michael's bed. She stared at it in disbelief. 'Look familiar?' she said, holding it out to Kingston.

'Those creeps!' Kingston exclaimed as he confronted his monster.'The whole thing's a fake! A big two-legged hoax with Gerard's and Michael's names written all over it!'

'And Kumi!' She's supposed to be our friend! They've been laughing at us the whole time. Probably hiding right now having a good old giggle!'

'Wait until I get my hands on them. Boy are they going to suffer,' Kingston said.

'Right! Let's find the rats!' Anna said determinedly.

'Not yet,' Kingston replied with a devious glint in his eye. 'Not until we know exactly what we're going to do.' He perched himself on Michael's bed and together they considered how they would take their revenge.

'There's got to be another way out of here,' Michael said as he searched the chamber for an alternative exit.

'You're wasting your time,' Kumiko grumbled. 'We're sealed in. Part of this sector must have been damaged by the asteroid.'

Gerard climbed out of his alien suit and slumped down on a nearby crate. 'Then I guess we just sit tight. Someone'll rescue us sooner or later,' he said. 'Anna and Kingston! They're going to miss us eventually.'

'You really think they'll want to help after what you did to them?' Kumiko replied, as she tried to patch her computer into the mainframe port tucked next to the door control circuitry.

'What are you trying to do?' Gerard asked.

'Use my brain. Something you pair wouldn't understand. It's a long shot but if I can hack into the central computer, maybe I can raise the alarm.'

'Look, what's the big panic?' Gerard asked.

'We could be in here for hours,' Kumiko said, as she continued with her computer. 'And in case you hadn't noticed, it's getting cold.'

Kumiko was right. The climate controls had shut down when the sector was sealed off and the temperature inside the observation chamber was dropping rapidly. If they didn't get out of there, they would eventually freeze to death.

Lazing in a couple of chairs in the warmth of the recreation room, Kingston and Anna pondered their revenge while they munched on lunchtime rations.

'Maybe we could sabotage his strawberries!' Kingston muttered, poking at his food.

'Or do something really horrible to his precious multi-mate,' Anna added.

'Or hijack her computer!'

As they continued to plot and scheme, Beth appeared at the doorway. 'So what's happening?' Kingston asked, leaping to his feet. 'Are we going to die slowly, or is it going to be quick and sudden? Smashed to bits by a rogue asteroid!'

'There's nothing to worry about,' Beth said, trying to reassure them. 'We're over the worst of it. The station is safe for the time being. But why aren't you with the others? Where's Michael and Gerard?'

'Oh don't worry, we'll look after *them*,' Anna replied, giving Kingston a significant look.

'Well, see that you do. I don't want you wandering around the station by yourselves.'

Behind them, Professor Ingessol rushed into the room and summoned Beth back to the control room. The lower levels of the station had lost climate control and she was needed to help locate the fault.

Kingston flopped back down on his seat. 'So much for being safe! We're going to freeze to death. Snap frozen human beans!' he exclaimed.

But Anna wasn't listening. She was more interested in what Professor Ingessol had said. Climate controls had been shut down on level five. 'Kingston! That's where we saw it! The alien.'

Kingston suddenly twigged. Gerard and Michael might still be in the observation chamber. Level five! If the climate control *had* shut down, they could suffocate, or worse still, freeze! Realising something terrible might be happening, they rushed from the room for level five.

Kumiko had finally managed to patch her computer into the chamber's main frame port but no matter which commands she keyed into her machine, she couldn't get a response. Checking the connection to the main frame, she tried again. Still nothing.

Gerard shivered slightly. 'Heating's off. Doors are sealed. Power's down. I'd say the computer doesn't want to know about us, wouldn't you?'

'We're not going to last in here more than an hour,' Kumiko said, giving up on the main frame.

'We'd better huddle together. Conserve our body heat,' Michael suggested and sat down next to Kumiko, wrapping his arm around her.

Tentatively, Gerard huddled next to them, inching closer, trying to soak up their body heat. They sat for several minutes, saying nothing, trying to get warm. Gerard continued to wriggle awkwardly.

'Gerard, will you sit still!' Michael complained.

'This isn't going to work,' Gerard grumbled and sprang to his feet, spotting some insulation fibre lining the outer walls of the chamber.

He quickly began to tear strips of the fabric from the walls. Here,' he said, tossing the fibre to Kumiko and Michael. 'Wrap yourselves in this.'

Draped in insulation fibre, they sat shivering from the intense cold. 'This stuff is useless. I can't even feel my feet,' Michael said through chattering teeth. 'It must be ten below in here. There's got to be something we can do.'

'Fire!' Gerard suddenly exclaimed to Michael and Kumiko. The answer was obvious and Gerard wondered why he hadn't thought of it sooner.

'We light a fire. It's simple!' he said, and began ransacking the chamber for flammable materials. 'I don't know about you pair, but I intend to see Christmas this year.'

Kumiko slowly climbed to her feet. The cold was beginning to take affect. 'You want to use up what oxygen we've got left?' she objected. 'You light that and you can forget about Santa Claus!'

But Gerard would not be dissuaded. 'So we either

freeze or suffocate. Personally I hate the cold,' he said, as he heaped a pile of sheeting in the centre of the room.

Kumiko picked up a piece of the material and examined it. 'We don't know what this stuff is made of,' she said worriedly. 'It might give off toxic fumes.'

'No! Gerard's right,' Michael said. 'Maybe the heat sensors are still working. It'll show up in the control room.'

'And how do you plan to light it?' Kumiko asked.

Gerard was one step ahead of her. He picked up the alien's headpiece and ripped its eyes from their sockets. Touching the wires to their power packs together, he produced a spray of sparks. 'You're not the only one with a brain,' he quipped.

Gerard put the power packs beside the pile of sheeting. As he touched the wires together again, sparks showered, electrodes glowed red hot and smoke began to rise from the sheeting.

'How long does it take to freeze?' Anna asked, as she and Kingston desperately tried to find a way down to level five and the observation chamber.

'Let me put it this way, I don't think we should stop to admire the view,' Kingston replied wryly as he led her into one of the old dismantled power reactor chambers. The chamber was lined with discarded machinery parts and cooling equipment. In the centre of the room was a deep well that dropped away several floors below them. Across the gap stretched a narrow, rickety old maintenance bridge. Kingston looked uneasily at the unstable gangway. 'There has to be another way around,' he said. 'I'm not going out there!'

'There's no time. We have to go on—or they'll freeze!' Anna said, bravely edging her way out onto the bridge. It began to creak and groan under her weight. Anna peered over the edge and her stomach tightened. The dirty brown rust-stained walls of the chamber seemed to drop away endlessly into the black space below.

Bathed in the flickering orange light of the slowly growing fire, the shivering children sat huddled around the flames trying to warm themselves. 'So who's the dumb one now?' Gerard said to Kumiko.

Before she could answer, fire extinguishers set in the ceiling suddenly erupted, blasting them with thick white cold foam.

'Gerard! The fire! Douse it!' Michael yelled, as the sticky retardant sprayed from the overhead nozzles, saturating him.

Gerard leapt to his feet, grabbed a pile of left-over insulation fibre, tossed it on the fire and smothered the flames. Too late. All three of them had been soaked to the skin and soon they felt the freezing air chill them to the bone.

Kumiko shuddered. That was all they needed.

Slowly, fearfully, Kingston followed Anna across the maintenance bridge. They were more than half way across when the bridge lurched under their combined weight. Kingston hung on desperately until the bridge settled. 'Kingston! Stop shaking,' Anna called back to him.

'Who's shaking?'

'You are!'

'And I wonder why?' Kingston replied, perched precariously over the deep reactor chamber. He looked down into the seemingly bottomless pit and muttered to himself. 'They're going to pay for this,' he said, inching slowly forwards once more.

Michael, Kumiko and Gerard continued to huddle

together, trying to conserve the last of their body heat. Kumiko knew that it was a hopeless gesture. 'We're going to die if help doesn't arrive soon,' she said, her voice slurring from the terrible cold. 'None of us is going to get out of here. All because of a stupid practical joke.'

Knowing she was right, Gerard looked around frantically and spotted the abandoned ZIT. Clambering slowly to his feet, he replaced the toy's power pack.

'Forget it Gerard,' Michael said. 'It's no good without the remote.'

'No, but it's got a camera in it. Maybe Kingston's got the remote. Maybe he'll see us,' Gerard replied and switched on the toy.

ZIT's remote control sat on a computer console on one side of the control room. Michael, Gerard and Kumiko appeared on its tiny screen, gesturing wildly for someone to see them. But the colonists were busy studying the trajectory of a new asteroid nearby.

'Professor,' Beth called from her computer console. 'Something strange. I've had a fire readout. It was there. Now it's gone.'

Ingessol turned to her and studied the readout on the computer's video mesh.

'Level five,' he said quizzically. 'Seems fixed. Keep tracking the asteroid.'

Gerard had been the last to give up on the camera. He huddled with the others, the three of them pathetically trying to keep warm. Time was rapidly running out. 'Cryogenics,' Gerard joked, forcing a smile. 'Maybe they'll be able to unfreeze us.'

Kumiko forced a smile, but as she shivered uncontrollably, her mind began to swim. Her legs buckled underneath her and she slumped to the ground.

'Get her to her feet,' Gerard instructed to Michael who rushed to her aid. 'Get her moving.'

'It's all right,' Kumiko said, still slurring her words

and struggling to get to her feet. 'But my legs are numb. I can't feel a thing.'

'Help me,' said Michael. 'I can't lift her.'

Gerard and Michael hauled Kumiko to her feet, and supporting her under each arm, began moving around the chamber trying to get her blood circulating.

'Stop! Listen. Both of you,' Kumiko whispered, thinking she'd heard a sound. She listened again. This time it was clearer, louder. A thumping on the door.

Outside the chamber, Anna and Kingston were hammering away with a length of pipe. Solid lumps of ice had built up around the door seals and over the control panel, sealing the door shut.

'Maybe we're too late,' Anna said fearfully, then smiled with relief as she heard banging from inside the chamber. The noise made Kingston chip even harder at the ice, trying to free up the door controls. Finally the ice fell away, and he stretched for the panel. Swinging it open, he thumped the door release override button.

The door edged open slightly, a few centimetres or more, and stopped. Kingston stuck his face up to the opening and called into the chamber. 'Push,' he yelled.

Inside Michael called back. 'We're pushing, we're pushing.' Relieved to hear Kingston and Anna's voices, they heaved on the edge of the door with all their strength. Again it refused to budge. 'On the count of three,' Kingston yelled from the outside.

'Do you think we could go on one,' Gerard exclaimed. 'We're freezing in here!'

Together they pulled and pushed the door and finally it gave way, ice cracking from the door seals. Michael and Gerard helped Kumiko to her feet and the three of them, still wearing their black insolation fibre, lurched awkwardly into the corridor.

Kingston watched, wide-eyed, as the three strange looking figures loomed out of the darkness. 'Aliens!' he muttered. 'They've mutated.'

'Relax!' Michael called out through chattering teeth, stepping into the light of the corridor. 'It's only us.'

'Hey! You think I'm stupid?' said a satisfied Kingston as they peeled off their insulation and made their way along the corridor.

Later in the medical bay, Helen gave them a full checkup. 'You're very lucky,' she said. 'Another ten minutes, and you'd have been in serious trouble.' Her sentence hung in the air—they knew just how close they had come to freezing to death.

Once the examination was over, Kingston and Anna took them to the recreation room for some warm soup. 'Sorry about the alien,' Gerard said, feeling contrite and grateful at the same time.

'Yeah. It was a stupid practical joke.' Michael added.

A smile flashed across Kingston's face. He looked to Anna and grinned cheekily 'You'll just have to make it up to us, won't you?' he said. Leaning back on his chair, he cupped his hands behind his head and stared off into space thoughtfully. 'Now let me think. What would I like for Christmas?'

'Yeah! And it better be good!' Anna warned, glaring mischievously at her brother.

'You know what I'd like?' Kumiko pondered. 'A hot shower, a three-course meal and a warm bed! And all of them on Earth!'

'An ore carrier would be nice,' Michael said ominously, as KL5 slowly left the asteroid belt and sailed on through space, still a long way from home.

CHAPTER NINE

THE SEASON TO BE JOLLY

The fuel reserves on KL5 had now reached critical level. As each day passed and the rendezvous with the ore carrier drew nearer, life on KL5 became more and more tense. With everybody busy, the children seemed to be the only ones looking forward to Christmas in space.

Michael was busy preparing a special surprise in the hydroponics lab. Snatching a few spare hours during their journey, he had managed to develop a secret stash of strawberries. The fruit was almost ripe and he intended to present them to the crew on Christmas morning.

As he tended his plants, Kingston sneaked up behind him and peered over his shoulder. 'What a rat!' Kingston exclaimed, catching sight of the bright, reddening berries. 'We've been starving on protein packs and you've got your own fruit salad plantation down here!'

'They're not just for me. And if you breathe one word!' Michael warned.

'Michael, it's almost Christmas. You know what that means? Being nice, giving and sharing.' Kingston's tone suddenly changed. 'Now hand 'em over, you rat!'

Michael refused. He slid the tray of plants back into his secret hiding place. 'And they stay there until Christmas, if you know what's good for you,' he warned, prodding Kingston in the chest.

'Great friend you are. You'd deny a dying man his last wish?'

'You're not dying rodent.'

'Oh yeah? I've got a sixth sense. What if they don't find the ore carrier? We'll drift off into space, slowly starving, living out our last days on algae!'

When a gloomy Kumiko arrived, with an unhappy Gerard and Anna in tow, Kingston's pessimism for once seemed justified. 'I'm just telling you what I heard,' Kumiko said in exasperation.

'Great! One chance in a thousand and we've just blown it. I knew the idea was crazy,' Gerard replied.

Kingston turned to Kumiko to see the worried look on her face. 'What's up with you?' he asked cheekily. 'Your computer blow up?'

'Worse. The ore carrier. It's not where it's supposed to be,' Kumiko replied.

Michael stared at them in disbelief. 'You're joking!'

'Yeah right. That would explain why we're all rolling around on the floor in fits of hysterics!' Gerard added sarcastically.

'I knew it!' Kingston exclaimed. 'It's been hijacked by space pirates. That's what's happened. Or it was swallowed by a black hole! See I told you, I've got a sixth sense.'

'Will you shut up, rodent!' Gerard said, threatening to cuff Kingston about the ear.

'This is going to be a great Christmas,' Anna moaned to herself. She'd been looking forward to Christmas, and this would ruin everything.

'It'd better be a good one. That's all I can say. It'll probably be our last!' Kingston predicted.

Several hours later, Duffy assembled the children in the recreation room for one of his famous announcements. 'Regrettably,' he began, 'I have decided that because of our current situation—'

Kingston was astounded by Duffy's sense of understatement. 'Situation,' he interrupted. 'It's not a situation! It's a crisis! Marooned, that's what we are. Stranded!'

Duffy ignored his outburst. Taking a deep breath,

he continued. 'And because your parents will be required to work double shifts—I have deemed it necessary to postpone Christmas.'

Kingston was mortified. He stared at Duffy in amazement. 'What!' he exclaimed. 'You can't do that!'

'You can't just forget about Christmas,' Anna added, equally horrified.

Duffy squirmed a little. 'Just for the time being,' he said uneasily.

Kingston got to his feet. He wasn't about to take this latest news lying down. Somebody had to take a stand. 'But that's criminal,' he objected. 'It's against the law.'

Duffy leaned forward and fixed Kingston in the eye. 'On KL5 I make the laws,' he said firmly. 'I'm sorry, but there you have it. There will be no Christmas until further notice.'

The announcement over, Duffy turned on his heel and hurried from the room. The children were flabbergasted. All except Gerard, that is. He leaned back in his chair and stretched. 'Suits me,' he said happily.

Anna glared at her brother. 'But it was the only thing we had to look forward to,' she said.

'Don't worry about it. The fat bloke in the red suit would never find us out here anyway.'

'He would so!'

'Yeah sure. I can just see it now. Speeding across the galaxy in a red suit going Ho, Ho, Ho with a bunch of reindeer all wearing breathing apparatus.' Gerard laughed at his own joke.

'That's not funny!' Anna exclaimed. She climbed out of her chair and marched out of the room, clearly upset. Kingston glared at Gerard and rushed off after Anna.

Kumiko was amazed that Gerard could be so insensitive to his sister. 'What do you do at Easter?' she asked. 'Rip the ears off the rabbit?'

'What did I do?' Gerard asked innocently. 'I can't

understand the big fuss about Christmas. Bunch of dumb relations just want to squeeze you and kiss you and pat you on the head and say how much you've grown!' he said, recalling a visit from Earthly relations some years back.

'Come on,' Michael said to Kumiko. 'Let's leave him to wallow in his own misery.'

'It was just a joke,' Gerard muttered defensively as he watched them leave.

Anna and Kingston sat in the viewing bubble, staring sadly out into space. The thought of missing Christmas was unimaginable. 'It's not fair. How would Duffy like it if he was a little kid?' Anna finally said.

'He was never a little kid!' Kingston replied. 'I bet they found him under a rock in some toxic wasteland.' The thought of Duffy being discovered in a pool of toxic sludge brought a smile to Anna's face. 'Yeah. Him and Gerard. They make a good pair,' she said. 'Scrooges both of them. Victims, that's what *we* are!'

Kingston agreed. 'You're looking at a man who's jingled his last bell, who's opened his last present, who's pretended for the last time that he actually *needs* another pair of socks and undies.' He sighed heavily at the hopelessness of their situation.

Anna was not so certain. She leapt up with a determined look on her face. 'I'm not going to give up my Christmas for anyone! Duffy included!' she exclaimed, grabbing Kingston by the shirtsleeve. 'Coming?'

They clambered down the central stairwell and raced towards the old virtual reality chamber. 'See it's perfect,' Anna said, as she led Kingston inside the chamber.

Kingston wasn't convinced. Duffy had banned them from the chamber and if he caught them, they'd be in big trouble.

'It'll be our secret. Just you and me,' Anna said, surveying the room.

'What's the point of that?' Kingston asked. 'Christmas on our own. That'll be even worse. No presents!'

But Anna had made up her mind. She could be very stubborn when she wanted to be. She wandered around the room formulating her plan. 'We decorate it. Collect presents. Nobody need know. Please Kingston, it'll be fun!'

Kingston stood in the centre of the room, shaking his head worriedly. 'Duffy'll be furious if he finds out. He can sniff out a good time a million miles away,' he said, slowly weakening.

'What's he going to do? Chuck us overboard?'

'Probably.' Kingston agreed, then suddenly burst into a huge grin. The thought of outwitting Duffy pleased him immensely. 'Let's do it!'

'And not a word to anyone. Whenever we run into our parents, we just look miserable.'

'Yeah! We'll give them the guilt treatment!' Kingston said happily, bouncing around the room, enjoying their conspiracy. 'Parent torture! The rack of guilt!'

While Kingston and Anna were settling down to formulate their plan, Michael was in the hydro lab, completing his chores and checking his berry plants. As he slid the last of the plant trays back into its hiding place, Professor Ingessol shuffled up behind him. He looked tired and dispirited. He had spent long hours in the control room trying to locate the ore carrier on the computer scanners.

'Sorry Michael,' Ingessol said, as he gave Michael a start. 'Just looking for a quiet corner.'

'They're meant to be a surprise for Christmas,' Michael said showing him the strawberries. Ingessol was pleased. 'Good. We need something to lift our spirits,' he said, slumping down on a nearby crate. 'I just don't understand it Michael,' he said. 'The ore carrier. I accounted for every possibility. I was so sure.'

'But it could be anything. Couldn't it? Something simple maybe?' Michael suggested, trying to be optimistic.

Ingessol shook his head. 'I've looked at it from every angle. Logically, laterally, mathematically, scientifically. But still nothing. It's impossible,' he said with exasperation.

Michael had never seen the Professor look so dejected. It worried him greatly.

Anna and Kingston began the first stage of their campaign of guilt with Gerard.

'Well Ronald,' Anna sighed, clutching her favourite dinosaur. 'I guess you'll never know what it's like to hang out your Christmas stocking.'

'Or to hang decorations on a Christmas tree,' Kingston added, with just the right amount of misery.

It was all too much for Gerard. 'Okay you guys, enough of the guilt treatment. I'm sorry, okay? You happy now?'

Anna looked at Gerard with her enormous eyes. It was more than Gerard could bear. He knew he'd have to do something to make it up to his sister. Kumiko, he thought. She'll know what to do, and he hurried off to ask her advice.

'You should see the way she looked at me. It was pure torture!' said Gerard, recounting the scene to Kumiko. Kumiko looked up and smiled at Gerard, amused by his suffering. 'You big softie,' she scoffed.

'Please,' begged Gerard. 'Okay, okay, I'll help you out,' Kumiko said. 'What about a Christmas tree?'

'As if,' Gerard replied. 'A tree in space!'

'No, a hologram of a Christmas tree!' she said, and Gerard smiled uncertainly, not sure what she had in mind, but if it would get Anna of his back, he was all for it.

Kingston and Anna hadn't wasted any time collecting bits and pieces to use in the virtual reality chamber. They emptied the sack out into the middle of the room and began pawing over the contents. 'For the person who has everything,' Kingston declared. 'Junk!'

Anna looked at him askance. 'Kingston. It's not the present, it's the thought that counts.'

'You sound like my mother,' Kingston laughed. 'And whenever she says that, you can bet you're about to get something totally useless. Like a brush and comb set!'

'Or shoes that are about five sizes too big. Designed to grow into,' Anna agreed.

While Anna continued to sort through her collection of junk, Kingston wandered over to the wrecked virtual reality machine. 'When Duffy says he wants something destroyed, he sure means it,' he said, holding up a strange-looking piece of circuitry from the machine. 'Maybe we could put it back together. We could have a virtual reality Christmas.'

'Don't even think about it,' Anna said, grabbing the component from Kingston. She held the crystals embedded in its centre up to her eye and the room seemed to do a multi-coloured swirl and dance for her. That'll make a great gift, she thought, and tossed it among her other bits and pieces. Then she and Kingston sprinted off in search of wrapping for the gifts and decorations for the room.

Gerard was waiting impatiently for Kumiko to key the last of the hologram program into her computer. He peered over her shoulder briefly. He couldn't understand why anyone would be interested in computers. He found them totally boring. As Kumiko made her final calculations, Michael entered the room and flopped down on a seat. 'Any word on the ore carrier?' Kumiko asked.

Michael shook his head. 'Nothing,' he said worriedly. He was still concerned about Professor Ingessol.

Kumiko keyed the final command into her computer and leaned back to give Gerard a better view. Suddenly, a bright beam of light shone from its projection port and a hologram of a tiny Christmas tree materialised in front of him.

'Pretty impressive eh?' Kumiko said proudly.

'That's not a tree!' Gerard exclaimed, peering disdainfully at the tiny tree. 'It's a weed. I thought your computer could do everything.'

Kumiko looked peeved by Gerard's insensitive outburst. 'Well it can't. You want a bigger tree, you'll need a bigger memory.' She switched off her computer and the hologram disappeared with a zap.

Gerard flopped down next to Kumiko annoyed by his own stupidity. For the second time that day he'd put his big foot in his mouth. 'Okay, so I've got a big mouth,' he said apologetically.

'What if we access the main frame?' Michael asked. 'Would that help?'

Kumiko nodded. Michael led them into the hydro lab, cleared away a stack of equipment from a bench top, and with a flourish revealed an old computer terminal. 'I found it the other day. Hasn't been used for years, but maybe it's still okay,' he said, making room for Kumiko.

Gerard wasn't impressed. 'They're going to know,' he worried. 'You start fooling around with the central computer and someone in the control room is bound to realise.'

'Well, we'll soon find out,' Kumiko replied, beginning to patch her computer into the main frame port.

'You can't just hack into the central computer and hope that nobody notices!' Gerard insisted. 'You know what happened last time you pair of genii hacked into the system. Virtual nightmare, remember?'

Kumiko looked across to Michael, raising an

eyebrow conspiratorially. 'How badly do you want the tree?' Kumiko asked, trying to tempt Gerard.

'Come on you guys! Duffy'll murder us! It won't be a medical this time, it'll be a funeral! Ours!'

'Leave it to me,' Michael said to Kumiko, making his way towards the door. 'Give me a couple of minutes, and I'll keep an eye on Duffy.'

'I'll need ten minutes. Maybe fifteen,' Kumiko said.

'Fifteen?' Gerard repeated.

Kumiko began keying in commands. 'Don't fret,' Kumiko said. 'I'll be in and out of there before they know it.'

'Tell that to Duffy when he's about to rip our heads off.'

'Come on Gerard, show some backbone will you.'

Michael arrived in the control room to find the colonists deep in argument. Duffy was insisting that since they hadn't been able to locate the ore carrier, they should use the little bit of remaining fuel to blast KL5 across the solar system as far as possible towards Earth.

While the argument raged, Michael moved across to Professor Ingessol, keeping one eye on Duffy. 'We have to wait. It's there. I'm sure it is,' Ingessol said to Michael.

'You're obsessed,' Duffy said, turning on Ingessol. 'We move on. I've made my decision!'

Michael placed a comforting hand on Ingessol's shoulder. 'I wouldn't worry about it,' he said quietly. 'He just likes the sound of his own voice. Dad's not going to agree. Nor Karl. They all trust you.'

Professor Ingessol was grateful for Michael's words, but he knew time was against them. If he couldn't fix the problem—and quickly—he'd have to give in to Duffy. 'There has to be an explanation,' he said, thumping his console.

'Maybe it's the computer,' Michael said. 'It's hardly reliable.'

Ingessol slowly shook his head. 'No, not this time. I've double-checked every calculation. The ore carrier's on fixed course, fixed speed. It's a simple problem of vectors,' he said, pointing to his calculations on the video mesh.

'Perhaps the asteroids put something out of alignment?' Michael suggested, getting so caught up in his conversation with Ingessol that he completely missed Tatsuya showing Duffy an unauthorised main frame access.

Michael suddenly looked up from Ingessol's video display mesh and noticed with alarm that Duffy had disappeared. He looked about anxiously but there was no sign of him. Where was he?

Kumiko had worked quickly and expertly, keying commands into her computer, but she still couldn't get the hologram projector to respond.

'You said it was simple,' Gerard said anxiously.

Kumiko threw her hands up in frustration. 'I'm doing everything right. The image assembler. It's not converting the commands.'

'And what's that in plain English?'

'It's there but it's not there,' Kumiko muttered cryptically. As she frantically re-keyed her calculations, a voice boomed out from behind them. 'You pair! What do you think you're doing?'

Gerard spun around to see Duffy striding towards them. 'We're dead,' he whispered.

'And what's this?' Duffy demanded, prodding at Kumiko's computer.

'It's a computer,' Gerard replied smugly.

'Don't try and match wits with me boy!' Duffy exclaimed, then turned to Kumiko. 'I want an explanation and I want it now!'

'I was just trying to make a hologram.'

'A Christmas tree for Kingston and Anna,' Gerard added.

The mere mention of Christmas sent Duffy's blood

pressure soaring. He reached down and ripped the computer from its connections. 'I told you, there will be no Christmas. And if I catch you hacking into the system one more time, I'll dispatch the lot of you down the waste disposal port!'

Gerard watched as Duffy marched from the room with Kumiko's computer tucked under his arm. As he disappeared into the corridor, something snapped inside Gerard. He'd had enough, and he raced after Duffy.

'We were just trying to do something nice. Not that you'd know the meaning of the word!' he exclaimed angrily, stopping Duffy in his tracks.

Duffy was speechless. Never before had he been spoken to in such a manner. 'How dare you!' he hissed.

'A simple Christmas tree. It's not as if we were going to blow up the station,' Gerard continued.

'That's not the point,' Duffy replied, trying to keep a lid on his temper.

'How would you like it if your Christmas was cancelled? Boy! Scrooge has got nothing on you!' Having said his piece, Gerard turned on his heels and marched back towards the hydro lab, half expecting Duffy to chase after him. His heart was pumping rapidly. He'd even surprised himself by his outburst.

Duffy stood staring blankly after Gerard, feeling more than a little stung by his attack. Turning to go to the control room, he almost managed to run down Michael.

'What are you staring at?' Duffy snapped, and without waiting for a response, pushed past him and stormed off.

Gerard marched up to Kumiko. 'Fair dinkum! If that guy wasn't so big, I'd deck him,' he said, still fuming. 'And thanks for the warning!' he growled at Michael as he entered the room.

'Hey back off. I'm sorry, I didn't see him leave,'

Michael said in his own defence. 'What about the hologram?'

Kumiko shook her head. 'And Duffy's got my computer,' she said with a heavy sigh, turning to Gerard. 'Looks like no Christmas tree this year.'

'Anna's going to hate me forever,' Gerard sighed, sinking down on a bench.

But at that very moment, Anna had a grin from ear to ear. She and Kingston were happily looping their special Christmas decorations about the virtual reality chamber. They'd collected rolls of bandages from the medical bay, dyed them with food colouring and baked them dry in the food reconstitution machines.

Standing back, they admired their work. Kingston was particularly impressed with his brilliant idea of the bandages. 'Okay, so tell me I'm brilliant,' he said, hoping his mother wouldn't miss them. Next, they sat down and began wrapping gifts in pieces of foil and plasti-film. 'Maybe we could give Duffy a bottle of cyanide,' Kingston joked.

'Kingston! That's terrible,' Anna replied, as she carefully wrapped a crystal component from the virtual reality machine and placed it on top of the large pile of gifts in the centre of the room.

'You're right,' Kingston agreed. 'He'd probably use it on us.'

'It's not *all* his fault. He's just trying to do his job. Deep down, he's probably just as worried as the rest of us.'

'Nobody's as worried as I am,' Kingston retorted.

Michael, Gerard and Kumiko sat dolefully in the hydro lab considering their next move.

'I'm really worried about the Professor,' Michael said to Kumiko. 'He's blaming himself.'

Kumiko wasn't listening. She hated being beaten by a computer and was still wondering why her hologram hadn't worked. Normally she could build them with her eyes closed.

'It's like he's given up!' Michael continued. 'He keeps babbling on about nothing is what it seems.'

'It's there but it's not there,' Kumiko muttered, lost in her own train of thought. 'What did you say?' she asked.

Michael looked confused. 'Ingessol. He keeps going on about nothing is what it seems.'

Kumiko thought for a moment, running the words over in her mind, piecing together parts of the problem. 'The Christmas tree and the ore carrier. What have they got in common?' she asked.

'This is no time for riddles,' Gerard said.

'Nothing is what it seems. It's there but it's not there,' Kumiko repeated. 'The computer's not converting digital commands into an image. That's why I can't get the tree to materialise.'

Michael still looked confused. Computers weren't his area of expertise.

'What if it's the same for the ore carrier. What if the ore carrier is actually out there but the scanners can't produce an image?'

'Sounds like science fiction to me,' Gerard scoffed.

But Kumiko was sure she was right, and given a few minutes on the central computer, she was certain she could prove it.

Despite Gerard's protestations, they made their way to the control room. Fortunately, the colonists were busy in one corner of the room, still arguing about the next step to take.

'We have no choice. We cut our losses. We can't waste any more time,' Duffy insisted. 'We use the fuel we've got and blast ourselves as close to Earth as possible. Hopefully we can get close enough and someone will pick us up on their scanners.'

'George's right,' Karl conceded. 'Maybe we can get close enough to Earth for a rescue ship to find us.'

Kumiko slid up to a console, while Gerard and Michael kept watch. 'If Duffy sees us now, we're dead,' Gerard whispered.

Kumiko quietly worked at the console, expertly keying commands into the computer. She looked up to the large video mesh to check the image. The star field on the screen distorted for a moment, and a second later it was replaced by a burst of noisy static.

It was enough to attract the attention of Duffy. At the end of his tether, he stormed over to them and demanded answers.

Gerard tried to speak, but hearing the word Christmas, Duffy cut him off mid-sentence.

'I am sick and tired of all this nonsense about a Christmas tree! I'm responsible for the safety of this station,' he said, and when Kumiko tried to explain her ore carrier hologram theory to him, he refused to listen.

'This pre-occupation with Christmas has to stop!' Duffy ordered in a raised voice. 'We have much more important issues to deal with!'

But Professor Ingessol interjected. 'George. Will you be quiet!' he snapped. 'Just for a moment, please.' He turned to Kumiko and gestured for her to continue.

'On my computer, it was fine,' Kumiko explained. 'But on the mainframe, nothing. The digital image assembler—'.

Professor Ingessol was one step ahead of her. 'Nothing is what it seems,' he muttered, then quickly sprang into action. Rushing to the computer stack, he slid out one of the circuit boards to examine it. Holding it up to the light, he looked through the strange coloured crystals embedded among the circuitry. 'It processes information from the long distance digital scanners,' he explained to Kumiko. 'And one of the crystals has shattered.'

'Can it be fixed?' Duffy asked.

Ingessol shook his head, defeated. 'And without it,

we're blind. But perhaps there's another, similar component somewhere on the station.'

Duffy quickly organised a search party. 'Right. Sam, you take stores. Karl, check the machinery bay. Tatsuya. You and Akiko try the mainframe bays. Find that replacement!'

As the colonists quickly dispersed, Kumiko turned to Michael and Gerard. 'What else on the station converts digital data into images,' she asked.

'Here we go, more riddles,' Gerard shrugged.

Kumiko looked at Michael. 'You should know,' she said. You've used it before. Virtual reality,' she said, and all three rushed away to the VR chamber.

Anna and Kingston had transformed the chamber completely. Red and green streamers hung around the walls, pieces of plasti-film cut into the shapes of reindeers and sleighs hung from the ceiling, and a large pile of Christmas gifts, all brightly wrapped, lay stacked in the centre of the floor.

'It's perfect, don't you think?' Anna said, as she proudly placed the last of the gifts on top of the heap.

'I suppose.'

'Kingston, you're supposed to be happy.'

'It's not going to be any fun without the others. And it would have been nice to have a Christmas tree,' he groaned as Kumiko, Gerard and Michael burst into the chamber. Gerard looked around surprised, then turned to his sister. 'What are you two doing in here?' he demanded.

'And what are *you* doing here? You've spoilt it now!' Anna replied.

Kumiko ignored them and rushed to the virtual reality machine. She searched through the dismantled bits and pieces, but couldn't find the image assembler.

'What have you done with it?' she asked, turning to Kingston and Anna.

'What have I done with what?' Anna replied, a little confused by all the panic.

Kumiko tried to describe the missing component. 'It's about so big. With crystals in it,' she said, trying to remain calm.

Kingston knew immediately what she was referring to. He'd seen it earlier. 'Nobody told us,' he said defensively. 'We thought it was junk.'

'It's all right. Where is it?'

Anna and Kingston pointed at the large pile of gifts on the floor and to their horror, Michael, Gerard and Kumiko quickly began to rip open the carefully wrapped presents.

'What are you doing?' Kingston protested, seeing all their hard work being destroyed in a matter of seconds.

'It's not time yet,' Anna pleaded.

'Sorry. Emergency,' Kumiko said, and continued tearing the gifts apart, ripping the wrapping into shreds.

Finally, Gerard held up the component. 'This what you're looking for?' he asked.

Kumiko nodded. She grabbed the circuit and raced from the room. Michael and Gerard followed close behind. As an afterthought, Gerard stopped and planted a kiss on Anna's forehead. 'Thanks,' he said, and disappeared.

'What was that all about?' Kingston asked, surveying the mess, feeling a little like he'd been hit by a hurricane.

Anna was too busy wiping Gerard's kiss from her forehead. 'Yuk! My own brother. I don't believe he actually kissed me!'

Kumiko rushed back into the control room and presented the component to Professor Ingessol. 'It's from the VR processor,' she reported.

'Kumiko, what would I do without you?' said Ingessol, taking the part and quickly connecting it to the system. After a few adjustments it was ready for testing, and everyone gathered around the video mesh in anticipation.

Duffy sidled up to Kumiko. 'It seems I *might* owe you an apology,' he muttered under his breath.

'It's okay. I guess you've got your job to do,' Kumiko acknowledged, letting him off the hook.

'Absolutely right!' he snorted self-righteously. 'And it's for your own good.'

'Okay everyone, cross your fingers,' Professor Ingessol said, giving Beth the signal to test the scanners.

Beth took a deep breath and began typing commands into her console. A hush fell over the room. Suddenly the image on the video mesh distorted violently and moments later the giant ore carrier miraculously appeared on the screen. The huge fully automated vessel, loaded with containers filled with ore, was a welcome sight indeed.

The room broke out into loud cheering and Kumiko, caught up in the excitement of the moment, threw her arms around Michael, hugging him affectionately. Just as quickly she let him go, feeling a little self-conscious.

Later that day, KL5 successfully docked with the ore carrier and the fuel from the giant craft was drained into the hold of the station. For the first time in many days, the colonists were able to relax. Their troubles would soon be over, they thought, and they'd be back home on Earth.

The next morning everyone was invited down to the virtual reality chamber, to Kingston and Anna's colourful wonderland and a surprise Christmas party. Michael handed round a bowl of strawberries, Kingston and Anna handed out their home-made, hurriedly rewrapped gifts, and Kumiko filled one corner of the room with a large sparkling Christmas tree hologram.

Duffy was the last to receive a present, and he looked a little embarrassed at the attention. Gingerly accepting the elaborately wrapped gift, he cautiously rattled it and sniffed at it.

'Go on George,' Beth said. 'It won't bite.'

Finally Anna grabbed the present and began ripping the wrapping off for him. Inside was the old digital image assembler. She held it up to the light and looked through the crystals. 'It changes everything,' she said, as the room danced and whirled before her eyes. 'Go on, try it,' she said, and Duffy, cautiously pleased, twirled it in front of him.

'Aren't you forgetting something George?' Beth said.

'Merry Christmas Anna,' Duffy said, shuffling uneasily and smiling awkwardly.

'Merry Christmas, Mr Duffy,' said Anna, giving him a hug.

DECOY

With its fuel reserves replenished, KL5 continued its perilous voyage across the solar system. While the colonists battled to keep the floundering craft functioning and on course, the children counted down the weeks, going about their chores, surviving on the last of the protein-packs and algae.

But there was a growing sense of excitement and anticipation among them as KL5 neared the end of its journey. Each hour seemed like a day, and each week a month, as they longed for the moment when they would finally set foot on Earth.

When Professor Ingessol reported that he'd sighted Mars on the digital scanners, the colonists celebrated, relieved that their journey was almost over. For the first time in months, the crew were able to relax, and Michael and Kumiko spent many hours together in the viewing bubble, searching the skies for glimpses of Earth.

One morning, they sat looking out at the red planet Mars, tiny and remote in the distance, unaware that Kingston had crawled through an air duct and was spying on them from a nearby grid.

Michael leaned close to Kumiko. 'When we do finally get to Earth, the first thing I want to do is see the ocean,' he said.

Kumiko looked at Michael sadly. 'I'll probably get dragged off again to some remote rock somewhere. Pluto probably. Be just my luck,' she replied. 'Just once I'd like to stay in one place so I can be with my friends.'

Kumiko looked across at Michael, who edged his

arm awkwardly around her shoulder. Kumiko smiled, a little bashfully. She slowly shuffled closer to him, resting her head on his shoulder.

Inside the air duct, Kingston couldn't believe his eyes. He lay dead still, watching his friends get closer to each other, trying desperately not to laugh.

In the control room, Professor Ingessol was trying to pinpoint KL5's position on a diagram of the solar system. 'According to my calculations, we should be here,' he said to Gerard and Anna, pointing to a spot between the asteroid belt and Mars.

'Give or take a few million kilometres,' Beth muttered as Ingessol finished wiring a strange looking electronic device—a collection of mismatched electronic circuits, switches and tiny lights, assembled within a makeshift metal frame—into her computer console. 'And with that transmitter,' he said, ignoring Beth and pointing to the device, 'we'll send an SOS signal. If we're close enough to Earth, and if it doesn't burn out ... '.

Gerard scowled at Ingessol. 'Here we go again. More ifs.'

Anna glared at Gerard. 'You're such a pessimist! Worse than Kingston. I told you,' she said, 'we're going to be rescued. We're going to phone home!'

'The moment of truth,' Ingessol announced to the control room as he completed the connections. Reaching down, he hoisted Anna up to the computer console and she proudly pushed the signal-send button. Immediately, the SOS beacon came to life, its network of tiny lights blinking haphazardly.

Kingston was trying not to make a sound. Inside his secret hiding place, he inched forward to get a better view of his friends. Peering through the air duct grate, his eyes widened in disbelief as Michael leaned over to kiss Kumiko. 'Oh spew!' he exclaimed loudly.

Startled by the noise, Kumiko and Michael leapt to their feet with embarrassment and looked around them. 'What was that?' Kumiko said.

Kingston reeled back from the air duct grid and slapped his hand over his mouth, trying to stop an overwhelming urge to laugh. He had to get out of there, but before he could retreat, the air duct grid was ripped from its fittings and Michael reached inside to haul him into the viewing bubble.

'How long has he been there?' Kumiko demanded as Kingston struggled to free himself from Michael's grasp.

'I haven't done anything,' Kingston said, protesting his innocence.

'You were spying!' Michael said, gripping him firmly.

'I never did. Ouch! Let go!'

Michael kept a firm hold on him. 'You were. You were spying, you little slime!' he said threateningly.

'It was just a joke. Where's your sense of humour?'

'Gone missing,' said Michael, marching Kingston into the corridor.

'You're such a juvenile,' Kumiko said, shoving the reluctant tunnel rat forward.

'Oh little miss grown up!' Kingston scoffed. 'I don't believe it. You were actually going to kiss her,' he said to Michael.

Kumiko turned to Kingston, her face red with anger. 'He was not!' she exclaimed.

Michael forced Kingston against a rocket backpack hanging on an adjacent wall. 'If you breathe one word, I'm warning you, I'll strap you into that thing and blast you into space,' he threatened.

'And you know what happens out in space, don't you? You start to swell up, your tongue gets really big and your eyeballs explode,' Kumiko added.

Kingston stared back at them in horror. 'They do

not! Do they?' he asked, imagining himself exploding into a million squishy bits.

Michael nodded ominously. 'And nobody can hear you scream,' he said menacingly.

Kingston was dumbfounded. He stood silently staring after Michael and Kumiko as they strode off down the corridor, glancing back occasionally to check they weren't being followed. He couldn't understand what all the fuss was about but he did know one thing. He was going to get even. 'Nobody tangles with Kingston Lewis,' he muttered.

The following morning in the recreation room, Michael collected his food wafer and placed it in the recon machine. He whistled to himself happily as he removed the food container from the machine and moved to a table, passing Beth on the way.

'Morning Michael,' she chirped, with a wide grin. 'You seem very cheery.'

Michael eyed her suspiciously. 'No I'm not. Why should I be?' he asked.

'Oh, no reason,' Beth tittered, as she moved towards the door, still smiling broadly.

Michael watched her go, wondering what he had missed, then sat down at a table with Anna who was finishing off her meal. She immediately began to giggle.

'What's so funny?' Michael demanded with growing frustration. But Anna shovelled more food into her mouth so she wouldn't have to answer.

Michael thought for a moment. Had Kingston opened his big mouth? If he had, he was dead meat! He lifted a spoon full of soya meal to his mouth, and as he glanced up towards the doorway, he saw it. Scrawled on a large piece of plasti-film, hanging from the ceiling, was a large sign in huge letters saying 'Michael loves Kumiko'.

Michael was furious! 'Kingston!' he exclaimed as he got to his feet and raced towards the exit, leaving Anna laughing loudly.

Gerard was in the control room checking progress on the SOS transmitter when Michael burst into the room. 'Gerard, have you seen Kingston?' he asked.

Gerard smiled knowingly. 'Maybe, what's it to you?'

'Have you or haven't you?'

Gerard toyed with Michael for a moment. 'Now let me think.'

'Don't strain yourself.'

'Well, I did see him in the rec room,' Gerard said cheerfully, playing Michael like a fish on a hook. 'That was earlier, then in the viewing bubble, but that was later ... '

'Don't get smart!' Michael warned.

'I'd try the hydro lab,' Gerard said.

Michael turned and rushed towards the door, and Gerard called after him. 'So how's Kumiko?' he asked cheekily, making exaggerated kissing noises.

Michael cringed, his face turning bright red. It seemed everyone had seen the sign. He raced off to find Kingston and exact his revenge. Kingston was going to wish he'd never been born.

Rushing into the hydro lab, Michael carefully searched for Kingston, checking between plant beds, under benches and behind the atmospheric purifiers. The tunnel rat was nowhere to be seen. 'Show yourself you little rodent!' he called loudly but there was no answer. Not a sound, then hearing footsteps, he turned to see Kumiko hurrying towards him. 'Michael,' she exclaimed. 'My computer. It's gone. I left it in the rec room.'

'Maybe Professor Ingessol borrowed it. For the transmitter,' Michael suggested.

'No, I traced it here,' she said, showing Michael her computer's small remote. 'You didn't borrow it?'

'No. I've been looking for Kingston,' Michael said, raising his voice threateningly in case the tunnel rat was nearby. 'And when I find him ... !'

'So you saw the sign too. The little deviant,' Kumiko

said as she checked her remote again. 'I don't understand it,' she said quizzically. 'It's on the move again. Now it's back in the rec room.'

Michael looked at the remote and back at Kumiko. 'I'll give you one guess,' he said.

'Kingston!' Kumiko exclaimed. 'I'll murder him!'

'Not if I do first,' Michael muttered as they raced from the lab.

Kingston's ZIT sped across the floor of the recreation room with Kumiko's computer strapped to its back. The tiny machine wheeled out of the doorway and sped off down the corridor, screeching excitedly.

Inside the viewing bubble, Kingston giggled maniacally, giving ZIT's remote control fierce space tug pilot tweaks and turns. As he looked at the remote's small screen, he had a bird's eye view of everything in ZIT's path through its tiny camera eye. 'Kingston, you may be juvenile,' he giggled, 'but you're a genius!'

As ZIT sped around a corner, Kingston saw Duffy and Tatsuya striding down the corridor talking and gesticulating excitedly. Intrigued by their behaviour, he turned up the volume of the remote to eavesdrop on their conversation.

'I've never seen anything like it,' Tatsuya reported to Duffy. 'It's heading straight for KL5.'

'Anything like what?' Kingston muttered to himself as Duffy wheeled around to Tatsuya.

'Where's Ingessol when you need him?' he exclaimed. 'You better find him. And fast!'

Continuing *their* search, Kumiko and Michael rushed into the rec room to find it empty. 'It's gone again,' Kumiko said, looking at her remote.

'He must be on the move all the time,' Michael said, as they charged out of the room following the remote's new signal.

Inside the control room, Duffy stood alongside Sam, Akiko and Beth staring at an approaching satellite on the video mesh. Silvery grey, the conical shaped craft had a lower section that dropped away like a whale's under belly. Manoeuvring rockets around its base encircled its main thruster. No-one had seen anything like it before, its presence a complete mystery to all of them.

'Any contact? A signal? Anything?' Duffy asked.

'Nothing. Not a peep,' Akiko answered, as the strange craft continued to close in on the station.

'I don't understand it,' Sam said, gazing up at the video mesh. 'They must have seen us. Somebody on that thing must know we're here.'

Duffy turned to Beth who continued to signal the craft from her computer console. 'Keep trying,' he ordered as Anna appeared with Gerard in tow.

'I told you,' she exclaimed, pointing at the craft. 'A rescue ship.' As they moved across the room, towards the video mesh, Ingessol and Tatsuya appeared behind them.

'Professor, look!' Anna exclaimed. 'It worked.'

Ingessol was beside himself with excitement. 'Yes! It actually worked,' he said happily. He hurried over to Beth without taking his eyes off the screen. 'How long's it been there?' he asked.

'We sighted it at about seven hundred hours,' Beth replied.

Ingessol stared at the craft. 'Any contact?'

'Nothing,' Duffy interjected.

Gerard and Anna watched the Professor as slowly he moved closer to the screen, seemingly mesmerised by the power of the craft, his expression changing from one of joy to one of concern.

Unaware of Ingessol's change in mood, Anna prattled away about being rescued. 'Ice cream. That's what I'm going to have,' she said. 'Buckets of it! All different flavours ... '

'Sssh! Be quiet,' Gerard said, trying to figure out what was on Ingessol's mind. Something was obviously troubling him.

As they watched the screen, the craft began an unusual transformation. As it neared the station, it slowly rotated, then the main pod began to open like the petals of a huge flower, revealing an ominous and threatening laser, pointing directly at them.

'Now what's it doing?' Sam asked Ingessol.

Ingessol, however, was in a world of his own. 'It couldn't be,' he muttered to himself. 'Surely not, not out here.' Suddenly he spun around to Sam and the others. 'We're in danger!' he exclaimed.

'What?' said Duffy, his body tensing.

'Sam, you remember, the Global Defence Satellites?' Ingessol said. Before Sam could respond, Duffy interjected. 'They were all destroyed. Every last one of them. Dismantled.'

'Yes. Supposedly. But what if one of them strayed?' Ingessol said, stumbling over his words. 'Or if it went off course?' Ingessol's questions hung in the air like a deathly cloud.

Anna immediately lost all interest in ice cream. She looked up at the screen to see the craft pivoting towards them, cautiously tracking the station, its systems seeming to come alive.

'Gerard. I'm scared,' she whispered.

Unaware of the danger, Kumiko and Michael were still hunting for Kingston. Consulting her remote, Kumiko crept inside the viewing bubble. 'He has to be in there,' she whispered. 'And there's no way out!'

'Maybe we should ignore him. He'll get tired of his stupid joke,' said Michael.

'No way!' Kumiko was not about to give in to Kingston. She keyed a command into her tracker, and after a second, a piercing tone sounded from the nearby computer.

Michael searched at the back of the bubble and found ZIT in hiding, the computer strapped to its back. 'Gotcha,' he exclaimed. 'Kingston! You're history. I'm going blast you out into space!' he said, peering down

183

at ZIT's eye camera, knowing full well that Kingston would be watching on the remote's screen.

But Kingston wasn't watching. From his hiding place in the air duct, he was staring out through the grid, past Michael and Kumiko, out into space. His eyes were fixed on the satellite that loomed up next to the station. 'Aliens! he shrieked.

He scrambled out of the air duct onto the floor and Michael and Kumiko rushed to collar him. Terrified, Kingston pointed towards the window, and Michael and Kumiko wheeled around just in time to see the satellite open fire with its powerful laser.

A dazzling beam of light bounced from its central nose cone, splitting back to its petal-shaped reflector shields, then reconnecting to create a blinding and deadly bolt of energy.

The laser blasted the station, destroying part of the lower superstructure. The shock waves sent the children sprawling to the floor.

'Aliens! We're under attack,' Kingston screamed as a loud explosion rocked the station.

Kumiko stared out of the bubble towards the craft. 'What is that thing?', she exclaimed, scrambling dazedly to her feet.

Kingston wasn't about to hang around to find out. 'Run for your lives!' he yelled, heading for the exit as a second explosion flung them against the walls. 'Don't just stand there. Run!' he shouted, dragging Michael and Kumiko into the corridor, racing for the control room as another loud explosion reverberated through the station.

The control room was in chaos. A loud siren sounded, warning lights flashed from the emergency systems, and everyone was rushing about frantically trying to stabilise the station.

'Sam! Level five,' Karl yelled above the noise. 'The fuel reserve! It's been ruptured. We'll have to seal it off.'

Anna stood in the centre of the room confused and terrified. 'Dad, tell it to stop,' she screamed, too frightened to move.

As he rushed towards the door, Karl grabbed her, thrusting her into Gerard's arms. 'Look after her,' he said, racing from the room with Tatsuya to seal off level five and contain the fuel leak.

Michael stared up at the video mesh as the satellite once more began to rotate, taking new aim at the station. 'What is that thing?' he yelled.

'Some sort of rogue satellite. It thinks we're the enemy,' Gerard replied, as the satellite blasted one of the solar sails.

'We're all going to die,' Kingston shrieked, ducking away from a nearby panel of power circuits as it exploded in a cloud of smoke and sparks.

Over the noise, Gerard could hear Ingessol yelling to Beth. 'The SOS signal. It's homing in on the signal. Shut it down!' he said, desperately trying to extinguish the fire in the power panel.

Beth quickly keyed commands into her console but the computer refused to respond.

'Shut it *all* down. Everything!' Ingessol yelled, seeing Beth was having trouble.

'The computers, they're jammed! Nothing's responding,' Beth shouted back, as another power panel exploded nearby.

'The beacon. Destroy it!'

'Mum! Smash the thing! Gerard yelled, rushing past his mother and grabbing the beacon. He ripped it from the console and hurled it to the floor, smashing it into a thousand pieces.

Almost immediately, with the signal gone, the satellite ceased its attack and the control room fell into an uneasy silence. Amid the smoke and confusion, Ingessol glanced around the room, surveying the damage. 'We were so close,' he muttered forlornly.

An hour later, after the colonists had assessed the

damage to the station, the children sat in the recreation room looking miserable. There was a feeling of defeat hanging in the air. The damage had been considerable.

'I can't believe they're just going to give in,' Kumiko said, breaking the silence.

'It *will* go away, won't it?' Anna said hopefully.

'Can't they send another SOS signal? Get help?' Kingston interjected.

Kumiko shook her head. 'We can't even use the computers. Nothing. If that thing detects any sort of signal, sound waves, electromagnetic disturbance, it'll blast us again.'

Kingston winced. 'Great! So while it sits out there, we sit in here and rot,' he said. 'Why does it have to attack us?'

'Yeah. Tell it to chase someone else,' Anna agreed.

'Like who? Let's face it, we're all about to die!' Kingston announced emphatically.

Michael turned on Kingston. 'Maybe we should blast you out there,' he said.

'Get lost. You're not using me as a decoy,' Kingston protested.

'But we could give it something else to hunt,' Kumiko said slowly, thinking aloud. 'Kingston, you're a genius.'

'Finally you realise,' Kingston said happily. 'Why? What did I say?'

But Kumiko didn't answer. 'Michael, I have to get my computer. It's still in the viewing bubble,' she said, leaping to her feet.

'No. It's too dangerous,' Michael warned, stopping her.

'I could get it,' Kingston volunteered with a sly grin. Michael shook his head. He wasn't about to let anyone go wandering about the station. 'Please. I want to help. It's my fault it's there in the first place,' Kingston pleaded.

But Michael was adamant. 'You're not going anywhere.'

Kingston produced the remote control to his ZIT. 'I don't have to go anywhere,' he said cheekily, flicking the power switch on the remote.

Inside the viewing bubble, ZIT came to life with a hapless squeal. It sped out the door and down the corridor towards the rec room, dodging fallen debris as it went. As it rocketed around a corner, with Kumiko's computer still attached to its back, it almost collided with Gerard and Michael.

'These things have got to be 50 years old,' Gerard said, as he and Michael lifted one of the rocket backpacks from its wall mount. 'How do we know they still work?'

'We don't. Now come on,' Michael said, as they struggled with the heavy appliance. 'I hope Kumiko knows what she's doing, or Duffy's going to be really peeved.'

Duffy strode down the corridor with a grim look on his face. Kingston ran along beside him with Sam, Ingessol and Anna in tow.

'What do I have to do? Nail you lot to the floor! You were told to stay in the rec room,' Duffy sighed.

'But it's brilliant,' Kingston boasted. 'And I thought of it! You'll be saying, why didn't I think of that?'

'I seriously doubt it,' Duffy replied between gritted teeth.

'You doubt everything,' Kingston mumbled, as they continued towards the rec room.

Moments later, everybody was clustered around the rocket backpack, and Kumiko stood in the centre, nervously outlining her plan.

'We attach my computer to the backpack. We blast both out into space, past the satellite—' she began, then reached for the remote tracker from her computer. 'When it's safely out of laser range, using my remote, I instruct it to transmit its homing signal. Simple.'

Kumiko looked up at the circle of blank faces. Kingston was first to break the silence. 'See I told you it was brilliant,' he said, not quite sure what was so clever about the plan.

Kumiko continued. 'The satellite will—'

Ingessol, who had been deep in thought, interrupted, finishing Kumiko's sentence. 'The satellite will home in on *that* signal. It will track the computer!'

'Of course,' Kingston exclaimed, everything becoming clear.

Duffy looked at Ingessol in disbelief. 'Do you seriously think a highly sophisticated Global Defence Satellite system is going to chase some kid's toy around the galaxy!'

'It's not a toy!' Kumiko snapped.

Sam turned to Duffy. 'We're fresh out of alternatives George.'

Ingessol agreed. 'We've shot our last bolt. This is our last chance. Come on Sam,' he said. 'We'll send that thing straight into the sun.'

Ingessol headed for the control room, while Sam took the backpack to a nearby airlock. Once the backpack had been fitted to a makeshift launch cradle, Kumiko strapped her computer on top, and sadly programmed it for the last time.

'You sure you want to do this?' Michael asked.

'It's only a machine,' Kumiko answered, putting on a brave face.

'Well I think you're really neat,' Kingston chipped in. 'I mean if it was me, I don't know whether I could send ZIT out there to be zapped.'

Michael glared at Kingston.

'And I'm really sorry I gave you a hard time. Nicking your computer and stuff,' Kingston continued, ignoring Michael's stony-faced look.

'It's okay. If you hadn't taken it, maybe I wouldn't have thought of this.'

'Oh yeah,' Kingston exclaimed, pleased with himself. 'You hear that Michael? Am I a hero, or what?'

'Don't push your luck rodent. There's still time to strap you onto this thing,' Michael said, gesturing to the backpack.

Preparing for blast off, Ingessol and Beth worked together in the control room, quickly hot-wiring Kumiko's remote into the central computer's transmitters. Duffy hovered nearby, clearly worried about the plan. 'This is crazy. Why can't we use the SOS transmitter? Strap *it* to the backpack?'

Gerard picked up the SOS transmitter from the floor nearby and held it up to Duffy. Bits and pieces of broken components hung from the damaged device, and Duffy lapsed into stern-faced silence.

Inside the airlock, the backpack was ready for blast off, the computer securely strapped on board. 'It was a birthday present from my Mum and Dad,' Kumiko said sadly. 'It's kind of like saying goodbye to a good friend.'

Kingston placed his hand on Kumiko's shoulder. 'You've still got us. I mean, well, we mightn't be as intelligent as a computer ... Well Michael mightn't be,' he joked, trying to lift Kumiko's spirits.

'You're really asking for it,' Michael said.

'Lighten up will you. I'm just trying to be cheerful. Kumi's favourite possession in the whole world is about to be blasted into a million bits!'

Michael glared at Kingston. 'You insensitive amoeba!'

Kumiko knew that Kingston meant well. 'It's okay Michael,' she said, as Sam entered the airlock and signalled that everything was ready for the launch.

Kumiko took one last long look at her computer, then turned and rushed off to the control room.

'Twenty seconds,' Ingessol announced as Kumiko settled down behind the console where her remote lay wired to the central computer. 'Stand by to boot up the central computer,' he said to Beth, then turned to Kumiko and checked to see that she was ready. Kumiko took a deep breath and nodded.

'Standing by, ten seconds,' Ingessol said, the countdown reaching Sam over the intercom.

Pressing the timer switches on the rocket backpack, Sam saw the digital counter begin to tick down towards zero. Quickly stepping out of the airlock, he shut and sealed the safety door. 'All clear,' he reported.

Inside the airlock, the backpack armed itself. As the timer switch clicked to zero, its rockets ignited. The airlock filled with light and fiery energy, and after a second or two, the launch cradle released the rocket backpack into the blackness of space.

On the large video mesh that overlooked the control room, the children watched anxiously as the backpack headed through space towards the Global Defence Satellite.

'Standing by. Wait for my order,' Ingessol said to Beth.

As Beth's hand moved to the power switches on the central computer, Kingston suddenly turned to Michael and Gerard. 'What's to stop the satellite from attacking us? When we signal Kumiko's computer?' he asked loudly. 'Has anyone thought of that?'

Michael and Gerard looked across to Ingessol, who shrugged uncertainly. 'Oh great! We're all going to get zapped!' Kingston moaned.

'The signal! What are we waiting for?' Duffy yelled anxiously.

'No, wait! Too early and the satellite will destroy it, and turn on us,' Ingessol replied. He placed his hand on Kumiko's shoulder. 'It has to pass out of laser range. Ten seconds,' he added, checking his timer. He turned to Beth and nodded, and she quickly reset the central computer, ready for the transmission.

The control room fell silent as the seconds ticked by.

All eyes were on the video mesh and the rogue satellite as it hovered close to the station.

'Now Kumi, the signal,' Ingessol instructed, and Kumiko began to key commands into her remote, instructing her computer to transmit its powerful homing signal.

'It's not working. It must be out of range!' she exclaimed.

Horrified, Michael and Kingston watched the video mesh as the satellite began to rotate slowly, homing in on the station, aiming its powerful laser at the heart of KL5.

Kingston was terrified. 'Kumi. Don't mess around. It's aiming at us!' he yelled.

'Do something,' Duffy barked. 'Or shut it down!'

'Beth, there must be a fault in the wiring,' Ingessol said. 'Gentle persuasion, Mum!' Gerard said and reaching forward, thumped the computer console where the remote was wired into the central computer. After a second, the tiny device began to flicker and, on the mesh, the computer showed clear connection status to the remote.

'There!' Gerard exclaimed. 'It just needed a little Koestler know-how!'

'Now Kumi! Before we're all blasted,' Kingston begged, as the satellite's laser locked onto the station.

As the satellite took aim at the station, Kumiko quickly punched commands into her remote. Immediately it began to transmit its signal.

'Quiet everyone!' Duffy ordered and the control room fell silent. Kumiko listened. 'There it is!' she exclaimed. 'It's working.'

Ingessol looked up to the video mesh to see the satellite closing in on the station. 'Come on, damn you! Take the bait,' he shouted.

'Shut it down. Shut it all down!' Duffy ordered, as the satellite continued to lock its aim onto the station.

'And do what George?!' Ingessol shouted, knowing that this was their only chance.

'Hang on everyone!' Duffy conceded. 'Prepare yourselves.'

But, as the children huddled together, bracing themselves for another attack, the satellite's manoeuvring rockets suddenly ignited and the ugly craft began to rotate. Its petal-like shields closed around the laser, it fired its main thrusters, and blasted away from the station into space, in hot pursuit of Kumiko's computer.

The tension in the control room gave way to loud cheers. 'That thing is so tiny, the satellite will be stalking it for months,' Ingessol announced to the room. 'It'll be like looking for a needle in a haystack,' he said, a broad grin on his face.

Michael and Kingston were the first to congratulate Kumiko. Then Akiko and Tatsuya threw their arms around her, hugging her tightly.

'I'm proud of you. You know that don't you?' Tatsuya said, smiling.

'We both are,' Akiko added affectionately.

Even Duffy tried to congratulate Kumiko. 'Not bad going, I suppose. For a small person,' he conceded.

Kumiko looked up to the video mesh and watched the satellite racing into the distance. She knew she would never see her computer again.

'Maybe I'll get to see the ocean after all,' Michael said, distracting her by placing his arm around her shoulder. 'Thanks to you.'

'Yes. Maybe,' Kumiko nodded, smiling a little sadly.

'So, do you want to teach me to swim?'

Kumiko looked at him in surprise. 'You can't swim?'

'I'm a space kid remember. I'd sink like a rock,' he said, a little embarrassed to admit it.

Kumiko smiled, and gave him a hug—cut short by a sudden, fierce explosion somewhere in the depths of KL5.

Alarms rang out, warning lights flashed, and on the video mesh, a red pictogram filled the screen, warning of a new emergency on level five.

'Level five! Something's happened on level five,' Duffy shouted, as he tried to get to his feet. Another explosion rocked KL5, hurling him to the floor. 'Stay down!' he shouted, 'everyone stay down!' For once the children were happy to do what Duffy said, crouching on the floor in fear.

CHAPTER ELEVEN

MISFIRE

G radually the explosions died away and the station stopped its destructive shaking. The control room was in darkness apart from the occasional spray of sparks from damaged power panels and the flashing pictogram on the video mesh, casting an eerie, intermittent red glow over the smoke-filled room. Slowly, the shaken colonists clambered to their feet and dusted themselves off.

'How much more can this bucket of bolts take?' Gerard exclaimed, as he crawled from beneath a pile of rubble.

'Michael! Are you all right?' Sam's voice echoed out of the darkness across the control room.

'We're okay!' he shouted back, helping Kumiko to her feet.

'It felt like half the station just exploded,' Gerard said, glancing around the chaos.

'Sam, what happened? Can you trace it?' Duffy's voice called out.

Sam fumbled his way to Beth's computer console and they quickly ran a damage assessment. 'It was the fuel, we've lost the fuel reserves on level five,' Sam replied, as emergency lighting returned to the control room, revealing the extent of the damage.

Power panels were scorched by the short circuits, one of the computer consoles buzzed unhealthily, and the air was thick with smoke. At the rear of the room, a section of ceiling and its supporting wall had collapsed into a pile of dusty rubble.

Kumiko looked around the room anxiously. Kingston

was nowhere to be seen. Quickly she and Michael began searching for him. 'There!' Kumiko pointed, seeing a small hand poking out of the collapsed section of wall.

Gerard reached down and hauled Kingston from the rubble. 'What are you doing down there?' he asked.

'Having a rest! What do you reckon?' Kingston replied sarcastically, shaking off the dust. 'Why is it that every time the ceiling caves in, I'm the one who ends up underneath it?!'

Nearby, Professor Ingessol keyed commands into his computer console. He looked up to the video mesh and a large image of the sun replaced the flashing red pictogram.

'Professor? What is it?' Kumiko asked, seeing the worried look on Ingessol's face.

'The explosions. It's the only explanation,' he muttered to himself, still staring up at the video mesh.

Immediately concerned, Duffy turned to Ingessol. 'Explanation for what?' he demanded to know.

'We've been blown off course. We're heading towards the sun,' Ingessol replied.

Kingston stared at the video mesh. 'Oh that's just great news! Now we're going to be burnt to a crisp,' he exclaimed.

While the colonists did what they could to restore the computers, the children retreated to the recreation room. It had survived the explosions better than the rest of the station. There they contemplated what might be done to stop the station plunging into the sun.

'Without any fuel for the tug?' Kingston said. 'We're doomed. Any requests for your last meal?'

'How can you eat at a time like this?' Kumiko asked.

'Don't want to die on an empty stomach, do I?' Kingston replied gloomily.

'Knock it off rodent!' Gerard said, as Kingston inserted a food wafer into the recon machine and it blurted out a pile of steaming lumpy green soup. Collecting the food, he sat down with Michael and the others.

'I thought condemned men were supposed to get one last special meal,' he said, screwing his face up at the bubbling ooze.

As Kingston tentatively lifted a spoonful to his mouth, Ingessol and Sam came striding into the room carrying piles of info-files and plasti-flim. Clearing some space on the tables, they set up a temporary work bench. 'We've got one chance,' Ingessol said to Sam as they sat down. 'It's a long shot but it just might work—if I can just find the right data to feed into the computer.'

'I'm still not sure what we're trying to do,' said Sam.

'Okay, this is us, KL5,' Ingessol said snatching a salt container from Kingston's table and plonking it down in front of Sam. Next he picked up an empty plate and put it down on the other side of the table. 'And that's Earth. Now over here—' he said, taking Kingston's plate of food, '—here we have the sun.'

Kingston looked relieved. 'Phew! Saved from a fate worse than death,' he muttered, happy to lose the unappetising concoction.

'And over here, coming up fast, we've got Mars,' Ingessol said, turning a pepper shaker into the red planet.

Ingessol moved the salt shaker towards Kingston's sludge to show KL5's route towards the sun. 'Now, we've lost the main fuel reserves, right?'

Sam nodded in agreement.

'But there's still a smidgin of fuel left in the tug,' Ingessol said, flying the salt shaker in a gentle arc towards the empty plate. 'It might be just enough to correct our course, bring us under the influence of Mars' gravity, and swing us back towards Earth. Then, if we're lucky, if we're close enough, Earth

Station One will spot us and send a rescue ship to collect us.'

'So what's the bad news?' Kingston chipped in.

'Kingston, you're such a pessimist,' Michael said, glaring across the table.

'There's always bad news,' Kingston continued defensively. 'And it usually comes right after the good news.'

Kingston was right. Ingessol hesitated for a moment. 'We only get one chance at this. In two hours we reach this point,' he said, moving the salt shaker closer to Kingston's bowl of algae soup.

'The point of no return,' Michael suggested.

'Correct. We go beyond that and we won't have the fuel required to blast us back on course. In that case—'

Kingston cut him off. He knew exactly what would happen. 'In that case, we drown in algae soup,' he said, watching as Ingessol plunked the salt shaker into the bowl of green ooze.

With no time to lose, Ingessol and Sam began preparations for the blast off. Michael and Gerard were to clean the debris from the atmospheric purifier and purge the filtration chambers to make sure their air supply would remain clean and intact for the rest of the voyage, while Kumiko took her usual place beside Beth at the computer console.

As Kumiko was preparing to switch on her video mesh, Beth leaned towards Ingessol and called to him urgently. 'Professor! The space tug's ignition. We've lost the interface.'

Ingessol turned in disbelief. The interface was critical if they were to have any control over the tug's ignition systems.

'It's dead. Not a flicker,' Kumiko confirmed from behind her console.

Professor Ingessol headed for the door. 'I'll check the

tug itself. Maybe the satellite attack has damaged the computer lines.'

Amidst all the activity, Kingston had been feeling left out. Now he saw his chance to make himself useful. 'I'll come with you,' he announced.

'We both will,' Anna chipped in.

'Don't even think about it!' Duffy said thrusting an arm out in front of them. 'Go back to the rec room and stay put.'

Before Kingston could argue with him, Michael rushed into the control room and told his father that the atmospheric purifier was malfunctioning. 'The pressure in the filter chamber. It's gone berserk!' he said, sounding panicky.

'Oh this is just great!' Kingston exclaimed. 'The place is coming down around our ears. Now we're all going to suffocate on toxic gas!'

Leaving the tug's ignition systems in Ingessol's hands, Sam hurried out of the room, taking Michael and Gerard with him.

'What about me?' Kingston pleaded as they left the room.

'Are you still here?' Duffy sneered.

'No it's my stunt double. What do *you* reckon?' Kingston said cheekily. 'It's not fair! Everybody else gets a chance. I want to help.'

Duffy thought for a moment. 'Kingston, you're absolutely right,' he finally conceded. 'Perhaps there is something you can do.'

Kingston's eyes lit up. 'Finally! Somebody recognises my immense talent!' he exclaimed to Anna as they followed Duffy towards the exit.

Duffy led Kingston and Anna towards the living quarters, and moments later, Kingston flopped down on Anna's bed, racked with disappointment. 'Child minding,' he said indignantly. 'What a loser.'

'I'm not a child,' Anna protested.

'Yeah right. You're a 25-year-old midget.' Kingston

was well and truly miffed. 'Half the station's been blasted, we're all about to be turned into toast, and we get stuck in here! Stay put he says! I hate being small,' he moaned.

'Maybe we could go out and sneak a look,' Anna suggested.

'And be stepped on by Duffy. No chance. Besides I don't want to *look*. I want to be in the thick of things!' Kingston said, leaping to his feet and barking out commands like a besieged ship's captain. 'Stand by ignition! Retract solar sails! Full power! Get outta my face rodent!'

Anna laughed, then looking to the air duct, said, 'They need never know!'

'Right,' Kingston nodded, deciding that watching would be better than nothing at all. 'The gallery. Above the control room.' He moved across to the air duct grid and removed the cover.

'Tunnel commandos are go!' Anna exclaimed, clambering into the gloomy shaft behind him.

Wearing breathing apparatus, Michael and Gerard worked with Sam in the hydro lab, trying to repair the atmospheric purifier. A blast of gas spewed from a ruptured valve and while Sam tried to shut it off, Michael checked the pressure gauges on the main filtration chamber.

'Can't we just shut it down?' Gerard yelled to Michael above the noise of the rumbling machine.

'And let all that stuff escape into the air?' Michael replied, indicating the gas spewing from the machine. He turned to his father and called out the readings on the gauges. They were steadily rising to critical level. 'The safety release valve! It hasn't opened,' he warned.

'The by-pass switches. The panel in front of you,' Sam shouted back. Michael opened the panel to expose a row of switches. He threw all three but still the machine groaned.

'One ninety. 195. It's still rising!' Gerard yelled, taking Michael's place at the gauges. With a loud roar, another valve erupted and a gas jet shot out from the side of the machine, sending Michael and Gerard reeling backwards, coughing and spluttering.

'Michael! Get out of here. The pair of you!' Sam yelled, as he wrestled with the damaged valve.

'We're all right,' Michael replied, rushing to his father's side.

'Don't argue! Behind the barriers. Now!' Sam ordered, pointing to the shelter behind them. Reluctantly, Michael and Gerard retreated to safety, ducking down behind a plasti-glass shield that protected the main filtration chamber.

Kingston and Anna clambered through the air duct towards the service gallery above the control room, but soon found their way blocked. Part of the shaft had been damaged by the satellite attack. 'I thought you knew these air ducts,' Anna said, as Kingston looked warily down two adjoining shafts.

'I do. I'm thinking,' Kingston said. After a moment, he pointed to the left shaft, but as they began inching along it, the shaft wobbled slightly on its moorings. 'Maybe we should go back,' he said worriedly.

But Anna was determined to get to the control room. She had come this far and wasn't about to turn back. 'No! I want to go on,' she said.

'But I'm supposed to look after you. Duffy'll murder me. What if we get gassed?' Kingston said, growing more afraid.

'Some tunnel commando you turn out to be. You're just scared.'

'I am not scared!' Kingston replied indignantly, and moved off down the duct with Anna following closely behind him. Kingston had not been in this part of the air shaft network before and he hoped he had made the right choice. Slowly and cautiously, he felt his way along the dark shaft, trying to ignore the distant rumbling sounds that echoed faintly up the shaft.

Groaning under pressure, the atmospheric purifier continued to spew gas from its breached valves. Yellow toxic gas blasted in jets from the breached pipes as Sam wrestled frantically with the release valves. As he struggled to divert the escaping gas, the machine began to vibrate, and the filtration chamber rumbled and creaked, straining from the increasing pressure.

Michael looked up at the gauges on the purifier and saw, to his horror, that they'd crossed into the red—and the pressure was still rising rapidly. 'Dad! Get out of there!' he yelled over the groaning of the machine, as a rivet exploded from the main chamber like a bullet.

Before Sam could move, a second rivet discharged and the filter chamber on the machine gave way, exploding in a cloud of gas, which pushed Sam over the safety railing and onto the hard floor of the level below.

'Dad!' Michael screamed, as he raced from behind the barriers to help his father, who lay semi-conscious on the floor.

'Dad! Are you all right?' he said, kneeling by his father's side.

'Michael! Get back! Both of you!' Sam mumbled, dazed and confused.

Michael quickly took charge. 'Gerard. Help me get him away from here.' Together they carefully dragged Sam behind the barrier.

'We have to get him out of here,' Gerard yelled, looking back at the purifier as the machine continued to rumble and vibrate out of control. 'We have to get him to the med bay.'

'No! We can't move him any more. We don't know what's wrong.' Michael replied.

'But the purifier!' Gerard shouted.

'We'll be all right. Go and get help. Quick!' Michael pleaded, and as Gerard raced from the room towards the medical bay, the purifier gave one last roar and shudder, then exploded in a mass of twisted metal.

Inside the air duct, Anna and Kingston heard the explosion and held on grimly as the duct began to shake violently. 'We have to go back!' Kingston yelled, watching sinister yellow gas billowing up the shaft towards them.

'I can't turn round,' Anna screamed.

As they tried to make their way backwards, the duct lurched violently and Kingston and Anna lost their footing. They slid towards a shaft opening, tumbled into it and disappeared down a vertical shaft.

As if riding a huge dark slippery dip, they slid down the shaft, shrieking with terror, bouncing from side to side, only slowing up as the shaft started to level out. Just as it seemed they might come to a halt, they came to another opening, and toppled over into an even bigger duct. Then, just as suddenly, the sounds of their sliding stopped.

Anna was the first to find her voice. 'Kingston!' she yelled, stunned and confused, her voice echoing up the shaft.

'Anna! Hold on,' Kingston yelled back.

Deep inside the air duct network, they hung together, dangling from a cross beam in one of the main vertical shafts. Dazed and frightened, Kingston looked down and saw only darkness. He looked up and saw smooth, black walls extending forever. 'I think we're in big trouble,' he said.

'I don't think Mr Duffy is going to be very pleased

with you,' Anna said, her voice shaking as she looked into the black hole below.

'You're the one who wanted to see what was going on,' Kingston retorted.

'And you're the one who wanted to be in the thick of things. Now we're up to our neck in it. I hate air ducts!' Anna said through gritted teeth. Looking up at the shaft towering above them, she saw a beam of light spilling into the gloom. 'There! Look,' she said, her eyes adjusting to the light. 'An opening.'

Peering inside the service access Professor Ingessol checked the last of the computer's circuit boards controlling the tug's ignition systems. Working in the docking room, where the computer cables from the space tug linked into the station's central computer system, he had traced the fault to the space tug's interface system. 'It's taken a blast from the satellite,' he said to Duffy over the static-filled communicator.

'The thrusters? Are they intact?' Duffy replied.

'They're fine. The cargo pod took the main blast. I've managed to redirect the ignition system. You'll have direct control.'

Duffy turned from the communicator in the control room and ordered Beth and Kumiko to lock in the ignition sequence.

'No turning back now,' Beth said, as she keyed the ignition codes into the central computer, then began the countdown to final blast off over the intercom.

'Kingston! Hurry up,' Anna pleaded, as Kingston clambered up onto the cross beam and tried to reach the vent further up the shaft. Beth's muffled voice echoed through the air duct, announcing that the ignition sequence was locked in. There were 15 minutes to blast off. If there was one place Anna didn't want to be when they blasted off, it was stuck inside an air duct.

Kingston stretched as high as he could and thumped the grid with his fist.

'You're too short,' Anna said, as she clutched grimly onto the cross beam.

'I am not short,' Kingston protested.

'Okay. You're very tall for your age. Now stand on your toes!'

Kingston stood on his tiptoes and thumped the grid again. This time it clattered from the vent and tumbled down the shaft, just missing Anna.

'You stay put,' Kingston said, as he hauled himself up to the opening.

'Where else am I going to go?' Anna replied, looking down the shaft. As she glanced down, she was shocked to see the cross beam beginning to bend.

'Kingston! Hurry,' she cried, as the beam began to give way.

'Hang on tight. I'll have you out of there in no time.'

As Kingston reached for the air vent opening, the cross beam gave way completely and Anna rocketed down the shaft into the black void below, her loud scream echoing up the shaft.

Kingston was horrified. Dangling by his finger tips, he glanced up at the opening, not sure what to do. Hearing Anna scream again he made his decision. Releasing his grip from the air duct, he slid down after her.

The countdown to firing continued over the intercom as Professor Ingessol made his final checks inside the docking room. Suddenly, Anna hurtled out of an air duct and crashed down into a pile of boxes behind him. Seconds later, Kingston landed right beside her.

Professor Ingessol stared at them in dismay as they scrambled to their feet.

'We were checking the air ducts,' Kingston said, quickly inventing an excuse.

'To see if there was air in them,' Anna added, pleased with her inventiveness.

Kingston looked at Anna incredulously.

'What's wrong with that?' she asked.

A bemused Professor Ingessol had no time to quiz either of them. The countdown was locked in. Twelve minutes to go. 'I think we'd better contact Mr Duffy,' he said, turning to the communicator.

'No I wouldn't do that,' Kingston said, diving to block Ingessol's path. 'He's very busy.'

'Right. Then you better stay with me,' Ingessol replied, as Beth's voice again echoed over the intercom. 'Countdown to firing, 11 minutes. Ignition sequence locked and ready.'

'You can watch the ignition from here,' Ingessol said, as he turned back to the computer console. 'And remember ... '

'We know. Stay put!' Kingston interjected, quoting Duffy's favourite phrase. They plonked themselves down and eagerly awaited the big moment when the space tug's thrusters would ignite and blast them back on course.

As the seconds ticked by, Michael and Gerard rushed along beside Helen, as Duffy and Akiko wheeled Sam into the medical bay. Still semi-conscious, Sam lay on the medical trolley groaning in pain. His clothes were scorched and ripped and blood oozed from a deep wound on his shoulder.

'I'll take it from here,' Helen said, taking control.

'But I want to stay with him,' Michael protested.

Helen looked to Duffy, signalling him to escort the boys outside. 'Better let Dr Lewis do her job,' Duffy said, ushering them out of the room.

'Come on. I'll wait with you,' Gerard said, and both boys slumped down on seats outside the medical bay to await further news.

'Your father's a strong man,' Duffy said, the level of concern and sympathy in his voice taking Michael by surprise.

'Yeah. Tough as granite. He'll be all right,' Gerard added.

Beth's voice continued counting down the remaining minutes to ignition as Kingston and Anna looked through the viewing port at the tug outside. 'Our own private cockpit,' Kingston said happily, as he settled back to watch the thrusters go to work.

Anna climbed up next to him and began playing one of their favourite games. 'Anna to tunnel rat,' she said, talking into her cupped hand, using it like a communicator.

Kingston was quick to join in. 'Rat responding,' he said into his hand. 'Come in launch control.'

'Stand by for launch.'

'Rockets armed and ready. Retract linkages,' Kingston ordered.

'That's a negative,' Anna replied, looking out at the tug's linkages that secured the craft to KL5. 'Linkage damaged. Direct hit!'

Overhearing the comment, Ingessol looked up from the computer console. 'What? Say that again,' he said to a confused Anna. 'What did you say about the linkages?'

'Typical. Invent a good game and everyone wants to play,' Anna muttered to Kingston.

'The linkages. What did you say?' Ingessol persisted.

Anna couldn't understand what the fuss was about. 'Direct hit,' she repeated. 'Now what have we done wrong?'

Ingessol didn't answer. He clambered up next to Kingston and Anna, stared out at the tug, and reeled back in horror. Anna was right. One of the space tug's minor linkages had taken a direct blast from the satellite's laser and was fractured. If the tug fired its thrusters now, it could break free from the station, and send both vessels somersaulting through space.

'We have to stop the ignition,' Ingessol shouted into the intercom, as Beth's voice crackled out. 'Countdown to firing, nine minutes.'

Michael sat with his head buried in his hands outside the medical bay. He looked up expectantly as Helen appeared through the examination bay doors. 'Your Dad's got concussion and a few broken bones, but he'll be fine.'

Michael breathed a huge sigh of relief. 'Can I see him?'

'Of course. And Michael, you did the right thing by not moving him,' Helen said, as she ushered him through the door.

Sam was lying stretched flat out on a bed. He'd been cleaned up and his shoulder was tightly bandaged. 'Hi Dad. How you feeling?' Michael said quietly, placing a hand on his father's good shoulder.

'Bit on the bruised side,' Sam answered rather groggily. 'Looks like I may be laid up for a while. You'll have to take over for me.'

'You name it. Anything,' Michael said eagerly.

'Michael, I know we haven't had much time together through all of this,' Sam said thoughtfully.

'Michael tried to brush off the admission. 'It's okay Dad,' Michael said.

'But I want you to know,' Sam continued. 'If we had to go through it all again, I'd want you by my side. I'm very proud of you son. Me and your mum, we both are.'

Michael tried to hug his father but there wasn't much of Sam that wasn't bruised. 'Sorry,' he said apologetically, seeing his father grimace a little.

'It's okay,' Sam said with a grin and took Michael by the hand. 'We're going to get through this,' he said reassuringly, looking up at Michael. 'We all are.'

'We're going to die,' Kingston muttered, watching anxiously as Ingessol tried to raise the control room over the communication system. Nobody seemed to be able to hear him but Beth's static-filled voice still crackled over the intercom. 'Countdown to firing, eight minutes.'

'What happens if he can't get through?' Anna asked, as she watched Ingessol thump the communicator in frustration.

'We end up with a space tug in our laps,' Kingston replied with a worried look on his face. 'Kaboom!' he exploded, just to emphasise his point.

'George! Come in. The space tug. It's broken free,' Ingessol called over the communicator. 'Abort the ignition.' Now there was nothing but static coming over the intercom, and Ingessol gave the intercom one last despairing thump. 'Come on you piece of junk!' he exclaimed. 'Work!'

Kingston turned to Anna with a worried look on his face. 'We're going to toast whatever way you look at it,' he said. 'If the space tug doesn't get us, the sun will.'

'I've lost Ingessol,' Duffy said, turning from the communication panel in the control room. 'I can't reach him.'

'We've got no choice,' Beth said. 'We have to go ahead with the ignition. If we delay by as much as a second, we'll pass the point of no return.'

Kumiko looked at her timer. 'Seven minutes.'

Duffy wiped the perspiration from his brow, then leaned across in front of Kumiko and Beth and opened a panel revealing the ignition safety switches. He turned the keys and a small safety light under each ignition button turned from red to green.

Ingessol continued in vain to raise the control room. 'Duffy! If you can hear me, stop the firing. Repeat, stop the ignition sequence.'

'Professor! Can't we stop it from here?' Kingston asked, pointing to the battered computer console.

'No time,' Ingessol said. 'I had to bypass this system. Now it's locked into the central computer.'

Beth's voice crackled over the intercom. 'Ignition sequence, six minutes.'

Ingessol groaned. The sequence was continuing and it had to be stopped. He turned to Kingston. 'You'll have to stop them,' he said.

'Me? What can I do?' Kingston said. 'I don't know anything!'

'You can run, can't you? Run to the control room. Tell Duffy, tell him to stop the firing.'

'He's not going to listen to me. I'm just a little kid,' Kingston objected.

'You can do it, Kingston,' Anna said encouragingly. 'Tunnel commandos never give up.'

'Run Kingston. Run. As fast as you can,' Ingessol said, pointing him to the door and the corridors stretching beyond. 'We'll follow. Run like you've never run before!'

Kingston took off from the docking room as fast as he could. His short legs pumping hard, he raced along the corridor, heading for the central stairwell that led up through the station to the control room above. 'Stop Duffy, stop Duffy,' he muttered to himself, as he clambered up the stairs two at a time.

Racing as hard as he could, he passed sign after sign. First level four, then level three, then he was charging towards the exit on level two. 'Stop Duffy, stop Duffy' he kept repeating, trying to encourage himself. 'How am I going to stop Duffy,' he groaned, as he reached a closed bulkhead door. As he slammed the controls, the door slid half open, and he squeezed through into a long dark corridor.

'Two minutes to firing,' Beth announced to the control room from behind her console. 'Let's hope the professor knows what he's doing,' she added as an aside.

'He hasn't been wrong yet,' Duffy answered sharply, reaching for the ignition buttons.

At the rear of the room, Gerard stood watching the proceedings. As he glanced up at the video mesh to see the sun glowing brightly, Michael appeared through the doors and joined him. 'Dad's going to be fine,' Michael said. 'Thanks to you.'

'Don't mention it. You would have done the same for me.' Michael grinned, feeling a lot closer to Gerard.

'Sixty seconds,' Beth announced.

'We're not going to make it,' Professor Ingessol gasped, stopping to catch his breath on the central stairwell.

'Quickly,' Anna said, taking him by the hand and urging him on. 'What's slowing you down?'

'Old age,' said the Professor with a sigh, puffing hard as he headed up the steep stairs.

Realising he was running out of time, Kingston raced down the dark corridor, and skidded around a corner. To his relief, he spotted the control room doors at the end of the long passageway. He sprinted off, running as fast as he could towards them.

As he reached the end of the passageway, he tripped and fell, sprawling along the floor. 'Thirty seconds,' he heard Beth say over the intercom. Now time was really short.

Clambering to his feet, Kingston summoned the last of his energy and sprinted the remaining distance, barging through the control room doors, yelling at the top of his voice to stop the firing.

Duffy stood at the ignition controls, his finger poised to hit the button. Kingston knew he had no time for explanations. He raced across the room, yelling wildly, took a flying leap across one of the computer consoles, and crash tackled Duffy to the ground.

The control room went into uproar. Sprawled on the floor in a tangle of arms and legs, Kingston rode the astonished Duffy like a bucking horse. Astounded by the attack, Michael and Gerard rushed forward and hauled him off. 'Kingston! What do you think you're doing?' Michael yelled above the commotion as the flabbergasted Duffy climbed to his feet.

'Get out of my way you imbecile!' Duffy shouted, as he pushed his way back to the computer console.

Kingston knew he had to stop him. He grabbed hold of Duffy with all his strength, clutching desperately to his leg. 'No! You can't. It's the tug, it's broken free,' Kingston panted, as he was dragged across the floor. 'You have to believe me!'

Duffy angrily wrenched his leg free, and marched across to the ignition switches. As he was about to hit the button, Professor Ingessol and Anna came rushing into the room, yelling as wildly as Kingston, stopping Duffy in his tracks.

'George! No! The linkages have been destroyed!' Ingessol gasped as Duffy's hand hovered over the switches.

'You press those switches—it's the end!' Ingessol exclaimed.

Kingston looked across to Duffy as Duffy's hand slid away from the computer console. The countdown reached zero.

'Ignition aborted,' Duffy announced quietly, realising that Kingston had saved the space station from almost certain destruction.

As the panting Ingessol told the others the full story, Kingston was hailed a hero and he enthusiastically soaked up the attention. The celebrations were shortlived, however, as the colonists realised they had been saved from one disaster only to plummet into another.

Michael moved slowly across to the computer consoles and looked up at the large video mesh. They were still heading on their course into the sun. They had missed the point of no return.

CHAPTER TWELVE

RESCUE

A sense of gloom and hopelessness shrouded KL5
and its crew. The dazzling light of the sun grew
brighter and brighter, as the crippled space station
sailed inexorably towards it.

It had been several days since the station had
passed the point of no return, and continuing to float
off course, the colonists realised there was nothing
they could do. After months of hardship, they had
come so close, but Earth remained beyond their reach.

'Slowly but surely we'll be sucked into its vortex. All
that'll be left of us will be a bunch of dried out, shriv-
elled up old mummies,' Kingston said dejectedly, as he
and Anna sat in the viewing bubble staring out into
space.

'Someone will think of something. Won't they?' Anna
said hopefully, as she looked out at the fiery ball in
the distance.

Kingston slowly shook his head. 'I don't want to
worry you, but if I were you, I'd break out your thermo-
proof undies,' he said, already feeling the intense heat
from the sun on his face.

'How long do they think we've got?' Gerard asked
Michael as they sat together, alone in the cockpit
of the space tug. Michael shrugged. They had
sneaked on board to escape the gloom, and were
quietly sitting behind the controls reflecting on the
past months, and contemplating their possible
future. Neither dared look at the other.

'In my last pictogram from Mum, before we left Io,

212

she said she'd got a dog,' Michael said, breaking a long silence. 'Guess what she called it?'

Gerard looked at Michael in disbelief. 'We're all about to die, and you're worried about a dumb dog!'

'Duffy. She called it Duffy.'

The thought of a dog called Duffy was too much for both of them. They burst into uncontrollable laughter.

They were laughing so much that neither of them noticed Duffy and Professor Ingessol enter the tug behind them. Duffy dropped his hand on Michael's shoulder and both boys leapt with fright. 'I want you to find Kingston and Anna,' Duffy said quietly, as both boys tried to control their urge to laugh. 'Stay with them. Look after them. Please,' he added.

As they made their way out of the tug, Gerard shot a questioning look at Michael. Duffy had actually said please.

A short time later, Gerard and Michael found the others in the recreation room. 'Duffy's hiding something for sure,' Gerard said, suggesting they climb up to the service gallery above the control room. 'He's never that nice.'

Kingston agreed wholeheartedly. The thought of Duffy saying please was totally foreign to him. 'Whatever happened to "get out of my face"!' he said as they clambered through the hatchway. 'It's definitely sus!'

Below them the adults had gathered together for a meeting, and crawling into the service gallery, the children settled back to listen. Duffy was on his feet addressing the others. 'We've considered every option. The tug's our only hope. With the cargo pod destroyed and the weight to fuel ratio as it is—' he said, looking around the circle of faces. 'It leaves five places. Five places, five children.'

The children sat dead still, confused, replaying Duffy's arithmetic over in their minds. Realising what he was actually suggesting, they looked at one another, wide-eyed and shocked. 'He can't be serious!'

Kumiko whispered to Michael, as they leaned forward to get a better view.

'I know it's a terrible risk, but KL5's finished,' Ingessol added. 'You know the outcome if they stay. George is right. With luck we can see them safely on their way to Earth.'

Gerard looked at Michael in surprise. 'They're mental!' he whispered, and Kumiko agreed. 'If he thinks I'm going anywhere in that flying tin can, he's out of his head!' she said.

Kingston felt his pulse quicken. 'Aren't they forgetting something,' he said, and all eyes turned to him. 'Who's going to fly the thing?' Michael sank back on his haunches. He knew exactly who would have to fly it.

An hour later and inside the medical bay, Sam lay propped up in his bed with Duffy, Ingessol and Michael by his side. 'You're deranged!' Sam exclaimed after listening to Duffy's plan.

'Please Sam. You're in no shape to go. The boy's the only one who can fly it,' Duffy said softly.

'In flight, yes. When I'm by his side, not by himself. He's taken off, but he's certainly never landed the thing,' Sam said, turning to Ingessol for support. 'You tell him.'

But Ingessol knew that Duffy was right. 'We can program the auto pilot. And we'll be in contact with them for most of the way,' he argued, hoping to get Sam's consent. 'Remember Sam, with the fuel shortage, the longer we wait—' Ingessol's voice trailed off.

While Sam lay silently considering their request, Michael moved in next to him. 'We have to try Dad. I know I can do it,' he said, trying to bolster his confidence.

'Have you seen the way Michael drives that thing,'

Kingston exclaimed, pacing up and down in the rec room. 'He's a speed freak.'

'Relax rodent,' Gerard said. 'There's no way Sam will agree.'

'Well, I won't be going. One chance in a million. That's what we're talking here,' Kingston muttered.

'Maybe one chance is better than none at all,' Kumiko said thoughtfully, despite her fear of flying.

'What about Mum and Dad,' Anna asked. 'If *we* leave, what's going to happen to them?' During all the excitement, no-one had really stopped to think about the others. The children looked at each other glumly as the realisation hit home. They might never see their parents again.

Their silence was broken when Michael appeared at the doorway. They looked up to see an enigmatic smile on his face. 'Better pack your bags,' he said. 'Lift off at sixteen hundred hours.' The decision had been made.

They had two hours until take off, and feeling overwhelmed by the ordeal ahead, the children reluctantly dispersed to prepare for their journey. Michael returned to his quarters and began packing a few belongings. While he sorted through his meagre possessions, he played the pictogram of his mother one final time. 'Give your dad a kiss for me,' he heard her say. 'And guess what, I got a dog—'

Michael quickly placed the pictogram into his pocket when Professor Ingessol bustled into the room.

'Toothbrush, socks, clean undies,' Ingessol said with a forced cheerfulness. Michael lifted a toothbrush from his pocket with a smile. For a moment the smile slipped from Ingessol's features. 'Who'd have thought, eh?' he said, reflecting on their adventures together.

'Yeah. Who'd have thought,' Michael replied nervously, thinking more about the journey that lay ahead.

Ingessol immediately turned the conversation to the business at hand. 'Right. I've programmed the auto pilot. The fuel should get you close enough to Earth

Station One. They'll pick you up on their scanners,' he said. 'You'll be rescued in no time.' Michael smiled tentatively.

'You'll be fine,' Ingessol added, sensing Michael's uncertainty.

'It's okay. I trust you,' Michael replied. Then unexpectedly, he wrapped his arms round Ingessol and hugged him affectionately, catching the Professor off his guard.

'You'll do just fine,' Ingessol repeated, clearly upset by Michael's imminent departure. They said goodbye and Ingessol hurried back to the control room. Time was pressing.

While Ingessol worked frantically to prepare the tug for blast off, Beth returned to the control room in a state of alarm. 'Professor! It's Anna,' she called. 'She says she won't go. Maybe she'll listen to you.'

Ingessol left his computer console and was almost at the door when Duffy intercepted him. 'I'll go. You're needed here,' he said.

'George, I'm not sure that's such a good idea,' Beth interjected. But it was too late. Duffy was gone.

When Duffy found Anna, she was sitting alone in the viewing bubble hugging her toy dinosaur tightly.

'Can I join you?' he asked tentatively.

Anna shrugged. 'If you want to.'

As Duffy clambered into a chair next to Anna, he pulled a bar of chocolate from his top pocket. 'I saved it for you,' he said quietly. 'For just such emergencies. For the flight.'

Anna eyed the chocolate suspiciously. 'There's no pilot,' she murmured quietly.

'But there'll be an automatic pilot. And Michael, he'll be with you.'

'I want a real one. I want Sam.'

'Sam's sick. He can't go. You know that,' Duffy said softly.

Anna looked up at Duffy, tears welling in her eyes.

'I'm scared,' she admitted, nestling in next to him. Rather awkwardly, Duffy placed his arm around her, trying to comfort her. 'You're allowed to be scared,' he said. 'But you want to help your Mum don't you?'

Anna couldn't see the connection.

'She needs you to go. We all do. We're relying on you to get to Earth Station One and send back help. It's a rescue mission.'

Anna eyed Duffy suspiciously for a moment, trying to work out if he was telling the truth. Finally she decided that he was, and she wiped away the tears from her cheeks. The thought of being involved in a rescue mission pleased her.

Duffy offered the chocolate to her again. 'I'd still rather have a pilot,' she said, accepting it this time.

The countdown for the space tug's departure began. Michael sat on the bed with his father, getting last minute advice. 'And don't forget, keep an eye on the thrusters. We've had trouble with them before,' Sam said, running a checklist through his mind.

'It's okay Dad,' Michael replied trying to put on a brave face.

'And the reverse thrusters. Short blasts only.'

'Dad! I'm nervous enough as it is!'

Sam wrapped his good arm around Michael. 'You'll do fine,' he said. Then after a moment, he tried to haul himself upright in bed. 'Maybe I should double-check the auto pilot.'

Michael placed his hand on Sam's shoulder and gently eased him back onto the bed. 'It's being done,' he said. 'Professor Ingessol knows what he's doing. I'll be okay.' Taking the pictogram from his pocket, he handed it to his father. 'My last pictogram from Mum. I want you to mind it for me.'

'I guess this is it,' Sam said, knowing he couldn't avoid the inevitable any longer. He hugged Michael tightly. 'Bye Dad,' Michael muttered, and rushed from the room towards the departure bay, tears welling in his eyes.

When Kingston's mother came to escort him to the space tug, he was lying on his bed, deep in thought. 'Haven't you packed your bag yet?' she asked, concerned that time was slipping away.

Kingston sat upright and held out a small bag. 'I have,' he said happily, and then produced a second bag from behind his back. 'And I've packed one for you too!'

'You know I can't go,' Helen said sadly, sitting down beside him.

'Well I was thinking,' Kingston said. 'Maybe we should have a doctor on board. Just in case one of us gets sick. I haven't been feeling very well lately,' he added, looking hopefully towards his mother.

'There's no room. You know that.'

'But Anna only counts as half a person. Me too. We're only small.'

Helen smiled, then grabbed Kingston and gave him a loving hug. 'Good try muscles. But no, I'm needed here.'

'But Mum,' Kingston persisted. 'What about you? Who's going to look after you?'

'I'm going to be perfectly safe,' Helen said. 'You know why? Because you're going to send back help.'

Kingston was not convinced. 'And what if we blow up? What if we take a wrong turn? Or disappear down a black hole?'

'Kingston, you have to think about the others. They're going to need you. The auto pilot has been programmed for a specific on-board weight. You have to go.'

'You're just saying that,' Kingston mumbled, flopping back onto his bed.

'Listen tough guy,' Helen said. 'If there was anyway you could stay with me, I'd want you to be here.'

Kingston eyed his mother for a moment. He knew

she was right. Picking up his bag, he hesitated by the door, and looked sadly back at his mother.

'You better get moving,' she said, trying to put on a brave face. 'You don't want to miss the boat.'

With the space tug checked and its auto-pilot locked in, Duffy strode out of the access tube and signalled to everyone that it was time for boarding.

'Now you behave yourself,' Karl said to Anna, as they ushered her towards the access tube.

'Yes Dad,' Anna replied automatically. It was the tenth time her father had said that.

'And do as Gerard says,' Beth chipped in.

'Yes Mum,' Anna replied again. It was the eighth time her mother had said that.

'And you do what Michael says,' Karl said firmly, turning to Gerard.

'Dad, will you stop fussing,' Gerard replied sharply. He hated goodbyes at the best of times, and now that it was time to leave, he just wanted to get on with it.

'I'll stop fussing when I know you're safe,' Karl replied, putting his arm around Gerard's shoulders. 'And don't go thumping anything. That tug's full of highly sensitive instruments!'

Beth placed a calming hand on Karl. 'They'll be okay. He's a big boy now,' she said, kissing Gerard on the cheek.

Gerard winced a little. All this emotion was too much for him. 'Better get on board,' he said, ushering Anna towards the access tube, passing Kumiko and her parents.

'I guess we'll see you on Earth Station One,' Kumiko said quietly to Akiko and Tatsuya.

Her mother nodded tearfully, and taking a comb from her hair, she handed it to Kumiko. 'It was my mother's,' she said sadly, as Duffy's voice boomed out loudly.

'The tug's ready. Time is pressing. Everyone on board please,' he announced, all in a fluster.

As everyone moved inside the access tube, Anna realised amid all the confusion, that Kingston was missing. She glanced around the room, searching for him.

'Please! Will you stop wasting time,' Duffy exclaimed.

'But we can't go without Kingston. We need him. He's part of the team,' Anna said, flatly refusing to enter the access tube.

At that moment, Kingston bounced into the room and smiled broadly.

'Someone call the genius?' he said cheekily.

'Will you get on board!' Duffy yelled.

The children waved their parents a final farewell, and as they made their way through the access tube, Gerard turned to Michael. 'I'm going to miss him bellowing at us all the time,' he whispered.

'Good luck,' Duffy said, as they disappeared through the tug door.

As the others climbed into the cockpit, Anna turned and rushed back to Duffy and threw her arms around his neck, taking him completely by surprise.

'Goodbye Mr Duffy,' she said, kissing him on the cheek, before rushing back to the access tube. Duffy lifted his hand and tentatively waved a fond farewell as the tiny traveller disappeared into the tug.

Karl turned to Duffy who had a tear in his eye. 'Careful George,' he said. 'You'll want some of your own soon.'

'Don't be ridiculous,' Duffy blustered, steeling himself. 'Glad to be rid of the little troublemakers.'

As the colonists made their way to the control room to monitor the launch, Michael climbed into the pilot's seat and quickly began to prepare the tug for take off. With mixed emotions, the other children buckled themselves into their seats and waited for the moment when the thrusters would ignite and blast them away from the station, never to return.

Michael flicked a switch on the communicator and Ingessol's image appeared on the small video mesh in front of him. 'Ten seconds remaining Michael. And may the force be with you,' he said jokingly.

Gerard turned to Michael, confused. 'What's he on about?' he said to Michael who shrugged. 'The man's flipped. And our lives are in his hands.' Gerard added nervously. 'You realise that, don't you?'

As Professor Ingessol counted down the final seconds to ignition, the children braced themselves for lift off, while Michael flicked the switches on the auto pilot. Immediately the roar of the thrusters filled the cockpit.

'I hate this machine!' Kumiko yelled over the noise, as the cockpit began to vibrate fiercely.

'Just hang on. It'll stop when we reach cruise speed,' Michael said, trying to reassure his passengers.

'We're about to fall apart, and he says relax. Typical!' Kingston said, offering his hand to Anna.

'It's okay,' she said. 'I'm not scared.'

But Kingston insisted. 'Hold my hand will you,' he said, gripping hers tightly.

As the tug's thrusters reached full power, the battered craft swung away from the ill-fated space station.

The remaining colonists watched in silence as the tug separated from the station. 'Good luck,' Beth murmured quietly, seeing the orange glow of the tug's thrusters vanish into the darkness of space.

The tug soon reached cruise velocity, and the vibrations in the cockpit died away. The children all relaxed a little. They were finally on their way to Earth Station One, and soon Michael began to feel more confident behind the controls. As the tiny craft blasted through space, he kept a watchful eye on the instruments panel in front of him, keeping a sharp lookout for any sign of trouble.

Occasionally, he would reach out to adjust a knob or switch or lever, and Kingston would bolt upright in his rear seat and demand to know what Michael was touching and for what reason.

As their trip continued smoothly, Michael stopped monitoring the tug's controls closely. There didn't seem to be any sign of trouble. 'Shouldn't you be doing something?' Kingston muttered from his rear seat.

'It's automatic, remember?' Michael replied. 'Everything's under control.'

Kingston wasn't convinced. 'Well you could at least look like you're doing something,' he replied, bolting upright again as a light began to flash on the main control panel and a piercing alarm rang out. Michael quickly searched for the problem, running his eyes over the instruments.

'We've only just got off the ground. I knew it. We're going to be blown to pieces!' Kingston exclaimed above the noise.

Ignoring Kingston, Michael quickly turned to the communicator and signalled for Professor Ingessol. The video mesh came to life and Ingessol's image filled the screen. 'We've got a warning signal,' Michael reported anxiously.

'It's all right Michael,' Ingessol said calmly. 'Tell me exactly which indicator it is.'

Turning from the communicator in the control room on KL5, Ingessol called to Tatsuya. 'Patch me down to the medical bay,' he said urgently. 'We need Sam in on this. And hurry,' he added, as Tatsuya began flicking switches to re-route the signal.

Professor Ingessol returned his attention to his video mesh. 'Michael? Have you got that location?'

'Top panel, second left,' Michael replied while his passengers watched on anxiously.

'I'm patching you down to your father,' Ingessol said, and Sam's voice crackled over the communication system. 'Michael can you hear me?'

'Yes Dad,' Michael acknowledged. 'What am I supposed to do?'

'The diagnostic switches! You know where they are?'

Michael reached up and flicked a bank of switches above his head. 'Got them,' he replied, and a small light began to flash red underneath the thruster controls. 'It's the thruster. Left centre,' he reported to his father.

'I want you to remove the security panel above you,' Sam said, trying to sound calm.

Michael turned to Gerard who was already on his feet, undoing the panel's locking clips.

Sam lay in his bed, Helen beside him, as he tried to talk Michael through the repair procedure. 'You'll have to replace the damaged circuit board,' he said.

Michael's voice crackled back over the communicator. The signal was weak and his voice, distant and thin, was beginning to break up. 'Dad ... You're break ... Hear ... can't ... you ... '

Sam knew they were running out of time. The space tug was almost out of range of the station's weak transmitter. 'Michael, just listen. Do as I say,' he said anxiously. 'Swap a matching circuit from the reverse thrusters. Acknowledge.'

Inside the tug, Gerard slid the damaged circuit board from the thruster controls and replaced it with a matching board from the reverse thrusters. 'Got it,' Gerard said, as he locked the circuit into position.

'Just remember ... It's important ... ' Sam's voice crackled intermittently over the static. With the signal getting weaker and weaker, Michael began flicking switches on the communication panel, trying desperately to restore contact with his father.

'Dad we're losing reception,' he exclaimed.

'Out of range ... remember ... reverse ... very important ... circuit ... ' Sam's voice crackled, before finally disappearing from the airwaves.

Anna looked up at Kingston and repeated Sam's final warning. 'What's very important?' she wondered gloomily.

Inside the control room on KL5, the unstable image on the video mesh distorted sharply and Michael's image disappeared forever. Professor Ingessol leant into the communicator, trying to restore contact but there was no response. The tug was out of range. Ingessol turned to the other adults. 'They're on their own now,' he said solemnly, looking up at the empty video mesh.

For the moment, the crisis on the space tug was over. 'Nothing to it,' Michael said with relief, as he engaged the thrusters again. Happy to hear the sound of the thrusters again, Kingston flopped back in his seat, momentarily relaxed.

'But what was so important?' Anna continued to worry as she tried to work out Sam's last words.

'Relax will you,' Kingston said, being surprisingly optimistic. 'We've had our disaster. Everything's going to be fine.'

Just as Kingston finished his sentence, another alarm sounded in the cockpit, different this time, more piercing, and he let out a yelp of fear.

'Is it the thruster?' Kumiko asked, as Michael searched through the control panel looking for the fault.

'No. Something else,' he replied, checking the diagnostic switches. 'The auto pilot.'

Michael pulled down on a lever and the tug began to vibrate severely. Anna let out a scream and reached out across to grip Kingston by the hand.

Quickly correcting his mistake, Michael returned the lever and pulled down on the one next to it. Much to everyone's relief, the siren fell silent.

Kumiko wiped her brow. 'What'd you do?' she asked.

Michael looked across to her and hesitated. 'Pushed the override,' he replied finally.

Gerard immediately sat up in his chair. 'Override to what?'

'The auto-pilot.'

Kingston stared open mouthed at Michael. 'So who's flying this tub?' he exclaimed.

'Relax will you. I've flown this thing lots of times,' Michael replied, taking the controls and trying to remain calm.

'And what about landing?' Kumiko asked hesitantly.

Michael ignored the question. Remaining silent, he concentrated on the tug's controls, intent on steering the craft towards its destination, Earth Station One.

The giant Earth station floated like a vast wheel in space, suspended miles above the Earth's surface. Inside the communications room, PJ, a young flight controller, swung away from her monitor and turned to Gilbert, her communications officer.

'We've got an unscheduled flight on scanners,' she reported. Gilbert quickly checked the scanners and confirmed the unauthorised visitor. He switched to broad band frequency and began trying to contact the approaching craft.

From their back seats, Kingston and Anna pressed their faces to the rear-side viewing port, straining to get a better view of the giant space station and Earth as they loomed out of the blackness like apparitions. 'It's fantastic!' Anna said, hoping that at last they were safely home.

As they peered out at the approaching station, the tug's communication system crackled to life. 'Earth Station One to unidentified craft, you are entering a controlled sector. Please identify yourself,' Gilbert's voice crackled.

Kingston was ecstatic. A great view, followed by a friendly voice. They were safe at last, he thought. 'Michael. Do something. Speak to the man,' he demanded excitedly.

Michael punched the controls on the transmitter, and after a couple of seconds the video mesh came to life. Gilbert's craggy face appeared on the screen. 'I repeat, please identify yourself.'

'This is a Gemini Series Tug. My name is Michael Faraday. We require emergency assistance,' Michael responded nervously.

Gilbert smiled broadly then turned to one of his colleagues off screen. 'Okay, which one of you lot's behind this?' he asked, suspecting the call was a hoax.

Pushing Michael to one side, Gerard leaned into the communicator. 'This isn't a joke, you peanut! We're from Io. It exploded. We've just travelled half way across the galaxy!' he said angrily.

'Yeah! And you'd better get help for my Mum!' Kingston added.

Gerard leant back into his seat. 'Duffys! They're everywhere!' he exclaimed.

Gilbert stared at the video mesh in front of him. 'It's a bunch of kids,' he said in disbelief. Kids flying a tug? Impossible, he thought. He wheeled around to PJ. 'Scramble the rescue unit and then take over. They're all yours.'

While PJ alerted the rescue crews, Gilbert turned back to the screen in front of him. 'Take it easy, Michael. I'm going to hand you over to one of our best pilots.'

Gilbert got up from his seat and handed control back to PJ. 'I'll check the personnel lists from Io. See if the kid's for real. It'll be amazing if anyone's survived.'

Michael took a deep breath and swung the tug towards Earth Station One. He knew he was about to have his first test of his tug landing skills, and the thought terrified him.

'Michael, my name's Peta Jamieson. You can call me PJ, okay? Now I'm going to get you down. Have you ever made a platform landing before?' PJ asked over the communicator.

Michael paused, then reluctantly shook his head. 'No, not a ship to station one, not without an auto pilot.' The others stared at him anxiously. They were stuck with a pilot who'd never made a proper landing!

'Well I think between the two of us we should be able to manage this,' PJ said to Michael, trying to reassure him.

'We're not going to make it,' Kingston muttered. 'I just know it.'

Anna turned and glared at Kingston. 'Kingston! You're making me nervous.'

'And you're not doing a whole lot for my confidence either,' Michael added, as he worked the controls to the tug.

'Now we're going to have to slow you down for approach,' PJ instructed.

Gerard crossed his fingers as Michael pressed the reverse thruster ignition switches. Immediately the green lights began to flash red and the warning siren rang out. Michael quickly searched the controls trying to find the problem.

'Talk to me Michael. What's wrong?' PJ called out.

'The thrusters, they're showing fault status,' Michael replied.

'Michael! You have to slow the tug's approach. Try the reverse thrusters again,' PJ ordered, as the tug sped directly towards the station.

'It's the thrusters. They've failed before,' Michael told her.

In the rear seats of the cockpit, Anna and Kingston sat huddled together watching through the viewing port as the giant Earth Station One loomed closer and closer.

'Michael,' Kingston asked, 'Aren't we going just a wee bit fast?'

Gilbert leant over PJ's shoulder and pressed a mute button on the control panel. 'Scuttle it. Now!' he commanded.

'But they're just kids!' PJ exclaimed.

Gilbert wasn't about to risk the safety of those on board the giant station. The space tug was on collision course. It either had to slow up, change course or be shot down. 'Do it!' he ordered, then released the mute button.

'Michael. You *must* alter your course,' PJ insisted.

'But we'll overshoot the station,' Michael replied.

Gilbert leaned down and whispered to PJ, 'I'm giving you a direct order. For the safety of the station! Scuttle it.'

PJ ignored him. 'Michael. We can rescue you. Alter your heading immediately! We cannot risk the station.'

Kingston went white with fear. 'They're going to blast us! We're going to be blown to space dust!' he exclaimed.

Kumiko turned to Gerard. 'What was it Sam said?' she recalled. 'The reverse thrusters.'

'What about it?' Gerard asked.

' "Important" he said. "Reverse thrusters!".'

'But that's all he said before we were cut off.'

'The security panel. Swap the circuit boards again!' Kumiko said realising what Sam was getting at. 'We have to swap them back!'

Gerard understood immediately. Reaching for the security panel, he removed the circuit board from the reverse thrusters and replaced it with the functioning one from the forward thrusters.

As Gerard replaced the security panel, Kumiko looked up to the control panel to see the warning lights return to normal. 'Michael now! Try it now!' she said, and Michael quickly engaged the reverse thrusters.

'Decelerating. Reverse thruster engaged. We're

landing!' Michael reported to PJ determinedly.

PJ looked up to Gilbert who, after briefly considering the consequences, nodded his permission. PJ smiled to herself and quickly and efficiently began to talk Michael down.

'Stand by. Prepare to come round to course three five zero.'

Michael complied. He quickly threw the relevant switches and the tug's thrusters blasted out loudly. 'Set on three five zero,' he said, and the battered craft began its descent. Michael held onto the controls, steering the tug towards the landing platform. On what looked to be a cargo dispatch wing of the station, a long stretch of platform descended like an open-topped tunnel into the space station. Numbers and arrows marked its surface and a row of bright blue lights illuminated the path, flashing like a pointer towards the landing cradle and access tubes.

'Keep her steady. Engage thrusters,' PJ instructed as Michael made his approach.

Kingston covered his eyes as they swooped down towards the platform. He peered out through his fingers. 'We're going too fast,' he yelled. 'We're all going to die!'

'Shut up rodent!' Gerard said, trying to help Michael concentrate. Beads of sweat appeared on Michael's brow as the tug moved closer to the landing platform. It zigzagged through space, and swayed up and down, and Michael had to battle to hold it to flight path. Trying not to over correct any movement, he struggled with the controls as the tug yawed, pitched, then swung back onto course.

'Hold on,' he shouted, as the tug skimmed over the platform, bounced once, twice and then skidded towards the access bays. The children hung on grimly, and as the tug ploughed towards the landing cradle and its protruding superstructure, Michael hit the reverse thrusters and they groaned to a dead stop.

The children sat silently in disbelief, unable to move, as the thrusters died away. Kingston slid his hand up to his chest to check his heartbeat and Michael looked across to Kumiko, a broad grin of relief filling his face. Kumiko couldn't help herself. She threw her arms around Michael and kissed him on the cheek. They were safe.

Michael just sat there. Stunned and relieved. He stared through the viewing port at the station's access bays. 'I did it, didn't I?' he muttered quietly, while the others clambered out of their seats, whooping with excitement.

'Hey, come on. Never doubted it for a second,' Kingston exclaimed leaping to his feet. 'I knew you could do it. We all did.'

Gerard playfully pummelled Kingston. 'Shut up rodent. Hey mate,' Gerard said. 'Put it there,' offering his hand to Michael, high five style, and Michael gave him a high five back. They were safe!

After being checked over by doctors and vetted by officials, the children gathered in the Earth Station One communications room for news of their parents. A rescue team had been immediately sent in search of KL5, and should have already reached the doomed station.

'We still haven't heard anything,' PJ reported. 'But don't worry, there's increased sunspot activity at the moment. It's interfering with communications.'

'We've getting something now,' Gilbert said, patching the transmission into the intercom.

'ES1 to *Odysseus*. We are having trouble receiving you ... hold on please ... ' said an anonymous voice. Then another voice came through, clear and strong and familiar. 'Hello! Hello! ES1. This is Professor Jacob Ingessol speaking from the rescue craft *Odysseus*—'

At the sound of Ingessol's voice, the children threw their arms around one another and leapt around the room cheering excitedly.

● ◐ ○ ○ ◐ ●

A week later, Michael was contentedly lazing on a beach with the others, enjoying his first contact with sand and surf, and his first holiday for what seemed like forever. 'I reckon I could get used to this,' he joked.

Gerard turned to Kumiko. 'So where to next?' he asked. 'You off to some barren rock somewhere?'

Kumiko was adamant. 'Absolutely not! I'm keeping my feet squarely on terra firma!'

An over-excited, slobbering pug-nosed dog rushed up to her, followed by Kingston and Anna.

'Sit!' Kingston commanded.

'Roll over,' Anna added, and the dog obediently tumbled in the sand.

'Fetch. Go on, fetch Duffy!' Kingston yelled, as he tossed a stick into the water. 'Go Duffy,' he shrieked, laughing as the mangy looking mutt bounded across the sand, collected the stick and came running back, its large ears flopping over its face.

'I've always wanted to do that!' Kingston chortled.

As the children joked about the dog's, and its similarity to Duffy, Kingston suddenly went quiet. He stood dead still, then bent down, putting his ear to the stand.

'Uh-oh! You feel that? Earthquake!' he exclaimed.

'Knock it off rodent,' Gerard said, looking about a little uneasily.

'True. I felt it too!' Anna said.

'And you know what happens in earthquakes?' Kingston continued. 'Tidal waves. Giant walls of water. Fifty metres high. And they come crashing down. Over the beaches!'

Gerard looked at Michael, and Michael looked at Kumiko. Together they leapt to their feet, picked the cackling Kingston up, carried him to the water's edge, counted to three and tossed him in.

'I've been waiting a long time to do that,' Gerard said, laughing as the rodent emerged spluttering and coughing. 'And now jungle boy,' he said, stalking Michael, 'it's time for your first swimming lesson.'